Ryan Meinerding concept art.

MARVEL STUDIOS

THE INFINITY SAGA

THE ART OF MARVEL STUDIOS AVENGERS: AGE OF ULTRON

WRITTEN BY
JACOB JOHNSTON

INTRODUCTION BY
JAMES McCANN

FOREWORD BY
JOSS WHEDON

BOOK DESIGN BY
JEFF POWELL

DUSTJACKET ART BY
RYAN MEINERDING

TITAN BOOKS

FOR MARVEL PUBLISHING
JEFF YOUNGQUIST, Editor
SARAH SINGER, Editor, Special Projects
JEREMY WEST, Manager, Licensed Publishing
SVEN LARSEN, VP, Licensed Publishing
DAVID GABRIEL, SVP Print, Sales & Marketing
C.B. CEBULSKI, Editor in Chief

FOR MARVEL STUDIOS 2015
KEVIN FEIGE, President
LOUIS D'ESPOSITO, Co-President
VICTORIA ALONSO, Executive Vice President, Visual Effects
JEREMY LATCHAM, Senior Vice President, Production & Development
JONATHAN SCHWARTZ, Vice President, Production & Development
WILL CORONA PILGRIM, Creative Manager, Research & Development
RYAN POTTER, Principal Counsel
ERIKA DENTON, Clearances Manager
RANDY McGOWAN, VP Technical Operations
ALEX SCHARF, Digital Asset Coordinator
MITCH BELL, Vice President, Physical Production
ALEXIS AUDITORE, Physical Assets Coordinator

MARVEL STUDIOS' THE INFINITY SAGA – AVENGERS: AGE OF ULTRON – THE ART OF THE MOVIE

ISBN: 9781803367866

First edition: January 2025

10 9 8 7 6 5 4 3 2 1

Published by Titan Books
A division of Titan Publishing Group Ltd
144 Southwark St, London SE1 0UP

www.titanbooks.com

A CIP catalogue record for this title is available from the British Library.

Printed in China.

Ryan Meinerding keyframe.

Jackson Sze concept art.

CONTENTS

FOREWORD 2015

I love comic books. I love movies. I love movies OF comic books. In many ways, they're a natural fit: super-hero comics are exciting, colorful modern legends—visual narratives of epic scale and intimate emotion in which every page turn might lead to a wonderful surprise. With the visual effects available today, any image can be thrown on the screen.

But with all they have in common, movies and comics are different languages. They need translators. Movies that miss the tone—or the visual template, or just the heart—of what makes a comic great are not rare. Some throw out the whole reason to use the source material. Some adhere so slavishly to it that they miss the fact that viewing and reading have very different effects on us. It's a marriage of mediums, and someone has to understand how they join. I've been privileged to work with a number of those people, and Ryan Meinerding is at the top of the list.

Ryan is an extraordinary artist, a painter of infuriating technical skill, and a sweet, humble guy. But first and foremost, to me, he's a translator. Not just between comics and film, but also between the real and the unreal, the fantastic and the mundane. He walks between the two mediums in a way few people ever have or will. His splash pages: dazzling concept-art pieces that contain, in a single frame, the essence of a moment—or possibly of an entire film. His costumes: designs that capture everything we love about an impossibly clad character, painted so that you not only see how it will fit, but also what fabrics will be used and where they will join. I think of Norman Rockwell, probably because the first stuff I saw of Ryan's were his period pieces depicting Captain America during World War II, which deliberately evoked Rockwell's style. But Ryan also shares Rockwell's eye for human detail—for idiosyncratic, unpolished truth.

Ryan's one of many who have shaped the Marvel Cinematic Universe. In this sketch, there's Kevin Feige, another born translator, and a handful of others—including Jeremy Latcham, Lou D'Esposito, Victoria Alonso, Chris Townsend, Alex Byrne and Charlie Wood—with Ryan in the front row (as if he ever stopped scribbling and posed for a picture). Ryan's also an impressive portrait artist. He's able to take my doodles and stunt gags and turn them into full-fledged concepts. Oh, did you want to see those doodles? They're in my safe. Okay, in my drawer—but if I had a safe, that's where they'd be. Point is, he understands his art, and he understands the costumers' art, the production designers' art—painting isn't supposed to be a collaborative art, and God knows Ryan spends more time locked in a tiny room by himself than most people. But he's more than a collaborator. He's a creator. A connector. A translator. He's the best at what he does, and he's humble about it. I guess what I'm leading to here is that I hate this guy. It's just obnoxious. Show off. But I owe him more than I can say (or type).

I swore I wouldn't put a cowl on Captain America ever again. The comic-book look hid all the best features of the particularly well-featured Chris Evans. Ryan heard that and locked himself in a room until he'd come up with a cowl that not only matched our childhood vision of the Captain, but looked great on Chris. He's a fanboy, after all. And he reminds me, time and again, why I am.

INTRODUCTION

AVENGERS RETURN!

"THEY'LL COME BACK...BECAUSE WE'LL NEED THEM TO."—NICK FURY

The man who assembled Earth's Mightiest Heroes to fend off the Chitauri invasion in *Marvel's The Avengers* wasn't just talking about a group of costumed champions eating shawarma together for the first time. As in most cases, Nick Fury would be proven right. Eventually.

But first, our heroes had their own journeys to make—and their own mistakes. At the end of *Marvel's The Avengers*, Tony Stark sees something in the wormhole to Chitauri space that rocks him to his core—so much so that his actions in Iron Man 3 lead him to question what it means to be Iron Man. In *Thor: The Dark World*, after losing his mother and putting his home at risk, Thor is forced to trust in Loki, the master of lies, to help him save both Asgard and Earth. Captain America, man out of time Steve Rogers, is convinced he can save a ghost—his best-friend-turned-assassin Bucky Barnes, aka the Winter Soldier. That faith nearly costs him his life. But perhaps more significantly, Steve discovers that Nick Fury's S.H.I.E.L.D. is not the protector of liberty he was led to believe, having been corrupted from within by the terrorist organization Hydra.

"They're abnormal people, and that's what's great about them. But it's also their weaknesses that spur them on to greatness." That's Joss Whedon's take—and he should know, having written and directed *Marvel's The Avengers*, the third-highest-grossing film worldwide to date. And now he's back to exploit those weaknesses in *Avengers: Age of Ultron*.

"We get to pull them apart as much as we put them together," Whedon says. "Obviously they're still the Avengers, and we hope that they'll save the day. But I think of movies like *The Empire Strikes Back* or *The Godfather: Part II*, where you get the same kind of movie, but something deeper, more personal. You get the same kind of movie that you loved, but you see a level beneath that, some sort of darkness."

By the time they come together to recover Loki's lost scepter in *Age of Ultron*, the Avengers already have survived the impossible—at a terrible cost to each of them. What now?

"Each of the individual Phase Two films helped to set the stage for *Avengers: Age of Ultron*," Executive Producer and Co-President of Marvel Studios Louis D'Esposito says. "In terms of global events and the overall paradigm of the MCU, clearly the events of *Captain America: The Winter Soldier* had the most impact on the Avengers as a team, but both the Iron Man and Thor films really helped establish where these characters are in terms of their individual stories and their places on the team. With *Iron Man 3*, you see the beginnings of Tony's obsession with protecting the world from what's out there. He saw something on the other side of that portal that profoundly changed him, and he's still coming to terms with that right up to the start of *Age of Ultron*. With Thor it was really about him finding his place in the universe and deciding he'd rather be a good man than a great king. He's got his own objectives, too, though. He still wants to know who controlled the would-be king.

"Now obviously *Guardians of the Galaxy* didn't include any of these characters," D'Esposito continues, "but in terms of expanding the universe and helping set up a great deal of the mythos that you see on screen in *Avengers: Age of Ultron* and will see as we go forward, *Guardians* was really an instrumental step. As with the first Avengers film, our goal is to make something that could be enjoyed by anybody, even if they've never seen another Marvel movie. But for those fans who are tracking all the moves, we think by the time they sit down to enjoy *Avengers: Age of Ultron*, they should have a good sense of where all the chess pieces stand."

"The biggest thing for Iron Man is he went through that portal to save the day at the end of the first *Avengers*. He saw what's out there. He knows that there are threats way bigger then we can handle," Executive Producer Jeremy Latcham says. "It's not the fear of the unknown. For Tony Stark, it's the fear of the known. He knows that there are bad, bad things, and they're five hundred feet above Stark Tower in a portal that can rip through space-time at any second, and that fear keeps him up at night, constantly tinkering, trying to improve—to protect Pepper, the life he's built, and the world, really."

In *Iron Man 3*, that fear—manifested in a series of panic attacks—drives Tony to the edge of recklessness, despite all his tinkering and improving.

It's not just Tony's past or his knowledge of what's to come that endangers him—it's what he's ignored. Like Aldrich Killian, the eventual founder of Advanced Idea Mechanics, at a 1999 New Year's Eve party. Fans of the comics instantly recognize the evil corporation A.I.M. and know this encounter will spell trouble—but the choice of talking to a hippie nerd or ringing in the New Year with a brilliant and sexy scientist looks like a no-brainer to Tony. It's a decision he'll

regret when the repercussions come rocketing through his Malibu home years later.

Killian's Extremis project—the one he pitched to Tony at the fateful '99 convention—uses a human bomb in a terrorist attack, nearly killing Tony's best friend, Happy Hogan. But Extremis is just the beginning of Tony's undoing. Perhaps it's the thought of nearly losing his friend, or the relentless threats by the Killian's puppet-terrorist Mandarin, or survivor's guilt and a bad case of PTSD from the attack by the Chitauri—but something snaps in Tony. Giving out his home address to the world, he invites the Mandarin's forces to attack him personally—and they do. The raid leaves Tony not only homeless, but also presumed dead.

Once again Tony is alone—stranded in rural Tennessee with a barely functional suit of armor. While not exactly a cave in the desert, Tony Stark has come full circle from *Iron Man*.

To save the day, Tony uses JARVIS to enact the "House Party Protocol," calling upon dozens of Iron Man suits that each operate independently. It's a huge leap in technology, inching further toward Artificial Intelligence.

"At the finale of *Iron Man 3*, in a big way it was JARVIS and the other suits that helped save the day," Producer Kevin Feige says. "Tony starts to realize: I don't have to be in the suit the whole time. In fact it might be more efficient if I'm not, so let me develop a system that can help do this for me."

And that's where we find him in *Age of Ultron*. "He is now funding the Avengers," Latcham elaborates. "He's funding this Iron Legion program, which is basically a proto AI program of these drone suits. He's looking for a solution that can keep the world safe. And he's carrying it all on his shoulders."

For a guy prone to panic attacks stemming from a paralyzing fear of an unknown threat that only he's seen, that may not be the best of ideas. But he's not the only guy who likes to fly solo.

The Avengers count among their ranks a demigod: Thor. And rightfully so, since it was the actions of another demigod—Loki—that brought them together. After his brother used the Tesseract and Chitauri scepter to open a portal between worlds, Thor decided it best for Loki to face Asgardian justice. What mortal would stand in the way of that logic?

Thor: The Dark World finds the Odinson challenged by uncomfortable choices that will only become more difficult in the face of escalating threats. "He's confronted by them everywhere," Executive Producer Victoria Alonso says. "He's such an honorable guy, and he's trying to do the right thing by everyone. His father has told him, 'You will be king. It's time.' But he doesn't feel he's ready. Although he wants to protect Asgard, he doesn't want to do it from the throne. He doesn't want any harm done to the people of Vanaheim, to Svartalfheim, or any other realm, including the human race. Specifically, he doesn't want any harm done to Jane Foster. And that protective nature keeps him from accepting the love of fellow Asgardian Sif."

The death of Frigga, Thor's mother, and the arrival of a common foe force Thor to seek an ally in Loki. Remembering their childhood and that spark of good he saw in his adoptive brother, Thor tries to believe he can rely on Loki, the only person who has lost as much as he. But like Tony Stark's declaration in *Iron Man 3*, Thor's invitation to evil could be his downfall.

"It's Thor's love for Jane and her life being in danger by being possessed by the Aether that causes him to bring her to Asgard. And her possession of the Aether is what allows Malekith to invade Asgard, putting everyone else in danger and leading to the sacrifice of Frigga," Alonso says. "Now with their mother dead, we're on this journey with the brothers—the two most unlikely people to be by each other's side—who have to get through it together, united by the common love of their mother to save the day, and fight not each other but also Malekith."

As in all great epics, the world is saved—but not without sacrifices. Loki seemingly dies to save his brother. Thor returns to Asgard and declines Odin's second offer of the throne. In the greatest lie of all, Loki still lives and has stolen Odin's form. The unknowing Thor chooses to split his time on Earth and Asgard, burdened by guilt, yet comforted by Jane Foster's love. Will it be enough?

Unlike Thor and Tony Stark, Steve Rogers seems ready for action—and the 21st century—in *Captain America: The Winter Soldier*.

But Steve's past won't stay buried. Where the others take on old enemies, Captain America faces his long-lost best friend—now a nearly indestructible assassin. And just when Steve turns to the one person he trusts, Nick Fury, he finds that even S.H.I.E.L.D. has become a lie.

"The comics had both the Winter Soldier storyline in *Captain America* and elements of a corrupt part of S.H.I.E.L.D.

another series," Feige explains. "We thought it would be the perfect moment to combine those two here. We'd been building to this, with S.H.I.E.L.D. as a 'Can you really trust these guys' agency, and even had the Avengers investigating that in the first Avengers film. So now, just when you think you can trust them, we pull the rug out from under the audience."

Latcham elaborates: "The revelation that Hydra was actually S.H.I.E.L.D. was there from the beginning. The choice to reveal it here in *Captain America* was perfect not just because it was the last movie of Phase Two before *Age of Ultron*, but also because it leaves Cap and Black Widow—and Falcon, who we meet here—out in the cold. And if that wasn't enough, we 'kill' Fury for most of the movie."

Cap has no one left to turn to but a fellow Avenger and a vet-turned-hero in the fan-favorite Falcon, who comic readers know becomes a partner as synonymous with Captain America as Bucky. With S.H.I.EL.D. dismantled, Cap is forced to face not only the demons of his own past—his feeling he failed Bucky and is responsible for the killer the Winter Soldier has become—but also the all-powerful beast that is Hydra. And he and his few allies must do it alone.

In a pivotal showdown, Cap attempts to reason with Winter Soldier by forcing him to remember the past. Steve hopes to convince Bucky he isn't merely the Winter Soldier, but a good man who can find redemption—and he doesn't have to do it alone. The former comrades-in-arms deliver blow after blow, physically and emotionally driving home this point, until both are near death.

In the end, Steve is left unsure whether he's gotten through, whether it's Winter Soldier or Bucky Barnes who has survived and—once again—disappeared. Nick Fury, too, has disappeared, erasing all traces of his existence. S.H.I.E.L.D. is nothing more than a handful of faithful agents ready to reclaim the name from Hydra. Captain America reports only to himself now, to his country and—most important—to his allies.

And so the call to assemble again goes out...

Kevin Feige says it best: "Making the *Avengers* films is just plain fun. Get these great actors together who had a great time on the first one, who have their own experiences filming their own movies, and bring them all back together. That's half of your magic right there. And Joss's dialogue, the way Joss can bring those characters to life—I could just watch the Avengers sit in a room and talk for two hours. I think a lot of people in the audience could, too. But we have to do more than that, of course, and you need a reason to have them all come together."

And what is that reason? "Tony Stark, in his effort to be a better man outside the suit, unlocks something that he should have never unlocked," Latcham explains. "He pulls open Pandora's box. And out comes Ultron."

But why Ultron now? Simple: This isn't just the climax of Phase 2 of the Marvel Cinematic Universe. Ultron—or some form of him—is a real-world concern.

"Ultron has been around 40, 50 years in the comic books, but is more relevant and more frightening than ever today, when we all have in our pockets technology that tells people where we are, what we're doing. And we're happy to do that, by the way," Feige says. "We all know that there are people listening, there are people watching. Now take that idea and think: What if people could control that—and what if that control went another few steps?"

The seeds of Artificial Intelligence have permeated the Marvel Cinematic Universe since *Iron Man's* introduction of JARVIS. The theme appears again in *Captain America: The Winter Soldier*, when Steve encounters the programmed consciousness of long-dead Hydra scientist Arnim Zola. Kevin Feige explains, "We wanted to see the notion that robotics and Artificial Intelligence as it is in the real world exists in the Marvel Cinematic Universe at a believable level before we took it to the Ultron extreme."

With such a real-world and well-seeded threat, and our heroes each facing crossroads in their own films, surely coming together as a team will solve everything. Right?

Not so fast, says Joss Whedon. "What's exciting about a sequel like this is an element of 'We put them together, lets tear them apart,'" he explains. "Once you have your 'origin of a team' story, you want the next story to be really about, 'Well can that paradigm sustain? Can these people actually stand each other once they have digested their shawarma?' It is interesting because we see a lot of new loyalties, and friendships, and conflicts. We get to get further into the heads of all the characters and see why they work as a team and why they don't, and the mistakes they are going to make and the solutions they are going to come up with."

One fact is certain: It's going to take a lot more than shawarma to survive this new Age.

Ryan Meinerding concept art.

Bryan Andrews storyboard.

Previs template.

Previs background.

Preliminary film look.

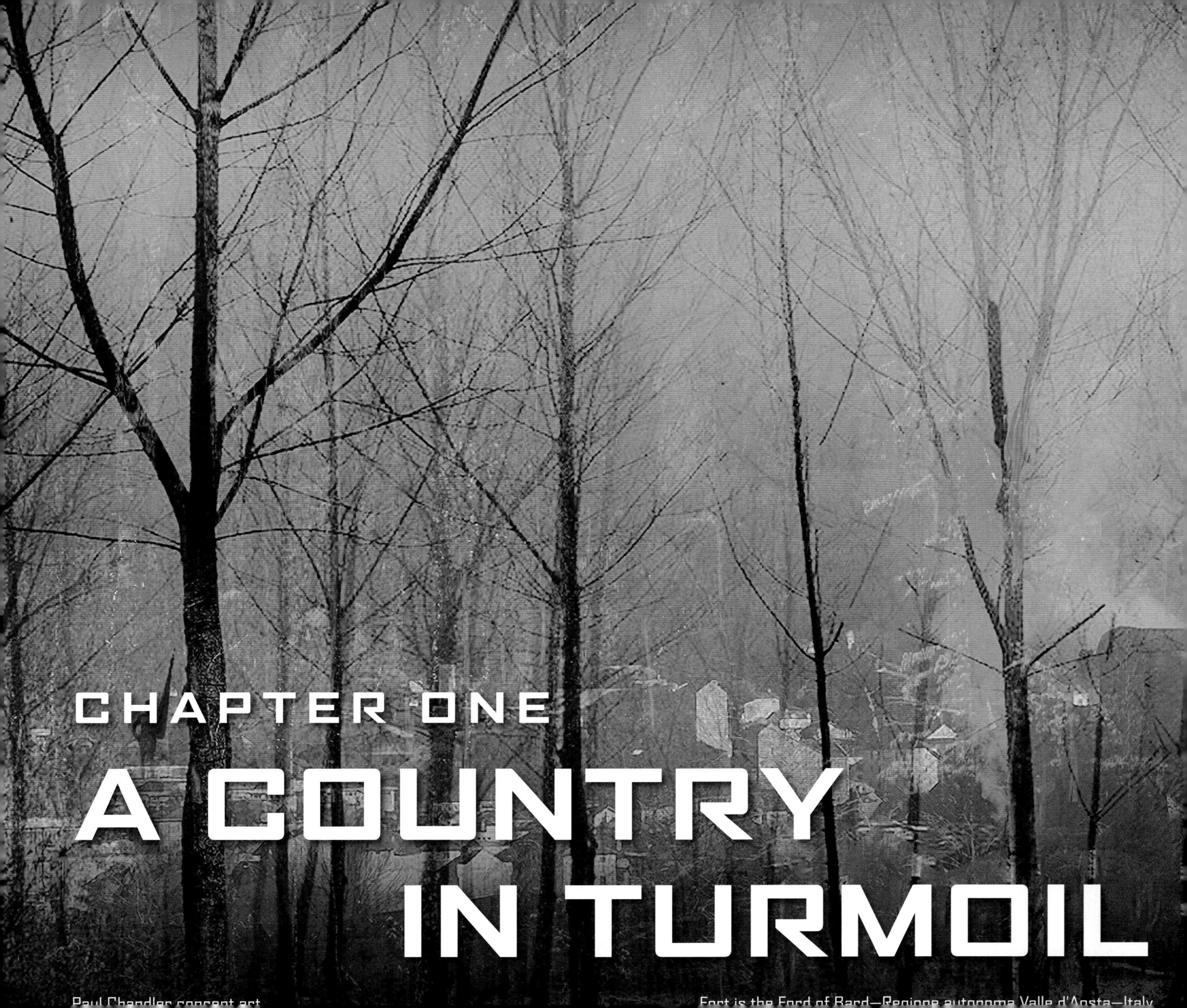

CHAPTER ONE

A COUNTRY IN TURMOIL

Paul Chandler concept art

Fort is the Ford of Bard—Regione autonoma Valle d'Aosta—Italy

A snowy mountainside complete with a towering, medieval fortress set against the backdrop of the rising sun. Majestic, peaceful—until the Avengers come bursting through the trees. "The idea of doing a whole recruitment scenario at the beginning of the film and starting with 'We gotta gather the team' seemed like ground we covered in the first movie. So the first frame of the film is the whole team, BOOM, coming at the camera together—working together as a well-oiled machine. And that is a super-exciting, powerful way to start the movie. It just announces to fans: This is an Avengers film, they are a super hero team, and they're operating at the top of their game," Executive Producer Jeremy Latcham says. "They have a mission—they're cleaning up S.H.I.E.L.D.'s messes. In particular for the opening in Sokovia, they're trying to find Loki's scepter. There's something different about the force they're up against this time: The tanks aren't quite conventional, there are soldiers with these weird Chitauri power suits, and they start looking around going, 'I think we might have found it this time.'"

The fortress itself was a happenstance find for filmmakers. Production Designer Charlie Wood worked with the Locations Department to scour the globe for a suitable fit. "I kid you not, we looked at 600 different locations at least before landing on Fort Bard," Wood recalls. "When I saw the photos originally, I couldn't believe we were looking at a location I wasn't already familiar with in Europe. I looked at it and said, 'Why haven't I seen this in other movies? Look how it sits in that valley, hidden in that gorgeous mountain range.' It was perfect."

SOKOVIAN FORTRESS

The fortress in Sokovia is a front for an underground Hydra base overseen by the infamous Baron Strucker. It stands as an imposing structure in architectural magnitude and geographical placement, two characteristics Charlie Wood knew were needed for a powerful opening sequence. "Ninety-nine percent of the locations we were looking at were wrong—they started to have a very Errol Flynn vibe to them, the danger being that having a stereotypical castle could almost become comedic," Wood says. "The location we ended up finding was brilliant as it wasn't a museum, it doesn't have that feeling to it—it really is a fortress. The location also served the story perfectly: It was alpine, it was cold, it presented a unique approach for the characters, it overlooks the city, and we were able to film completely practically there except for all of the snow we brought in."

Paul Chandler concept art.

Fort is the Ford of Bard—Regione autonoma Valle d'Aosta—Italy.

Fort is the Ford of Bard—Regione autonoma Valle d'Aosta—Italy.

Paul Chandler concept art.

"It's important to remember that these are concept paintings trying to establish a visual language that work for the film: the right sense of place, the right architectural notes, the right color palette—the difference between a cool gray, an ochre or blue brick can make a surprisingly big difference—the right lighting, the right proportions, textures, etc. Sometimes even the right time of day. There are many visual plates to spin simultaneously," Concept Artist Bob Cheshire says.

Bob Cheshire concept art

Fort is the Ford of Bard—Regione autonoma Valle d'Aosta—Italy.

IRON MAN MARK 43

The Mark 43 armor carries the same intricate design lines and breakups as the Mark 42 from *Iron Man 3*. Head of Visual Development Ryan Meinerding, who designed the Mark 42 with Phil Saunders for *Iron Man 3*, began experimenting on new color breakups for the Mark 43. "The heavy use of gold we brought in for the Mark 42 was a strong choice and made sense for *Iron Man 3*," he says, "but for *Avengers: Age of Ultron*, we decided to reintroduce the red and bring back the more iconic Iron Man visage."

Ryan Meinerding concept art.

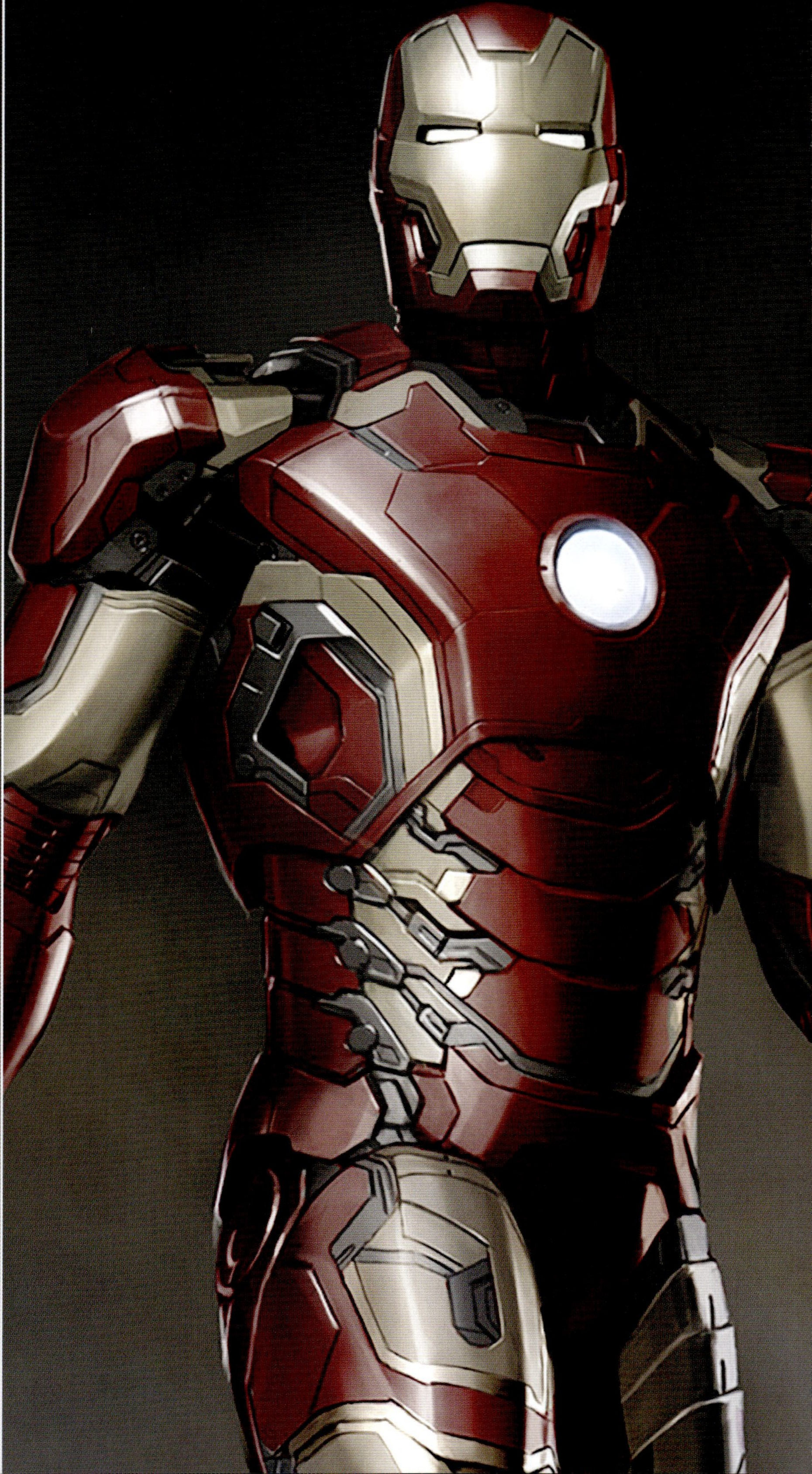

Ryan Meinerding concept art.

CAPTAIN AMERICA

"The *Captain America: The Winter Soldier* stealth-suit design worked so well because it was Captain America working for S.H.I.E.L.D.—he was doing black ops, or rather, things he may not have been comfortable with. As far as design goes, it made us subdue the stars and stripes, subdue elements of his history, and find ways of making a traditional Captain America suit work under astringently tactical guidelines," Ryan Meinerding says. "In *Avengers: Age of Ultron*, we find Cap is wholeheartedly the leader of the Avengers with the fall of S.H.I.E.L.D. in the previous film. We tried to take a lot of the cues from the stealth costume and still apply it to his new suit, but really focus on making him a leader of the Avengers and not just an agent of S.H.I.E.L.D. This meant bringing the stars and stripes back—similar to the stealth suit—keeping it tactical, as well as applying a darker blue than we used in the first Avengers film."

Ryan Meinerding concept art.

Ryan Meinerding concept art.

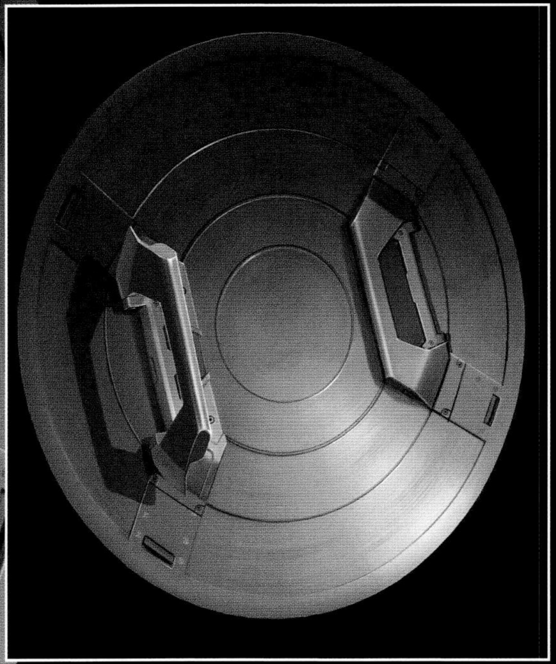

Ryan Meinerding concept art.

"When Joss Whedon watched *Captain America: The Winter Soldier*—there's a scene in there where Cap kicks up the shield, and it attaches to his arm. The idea behind this image sort of inspired the idea of, 'What if there weren't straps? What if it was attached magnetically?' It would not only offer an innovative visual, but also allow for different and new actions with the shield," Meinerding says. "We began conceptualizing this idea and came up with two magnetic connections on the back of his wrist and the back of his forearm that are actually visible on the costume. We also added a foldout handle so if you wanted to have him pick up or whirl the shield around in a new way, there's actually a metal handle that folds over one of the magnetic action points, as well."

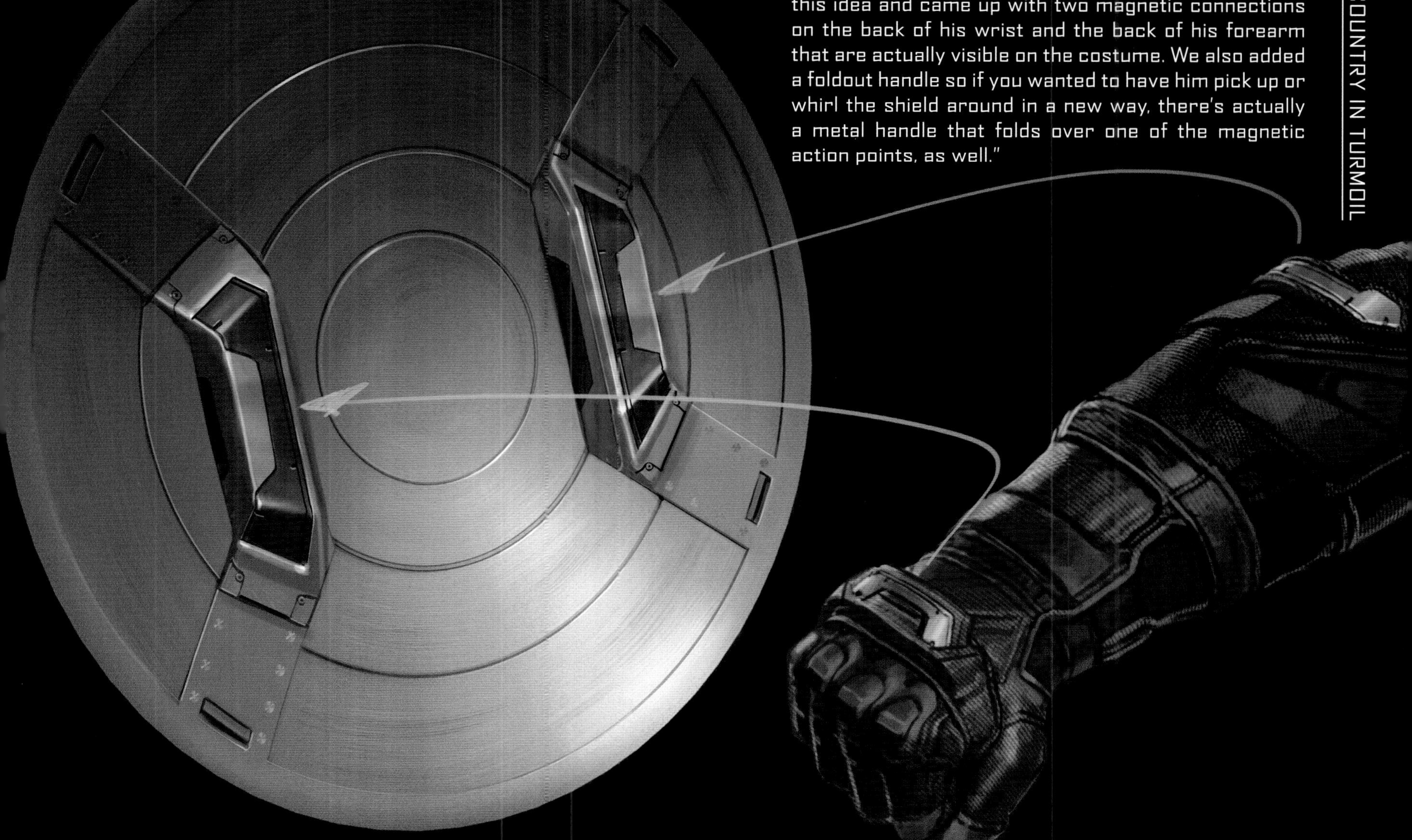

THOR

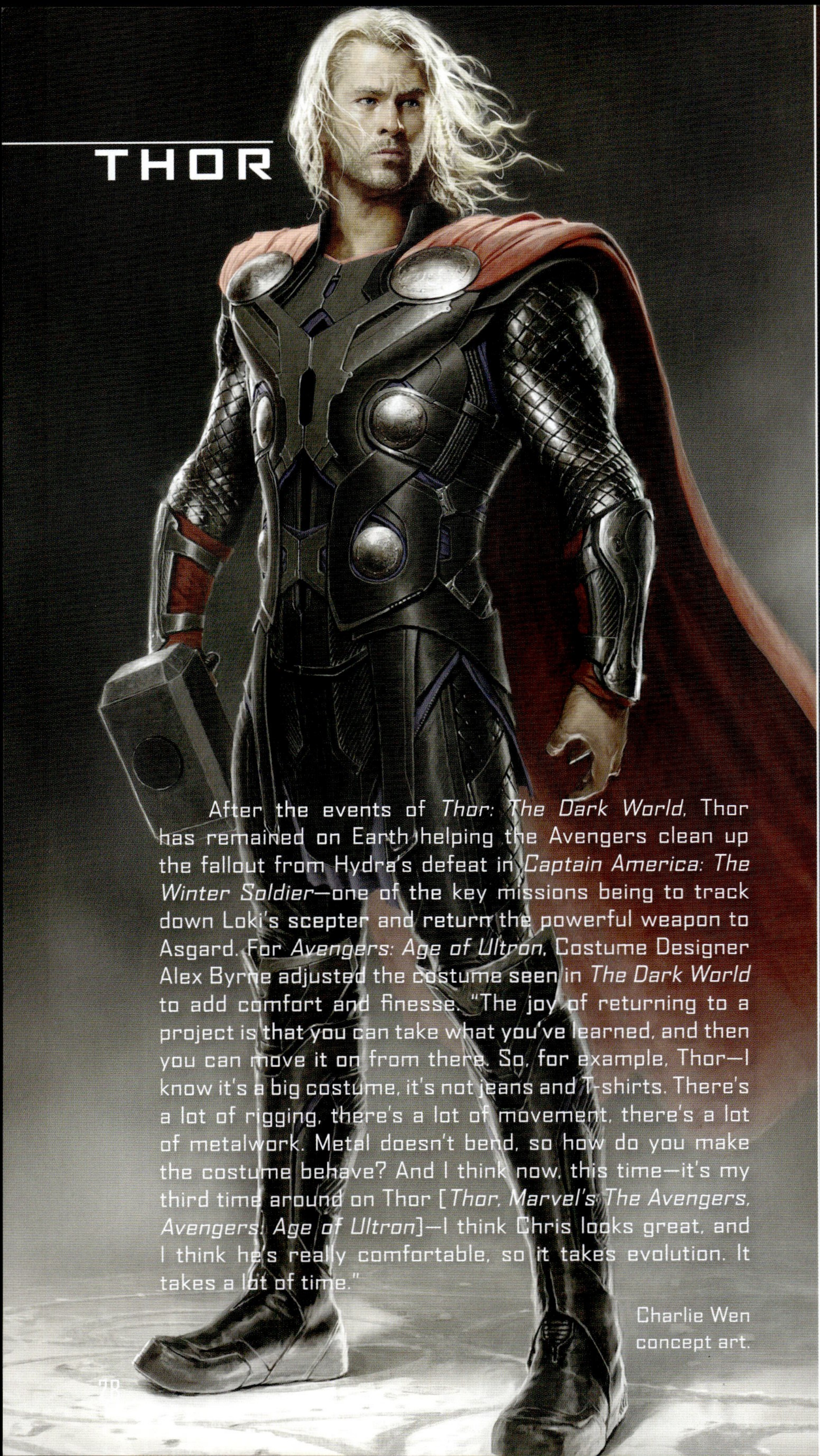

After the events of *Thor: The Dark World*, Thor has remained on Earth helping the Avengers clean up the fallout from Hydra's defeat in *Captain America: The Winter Soldier*—one of the key missions being to track down Loki's scepter and return the powerful weapon to Asgard. For *Avengers: Age of Ultron*, Costume Designer Alex Byrne adjusted the costume seen in *The Dark World* to add comfort and finesse. "The joy of returning to a project is that you can take what you've learned, and then you can move it on from there. So, for example, Thor—I know it's a big costume, it's not jeans and T-shirts. There's a lot of rigging, there's a lot of movement, there's a lot of metalwork. Metal doesn't bend, so how do you make the costume behave? And I think now, this time—it's my third time around on Thor [*Thor*, *Marvel's The Avengers*, *Avengers: Age of Ultron*]—I think Chris looks great, and I think he's really comfortable, so it takes evolution. It takes a lot of time."

Charlie Wen concept art.

Jack Dudman concept art.

Jack Dudman
concept art.

HULK

Captain America wasn't the only hero for whom Ryan Meinerding was developing a new look. Hulk comes storming into the film with a new pair of Stark-issued pants, specially tailored for Bruce Banner—and his monstrous counterpart. "Honestly, the stretchy pants came from Joss Whedon. He wanted to do it on *Marvel's The Avengers*, but we just couldn't do it—there wasn't really a place where he could have obtained them in the movie," Meinerding says. "So now that he's an official member of the Avengers team and Tony could help him develop a pair of pants that wouldn't rip when he became the Hulk, that would probably be one of the first things Banner would ask for. In the design, we treaded a few lines—trying to make it feel like he was a super hero; making them feel like they fit with the Hulk, but not feel like generic sportswear or active wear, which was challenging because inherently they would have to be some kind of spandex material."

Ryan Meinerding concept art.

Ryan Meinerding concept art.

HAWKEYE

"Joss Whedon liked Hawkeye's hero costume we designed for the first Avengers film, so we didn't mess with that," Concept Artist Andy Park says. "But this time, the mandate was to give him a sleek, new jacket he could wear as he faced colder climates during his missions. Unlike Thor, Hawkeye doesn't have the ability to call on metal chicklets for warmth!"

After the concept was set, Alex Byrne set out to bring the jacket to life. "It was a difficult one, even just being a jacket. There's a limit to the number of shapes that work, and it could have gotten very cliché . So we began with the design and just started building it, finding the materials, looking at what worked and what didn't," Byrne describes. "Even though it looks relatively simple in black, the jacket itself has a hundred and forty-five pattern pieces. Just to cut out the pieces of that jacket takes one cutter two days—so it's very, very labor-intensive. You know, there are high-tech methods that we can use—but at the end of the day, these garments are sewn, and sewing is a hand-finished job."

Andy Park concept art.

Andy Park concept art.

"Everyone loved the bow, but they just felt perhaps we should change the color of it. So instead of it being black so it just goes into the background, we bring color into it. We've done a very subdued maroon, which blends in with the costume," Propmaster Barry Gibbs says. "Hawkeye does exactly the same thing: He carries a small bow, flicks it out, and it becomes a larger version. However, we have streamlined it a little bit and added a few more features, so it has an infrared- and sonic-sighting device, but still retains the features of the buttons that dial in the arrow tip."

Josh Nizzi concept art.

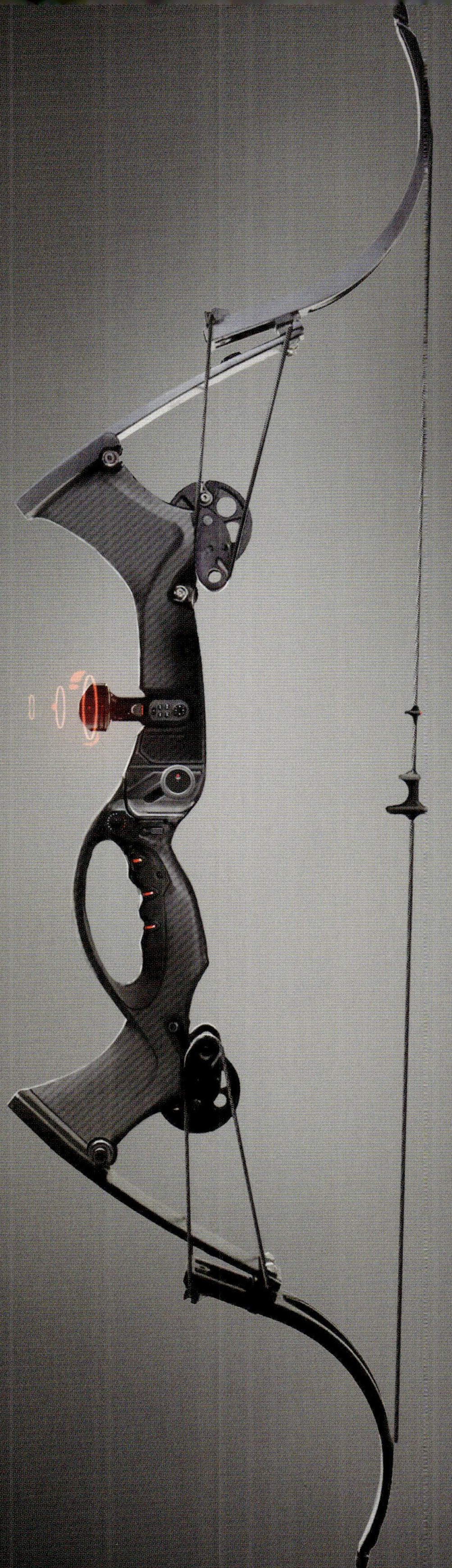

Josh Nizzi concept art.

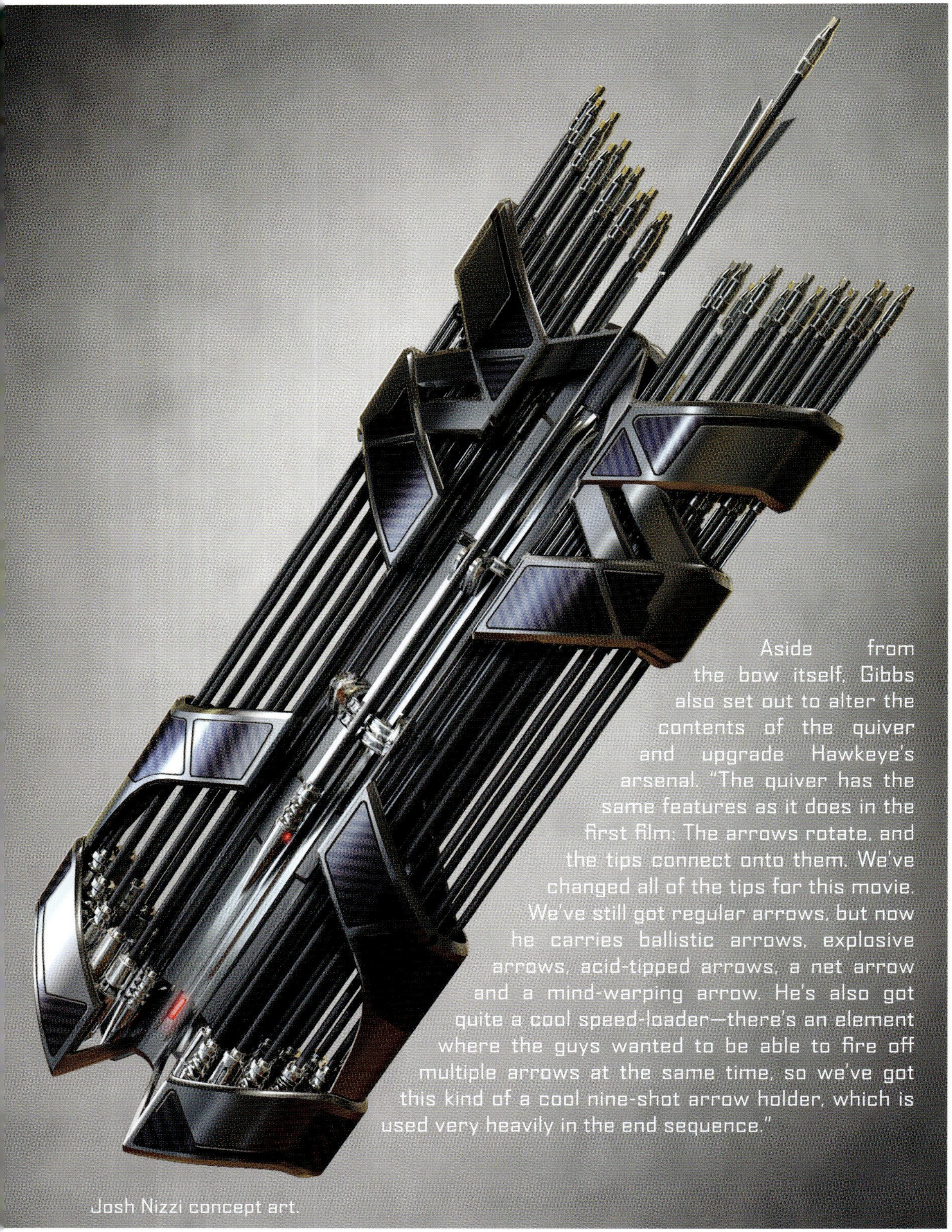

Aside from the bow itself, Gibbs also set out to alter the contents of the quiver and upgrade Hawkeye's arsenal. "The quiver has the same features as it does in the first film: The arrows rotate, and the tips connect onto them. We've changed all of the tips for this movie. We've still got regular arrows, but now he carries ballistic arrows, explosive arrows, acid-tipped arrows, a net arrow and a mind-warping arrow. He's also got quite a cool speed-loader—there's an element where the guys wanted to be able to fire off multiple arrows at the same time, so we've got this kind of a cool nine-shot arrow holder, which is used very heavily in the end sequence."

Josh Nizzi concept art.

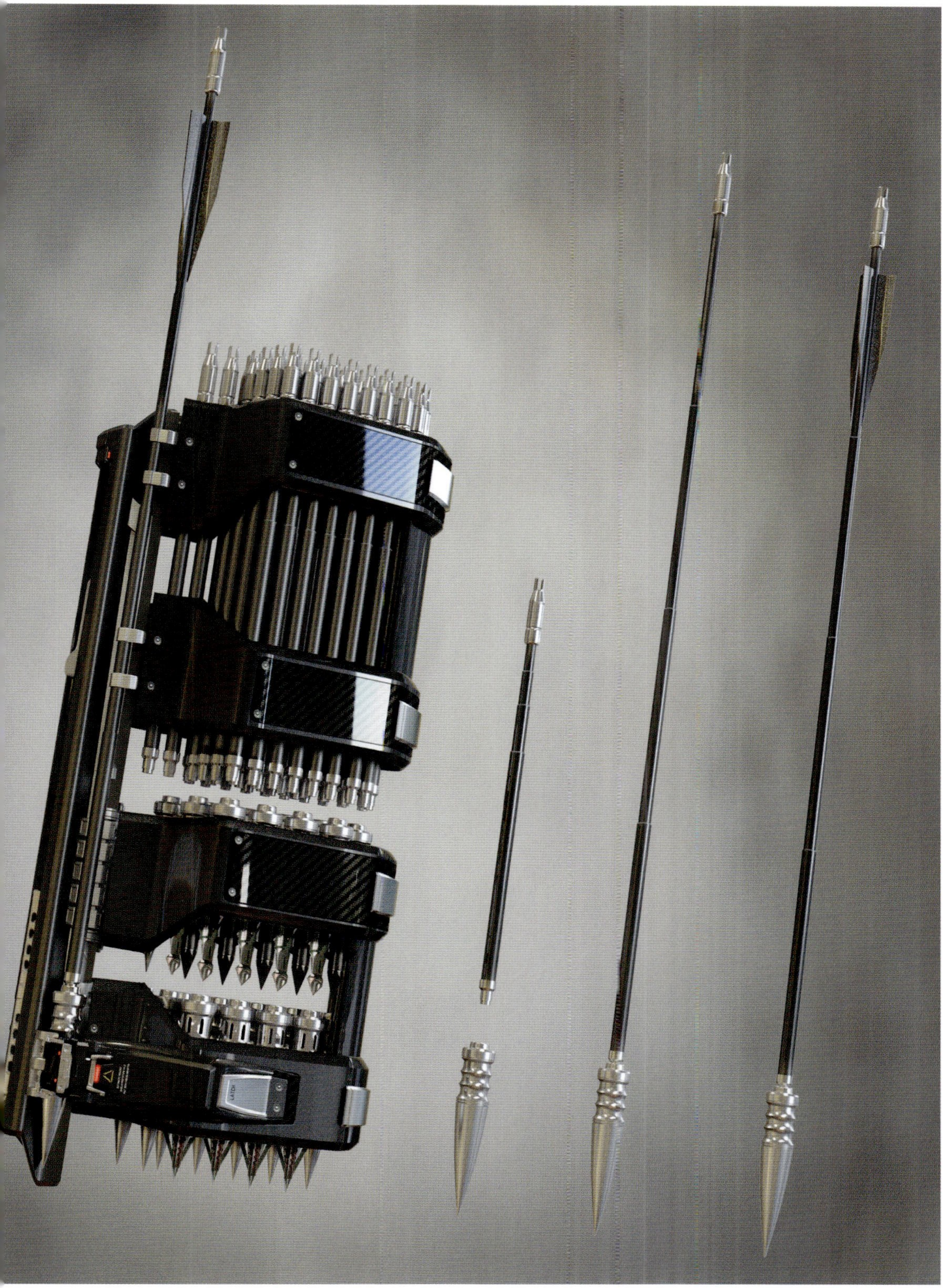

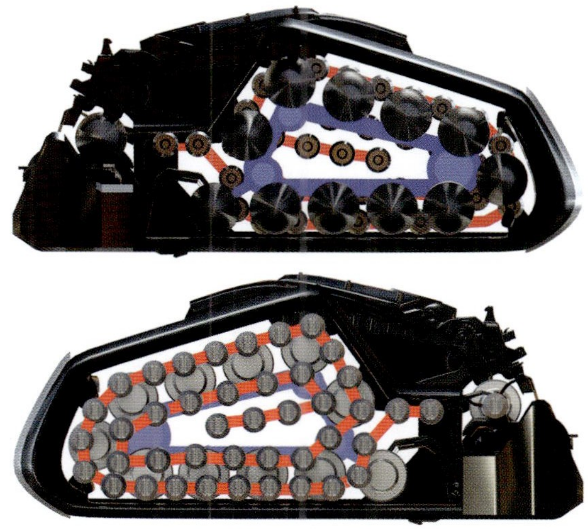

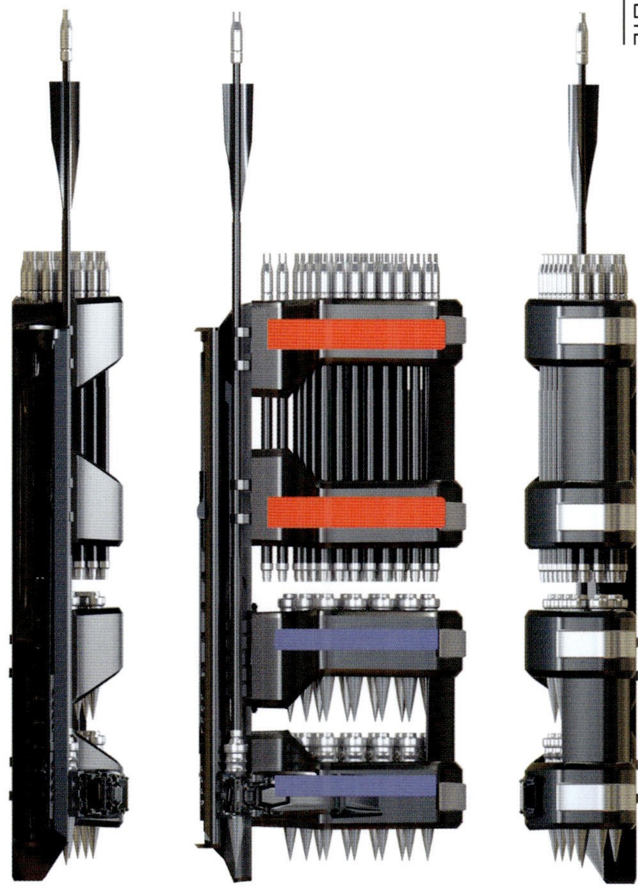

Josh Nizzi concept art.

STANDARD TIP / "THROUGH THE BULLET HOLE TIP"

DRILL TIP

EXPLOSIVE TIP

ACID TIP

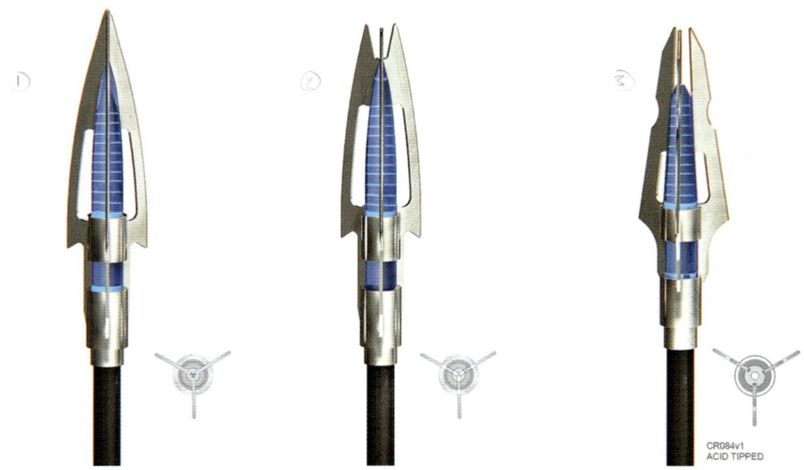

Chris Rosewarne concept art.

NET TIP

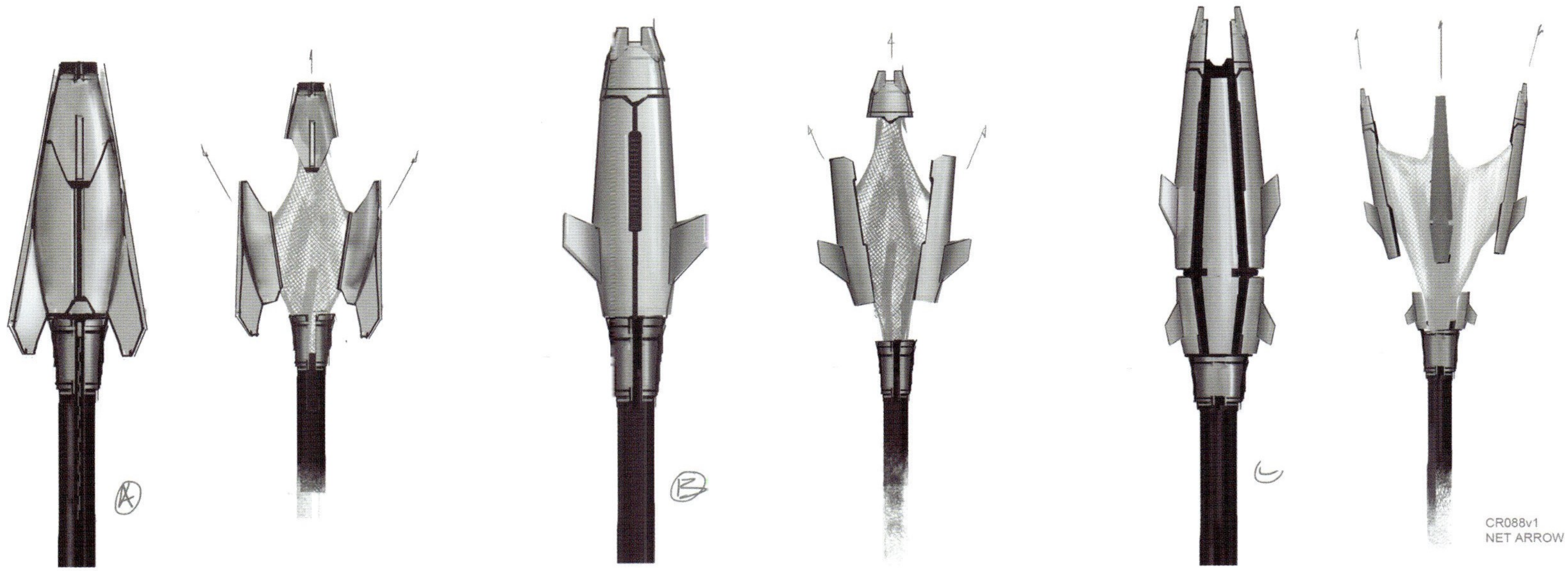

BLUNT TIP

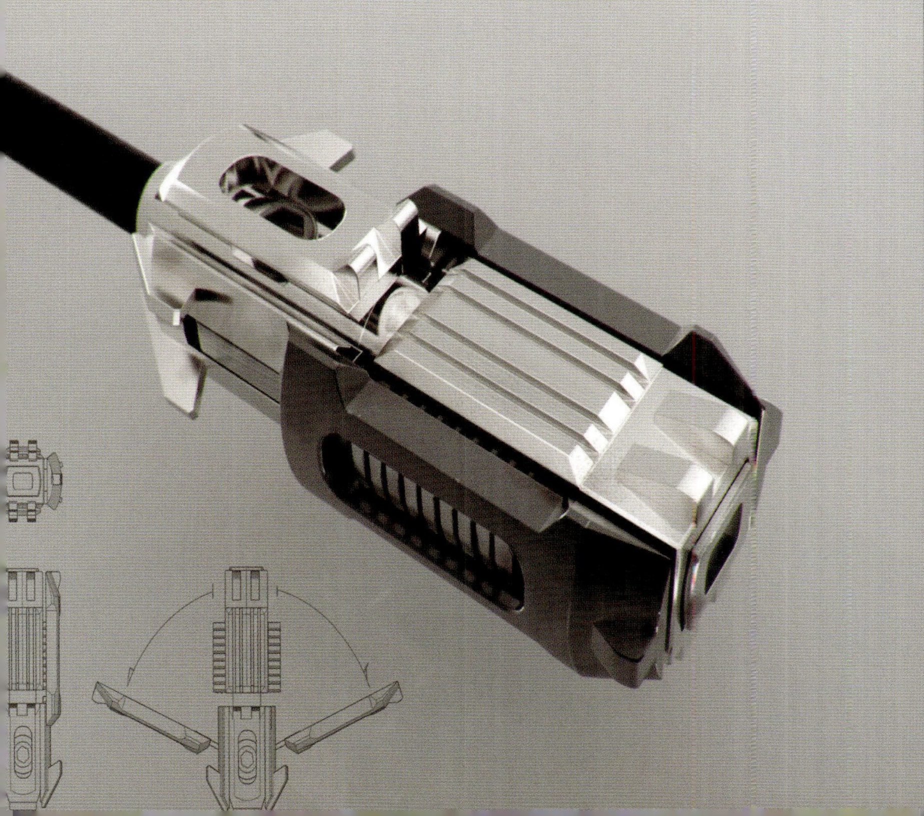

Chris Rosewarne concept art.

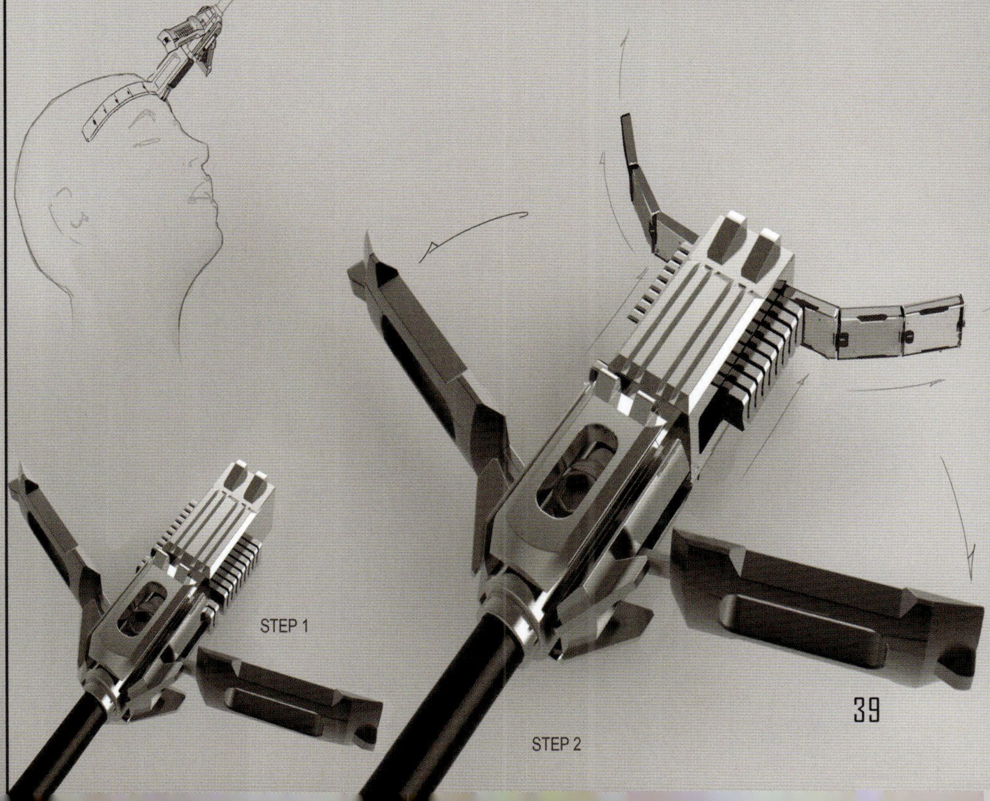

BLACK WIDOW

Andy Park was anxious to redesign Black Widow for *Avengers: Age of Ultron*. "I've had the honor to design Black Widow's look in all of her appearances except for *Iron Man 2*. It's a fairly consistent design due to her iconic look in the comics," Park recalls. "The idea behind this particular suit was to go more super hero. We wanted to give her obvious upgrades with the 'Widow stings' coursing throughout the suit to be utilized in hand-to-hand combat—and possibly for long-range combat, as well. Her gauntlets are far more advanced this time around, as well. Her character is more of a femme fatale, so keeping the rest of the suit as minimal as possible is really the way to go."

Andy Park concept art.

One of the more flashy elements of the new design was a "powered-up" mode, as noted by the lights that run from Black Widow's ankles up through the suit. "For the first time, we had a team of electricians in our department," Alex Byrne says. "There is an operating board that goes with her costume because she has different modes of 'off' and 'standby' and then 'fully powered-up.' In previous Widow costumes, we used a pleasing sort of stretch suit that could breathe much easier. Now, the electrical cables obviously don't stretch, so the making method of that had to change completely. That big rethink led us to a completely new method of using fiber optics."

Andy Park concept art.

Andy Park concept art.

Black Widow expands her arsenal in *Avengers: Age of Ultron* with a set of batons that accentuate her abilities in hand-to-hand combat. The design, originally created by Andy Park, was further detailed by Concept Artist Chris Rosewarne. "In Park's concept, the batons appeared to be more of a blunt-force weapon, so I developed them to be used like a set of Kali sticks with the potential to emit an electric shock that could either help stun or just add extra punch to a blow. I imagined that the black handle and black machined casings down the stem were the electrically insulated areas—you wanted to avoid touching elsewhere! It definitely looked like a weapon that needed extreme skills to brandish."

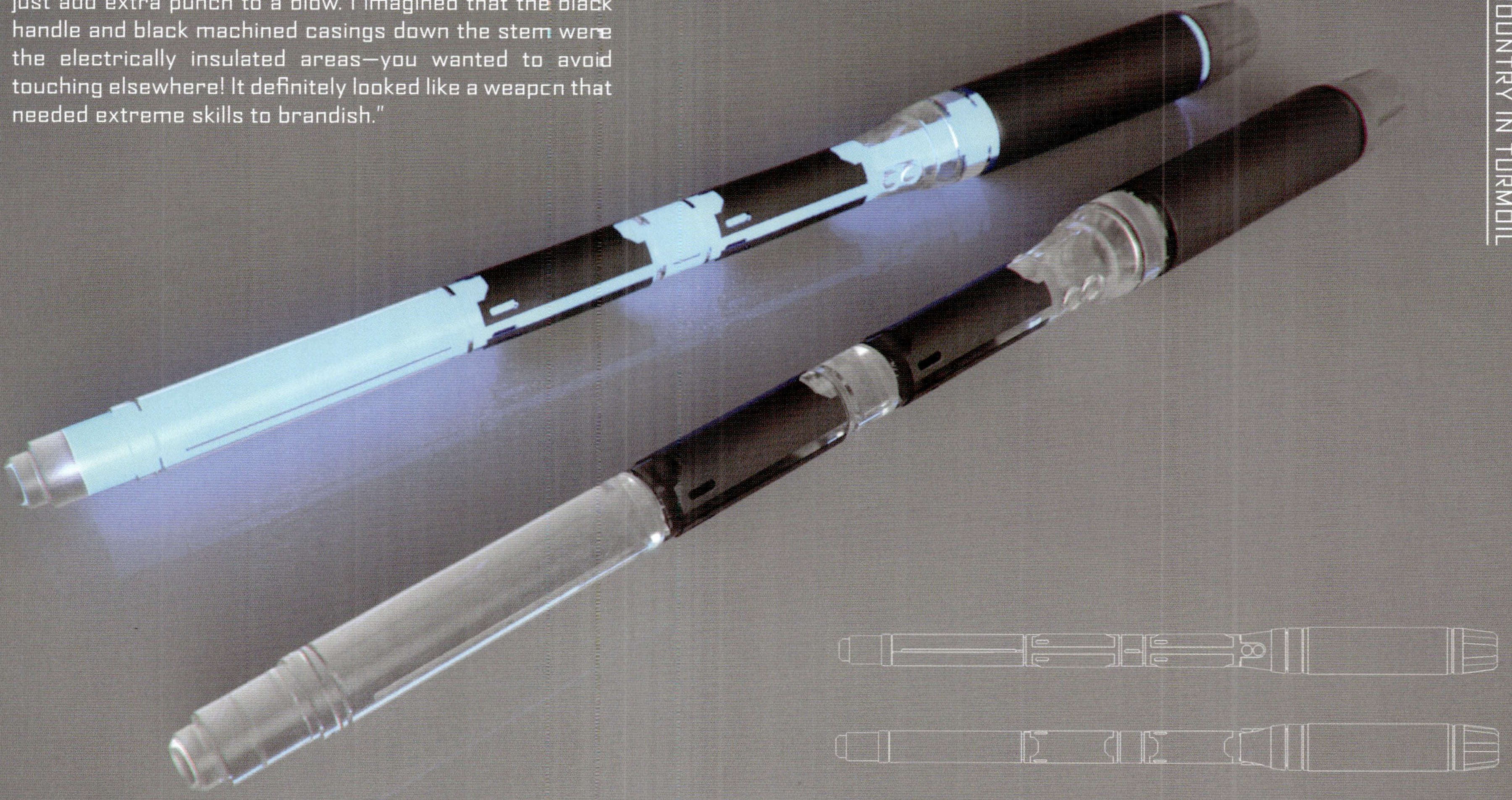

Chris Rosewarne concept art.

THE IRON LEGION

Rodney Fuentebella concept art.

"The concept behind the Iron Legion comes from Tony's prolific experimentation building suits for unique situations," Concept Artist Josh Nizzi says, adding that Stark is trying to help keep the world from spiraling into chaos any way he can. Executive Producer Louis D'Esposito elaborates, "As we began thinking about how the Avengers are seen in the world, the idea came up that as they are deploying across the globe on these missions like you see in the beginning of the film, they may need some help. So the idea of these peaceful, non-threatening drones was really a natural extension of that. Joss Whedon's ability to weave them so perfectly into the narrative of the film is what makes him a great writer."

Josh Nizzi concept art.

Josh Nizzi concept art.

Concept Artist Rodney Fuentebella was one of the many illustrators attempting to crack the Iron Legion's look. "The real challenge came from trying to find the blend of making it feel like an autonomous Stark-tech drone, but also having the appearance of a distinct and offensive Iron Man armor—all without a pilot inside," Fuentebella describes. Concept Artist Josh Herman also aided in the early designs. "I tried keeping the mechanics exposed, especially in the joints, to show that there was no way for a person to fit inside the suit, as well as moving the eyes slots on the helmet to a non-human proportion, or removing them entirely," Herman says. "Shifting away from red and gold also helped to push it further away from an Iron Man suit that Tony would wear, and using neutral colors made them read more military and less flash."

Rodney Fuentebella concept art.

Rodney Fuentebella concept art.

Rodney Fuentebella concept art.

Josh Nizzi concept art.

Josh Herman concept art.

STRUCKER'S ARMY

Strucker's army blends arctic military wear with stolen Chitauri technology. Exo-suits grant Strucker's soldiers superhuman abilities made possible by alien science. The Chitauri tech provides a vast source of power, durable materials and potent energy weapons. "The mechanics of the suit are based on modern military research, which allows the soldier to have full range of motion while increasing strength and protecting bones," Josh Nizzi explains. "The suit is controlled by a neural interface that gets input directly from the brain. The suit also has energy-discharge capability on each fist, enabling it to deliver powerful blows."

Josh Nizzi concept art.

"The design was challenging in many ways because exo-suits have become so popular in film and video games," Nizzi continues. "The design needed to have the same functionality and interesting technology as other popular designs, but stand out as something belonging to the Marvel Universe. Concepts explored mixing the Chitauri technology with Hydra design elements in the age of Iron Man. Eventually, we established the backstory that scientists were just starting to understand the alien technology so they used it as a way to amplify modern cutting-edge designs. This helped to direct the final design by having modern technology as the starting point and augmenting it with Chitauri."

Josh Nizzi concept art.

"It was a lot of prototyping, a lot of trying them on the guys in our department who would clunk around and say, 'This works, this doesn't work.' FBFX did a great job making a very lightweight, moveable exo-suit that contained almost all of the elements from the original design," Alex Byrne says. "It wasn't without its challenges, though, especially with finding ways to integrate the tech practically. A human body moves in a certain way—our joints only move in certain directions—so the practical aspects really guide everything you do on this."

Josh Nizzi concept art.

Josh Nizzi concept art.

Soldiers in exo-suits aren't the only ground troops Strucker has at his command. Costume Illustrator Jack Dudman's design for Hydra's makeshift army was inspired by previous Marvel films. "The idea was that there was a general uniform, but discipline was lacking. These were the mixed remnants of Hydra, gathered from all over—a force that had once been more organized, but with the previous events had become almost mercenaries in their behavior," Dudman says.

Jack Dudman concept art.

Jack Dudman concept art

"The Chitauri guns were a hybrid mix of existing weapons that were enhanced to fire the powerful blasts of Chitauri weaponry," Chris Rosewarne says. "Joss Whedon had chosen three different types of assault weapons that I could begin working on. I pulled some of the textures and materials over from the Chitauri tech in the first Avengers film and began to make them look more machined, like the tech had been stripped down and repurposed within manmade components that could work over the chassis of existing weapons. The look was pure hard-surface technology with subtle indicators of its alien origin—gold-plating conducers and visible blue energy glowing from within the guns."

Chris Rosewarne concept art.

Chris Rosewarne concept art.

When the Avengers arrive in Sokovia, they come face to face with more than just ground troops. Tearing their way through the snowy forest are hybrid tanks that radiate an air of both military and Chitauri weaponry. "We looked at many different types of tanks," Chris Rosewarne says. "Charlie Wood was very keen to make them look fully loaded with cool tech, reactive armor panels, electrical-jamming equipment, various camera and sensor arrays and additional weapons that made the tanks look capable of taking on anything or anyone!"

Chris Rosewarne concept art.

Chris Rosewarne concept art.

Chris Rosewarne concept art.

Chris Rosewarne concept art.

Chris Rosewarne concept art.

If the tanks and exo-suits weren't enough, Strucker also employs antiaircraft guns refined with Chitauri tech. "The antiaircraft guns were a larger assimilation of the same approach I took with the Chitauri guns—the blending of alien weaponry into manmade components that could harness the Chitauri power," Rosewarne describes. "The barrels were very similar to those on the tanks, conveying the look of a weapon that has to channel heavy-caliber blasts. I looked at both older and modern versions of antiaircraft guns. I experimented with a different array of barrels—something that was more reminiscent of World War II—and I liked the heavier look of the designs. But I also saw how modern antiaircraft guns were put together, with less armor and more mobility. In the end, I took the older, heavier, industrial aesthetic as the weight it gave to the silhouette of the design just made it look like it could really punch hard!"

Chris Rosewarne concept art.

BARON STRUCKER

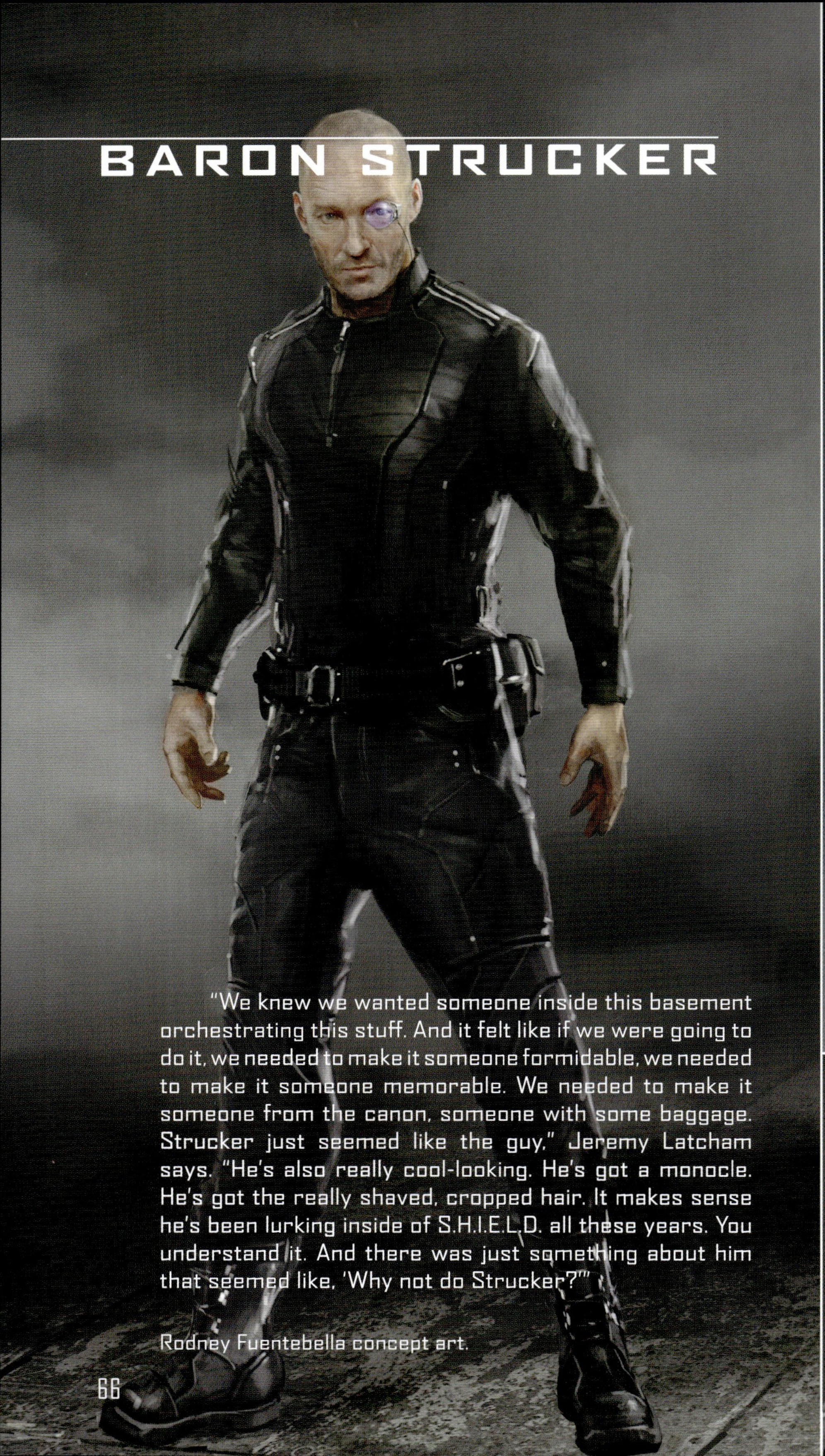

"We knew we wanted someone inside this basement orchestrating this stuff. And it felt like if we were going to do it, we needed to make it someone formidable, we needed to make it someone memorable. We needed to make it someone from the canon, someone with some baggage. Strucker just seemed like the guy," Jeremy Latcham says. "He's also really cool-looking. He's got a monocle. He's got the really shaved, cropped hair. It makes sense he's been lurking inside of S.H.I.E.L.D. all these years. You understand it. And there was just something about him that seemed like, 'Why not do Strucker?'"

Rodney Fuentebella concept art.

Josh Nizzi concept art.

Rodney Fuentebella concept art.

Rodney Fuentebella concept art.

WEAPON STORAGE FACILITY

Pete Thompson concept art.

COMMAND CENTER

The majority of the interiors of Strucker's base were shot on location in Italy, with virtual set extensions added in postproduction. The foundation for those virtual sets comes from the combined efforts of the Art Department and the Visual Effects team. "There are different stages to creating concepts. Sometimes, later on in the process, visuals are required that combine existing sets with virtual spaces and models designed by art directors," Concept Artist Bob Cheshire explains. "The visuals join these up for everybody to visually communicate how, for example, the existing set will look with the virtual set added on. This can help everybody involved, but can also support the actors sometimes when confronted with a green-screen extension to a set to help illustrate what they're looking at and reacting to."

Pete Thompson concept art.

HALLWAY

Bob Cheshire concept art.

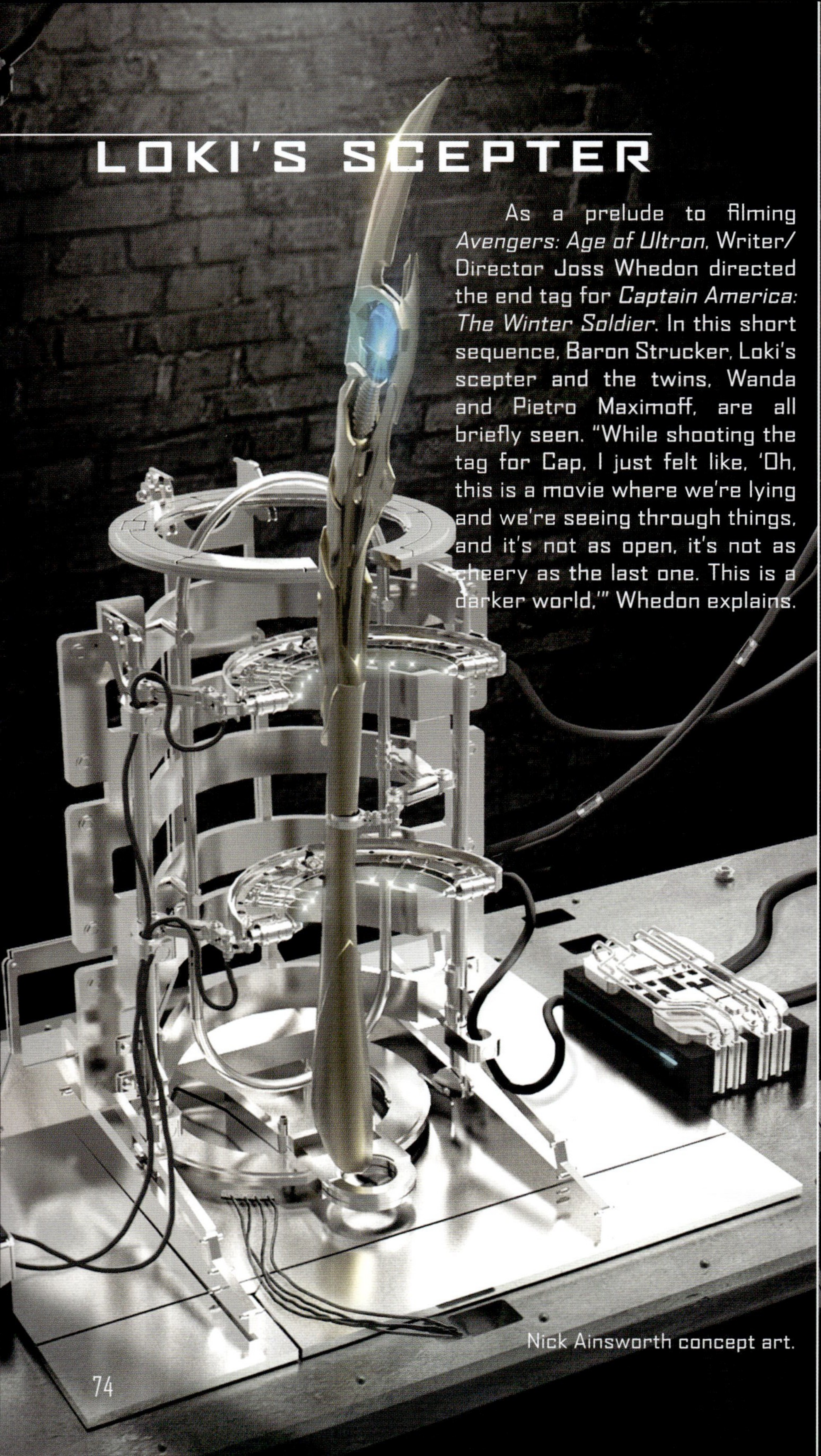

LOKI'S SCEPTER

As a prelude to filming *Avengers: Age of Ultron*, Writer/Director Joss Whedon directed the end tag for *Captain America: The Winter Soldier*. In this short sequence, Baron Strucker, Loki's scepter and the twins, Wanda and Pietro Maximoff, are all briefly seen. "While shooting the tag for Cap, I just felt like, 'Oh, this is a movie where we're lying and we're seeing through things, and it's not as open, it's not as cheery as the last one. This is a darker world,'" Whedon explains.

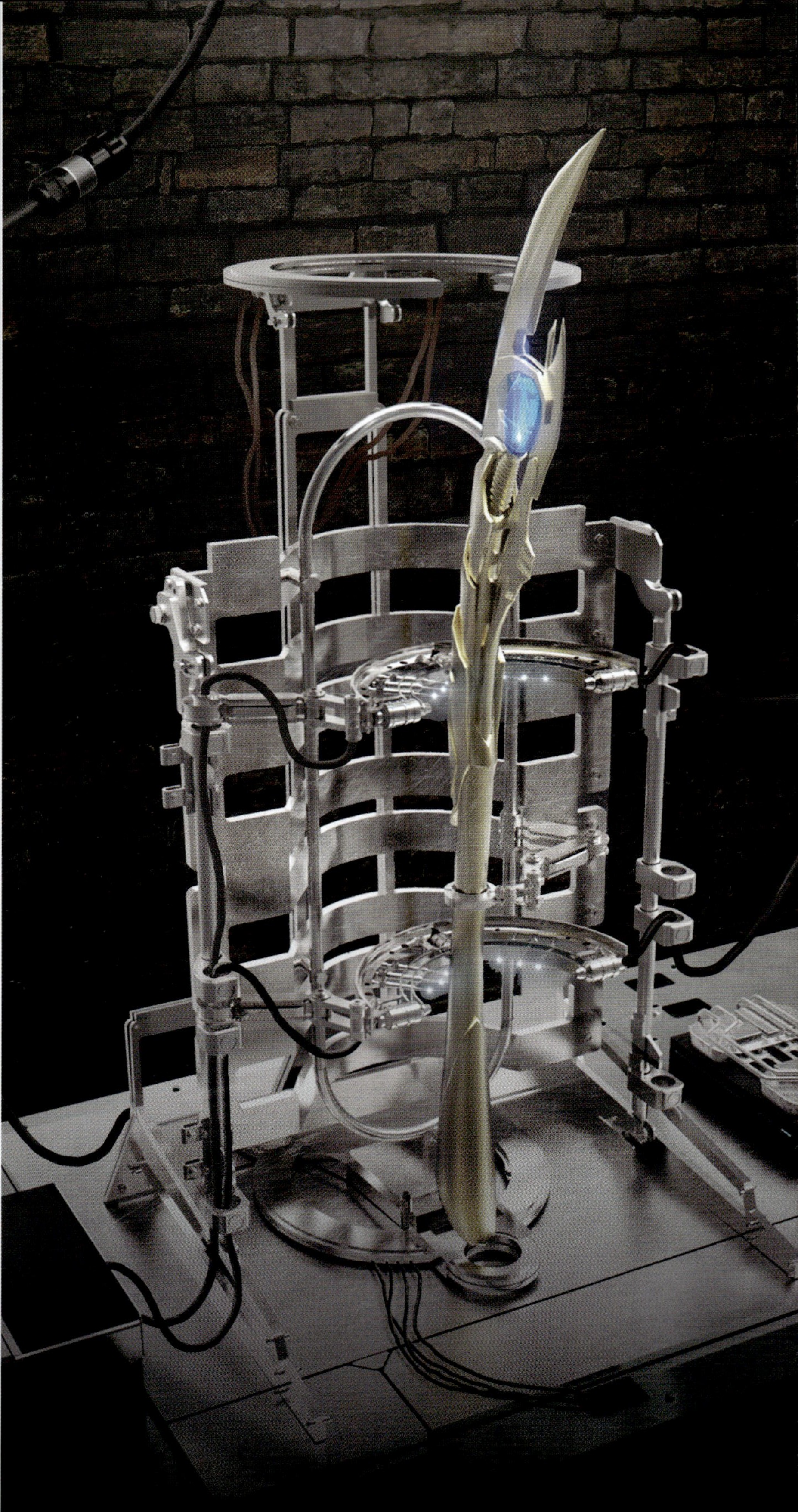

Nick Ainsworth concept art.

THE TWINS

Wanda and Pietro are new additions to the Marvel Cinematic Universe. Alex Bryne recalls the origin of the design process for the twins and their visual progression during the film: "I think for both Pietro and Wanda, the point was that we needed to start them off in Sokovia, in Eastern Europe. We needed to believe that they were orphan children living there, and then gradually to move them toward the roots of their super hero look in their ordinary clothes. There is a kind of evolution."

Concept art by Jack Dudman and Darrell Warner.

PIETRO

"For Quicksilver, it's all about speed and being aerodynamic in the way he moves," Alex Byne says. "He's incredibly athletic—balletic, really. He's very graceful in the way he moves, so you know that you can really use the lines down the body and streamline him." Byrne's team created multiple, but subtle, changes in Pietro's pants throughout the film. "There was a phase of jeans in the 1980s that had everything but the kitchen sink on them. And we bought some amazing pairs on eBay and took the bits we liked and just evolved from that. He's actually got four different pairs of trousers—but then again, you don't really notice because they evolved from a pair of stretch jeans where we put colored stitching down the sides."

Jack Dudman concept art.

Jack Dudman concept art.

QUICKSILVER

Ryan Meinerding concept art.

Andy Park concept art.

WANDA

Wanda Maximoff, the Scarlet Witch, went through an enchanting design process that became more about capturing her personality and history than alluding to her comic-book counterpart. Alex Byrne was quick to point out this was her favorite look to create. "I really like Wanda's clothes. I like the way her clothes evolve and end up as Scarlet Witch. It was a very interesting mixture of clothing meets costume meets super hero, and it was a great kind of journey through her character," Byrne says. "I looked at a lot of Eastern European fashion and models, contemporary and traditional, and it's that kind of mixture of that, even though we talk about them as clothes, they need to be slightly heightened. It's not day-to-day—it's got slightly heightened levels—so it's finding that balance."

Andy Park concept art.

Jack Dudman concept art.

SCARLET WITCH

Andy Park began the design phase for Wanda even before there was a finished script. "I did some early passes of her that were far more super hero and harkened back to her comic-book roots. However, as we received the first draft of the script, it was very clear we wanted the character's direction to veer a bit more real world, a bit more bohemian."

Andy Park concept art.

Andy Park concept art.

UNDER THE FORTRESS

Tim Hill concept art.

Tim Hill concept art.

Tim Hill keyframe.

Tim Hill concept art.

Tim Hill concept art.

Bob Cheshire concept art.

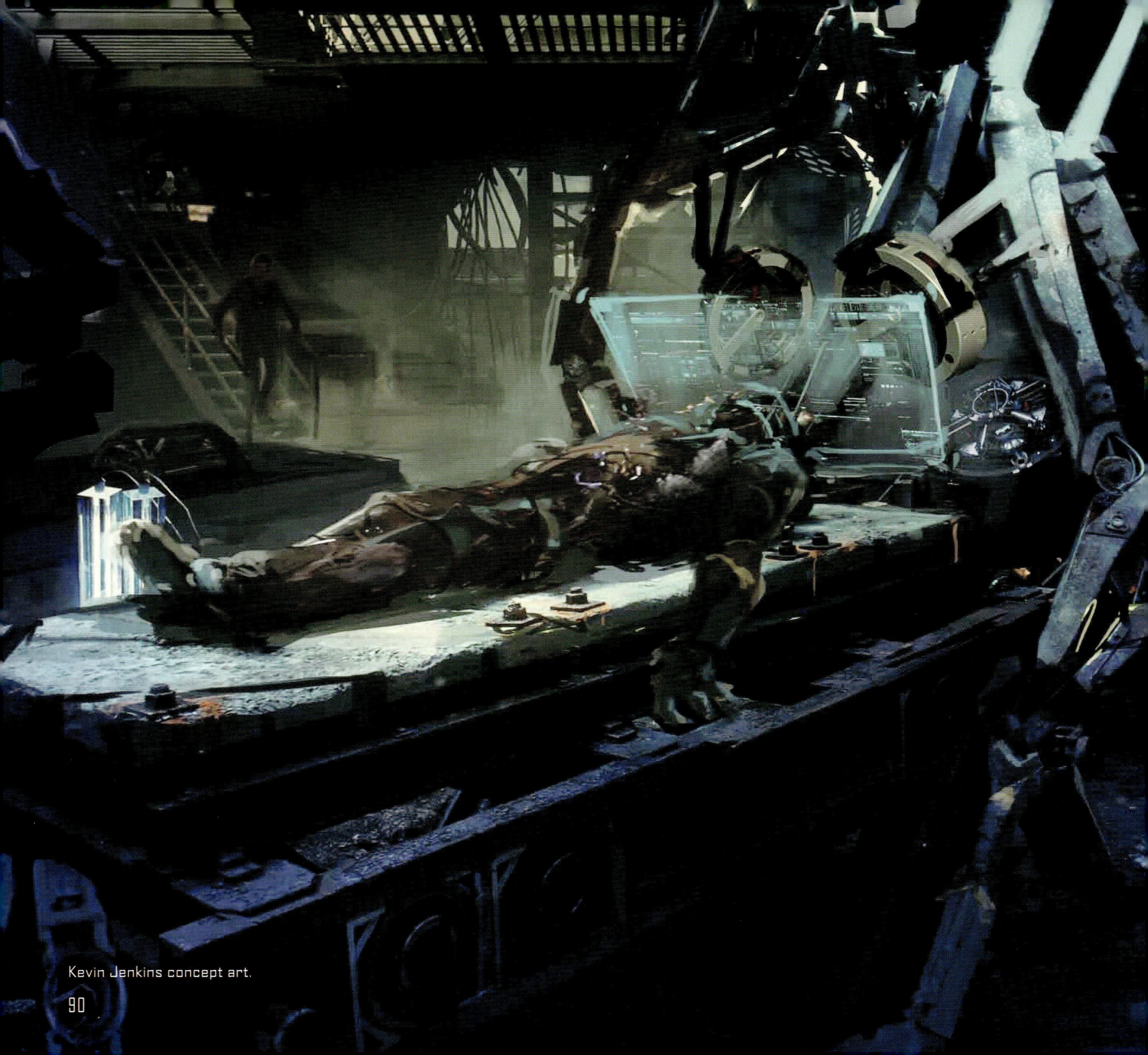

Kevin Jenkins concept art.

Kevin Jenkins concept art.

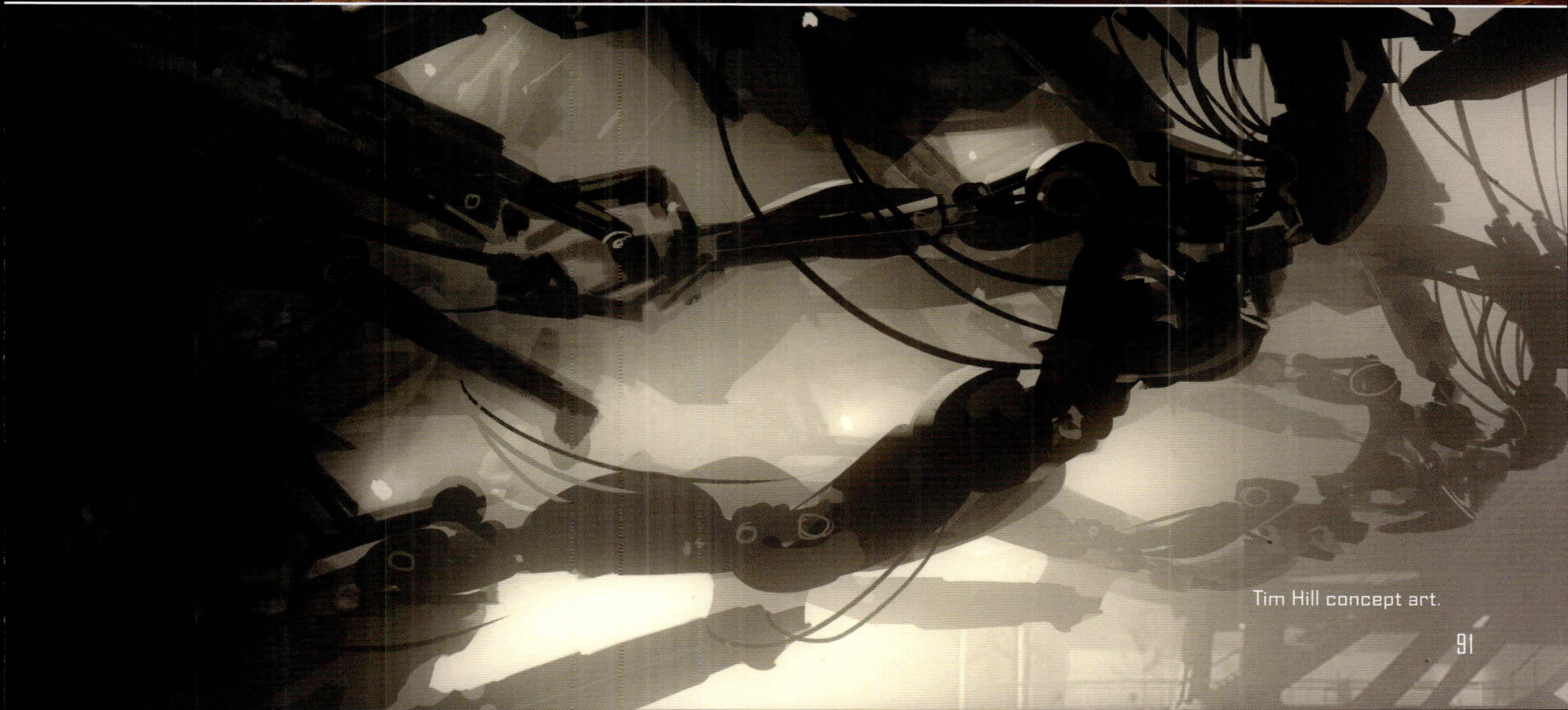

Tim Hill concept art.

LEVIATHAN CHAMBER

As Tony makes his way deeper into the fortress, he discovers that Baron Strucker has been housing not only Loki's scepter, for experimentation and weaponization, but also a full-size Leviathan strung up and torn apart. The chamber itself is dirty and mobile, mirroring the subterranean horror of the discovery. "The inspiration for this room came from asking in our head, 'What environment would ever exist to house such a massive thing?' while still keeping in mind it needed to be underground," Charlie Wood says. "We began looking at German V-2 factories from World War II. Below the factories would be colossal spaces where they would build ballistic missiles. They were creating armaments in these secret military environments. We drew a lot of inspiration from that."

Tim Hill concept art.

LEVIATHAN MODULE

Kevin Jenkins concept art.

Andy Park keyframe.

WANDA INVOKES TONY'S DREAM

STORYBOARDS BY BRYAN ANDREWS

Storyboard Artist Bryan Andrews had the opportunity to visualize multiple sequences in *Avengers: Age of Ultron*, including this key moment in which Wanda gets inside Tony Stark's head. "Joss Whedon had the sequence written by the time it was handed to me," Andrews says. "There were a couple versions, but only with very subtle differences in key parts. How Tony enters the room, does he still have a glove on for a flashlight—things like that. But all of that can change quickly. Once Joss sees the first pass or two, as well as how the set design is coming along, he can then make more detailed calls about how he wants to shoot it."

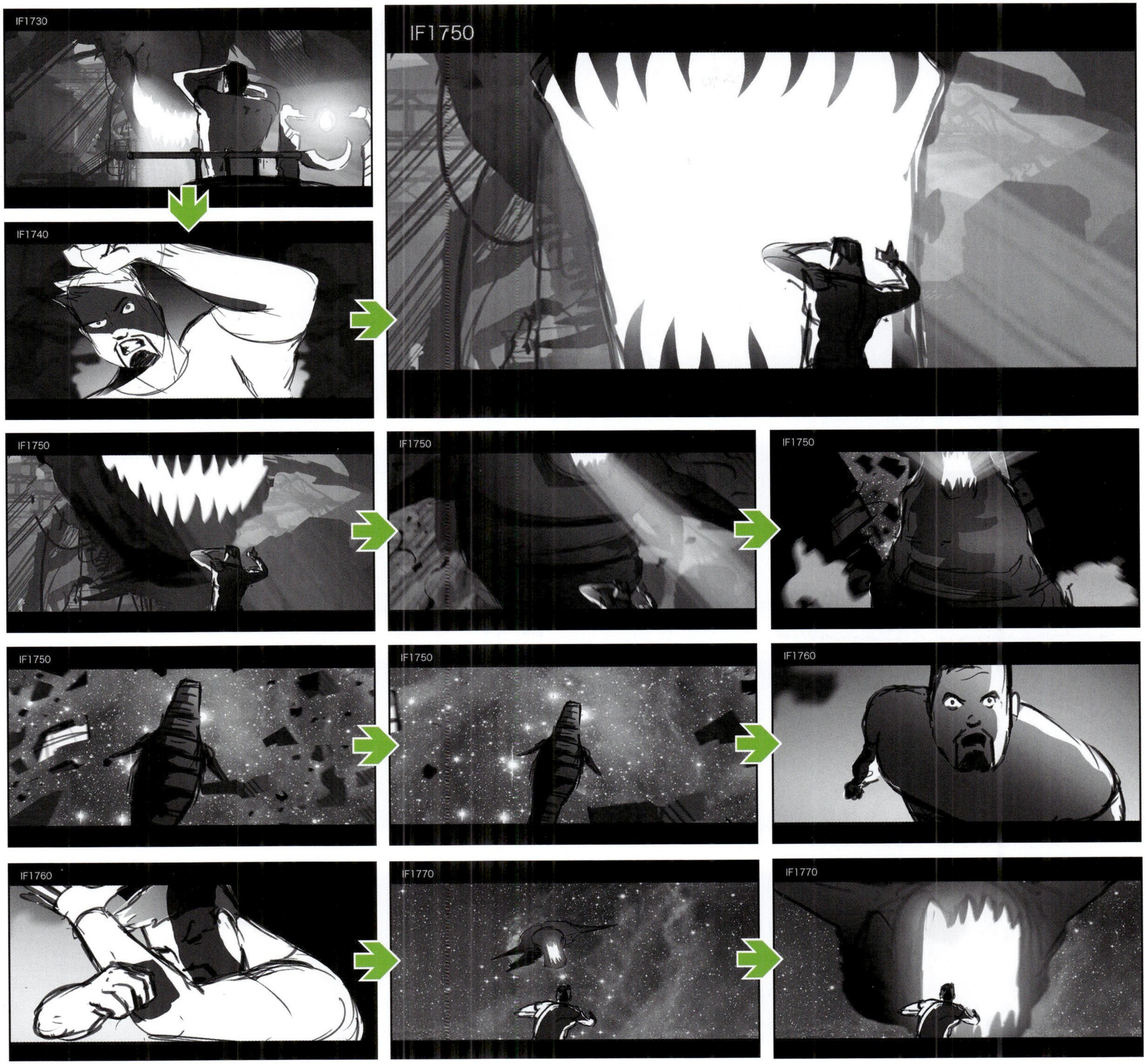
IF1730
IF1740
IF1750
IF1750
IF1750
IF1750
IF1750
IF1750
IF1760
IF1760
IF1770
IF1770

"I had examples of the set and development ideas to use as reference, and I just riffed off that," Andrews continues, describing the tone Whedon sought to establish with this beat. "He stated that it should be spooky, moody—and it was written as such—so I just added what I could to help visualize the creepiness, then brought a few extra staging bits to the scene."

"There were a few bits that were fun to explore in particular about this sequence," Andrews says. "The part of the vision that shows all the Avengers dead and blasted was cool. I believe I added the shield totally broken in half. Joss dug it, and there was the idea then to match the broken edge to the shattered chest of the villain in the finale—it was rad to be playing with such imagery. Another fun and challenging bit was when Wanda is supposed to get into Tony's mind. She's been popping up randomly at a distance throughout the sequence, all horror-movie-style—so to finally get her close, we do a slight cam drift off Tony's close up, and she's right behind him. Then her hands could pop up next to his head, working their magic. It was different than the script, but Joss liked it, thought it was a spooky and elegant way to go. Then the beast's mouth opening full of light behind Tony, which was fun. Giant glowy monster mouths behind people are always cool."

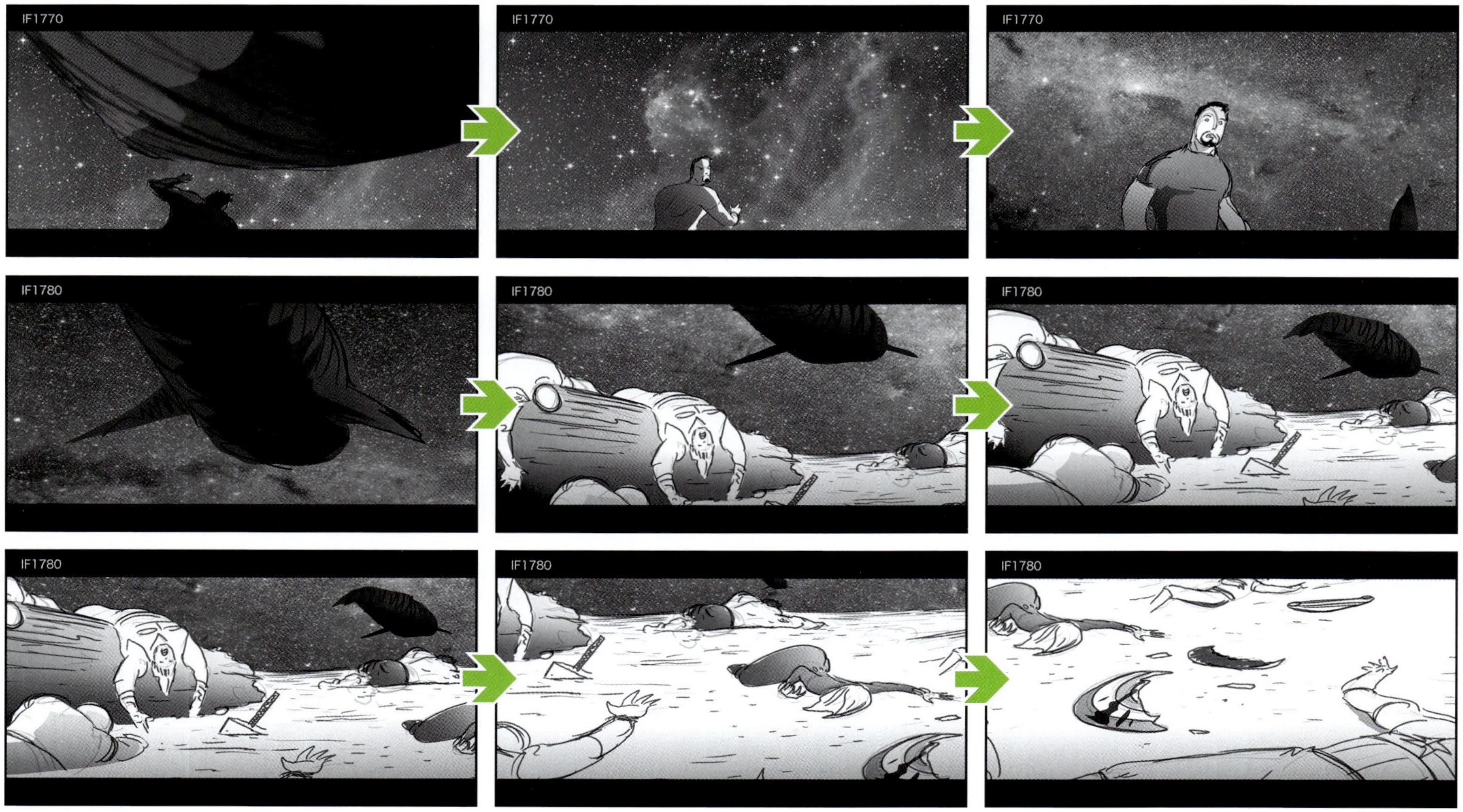

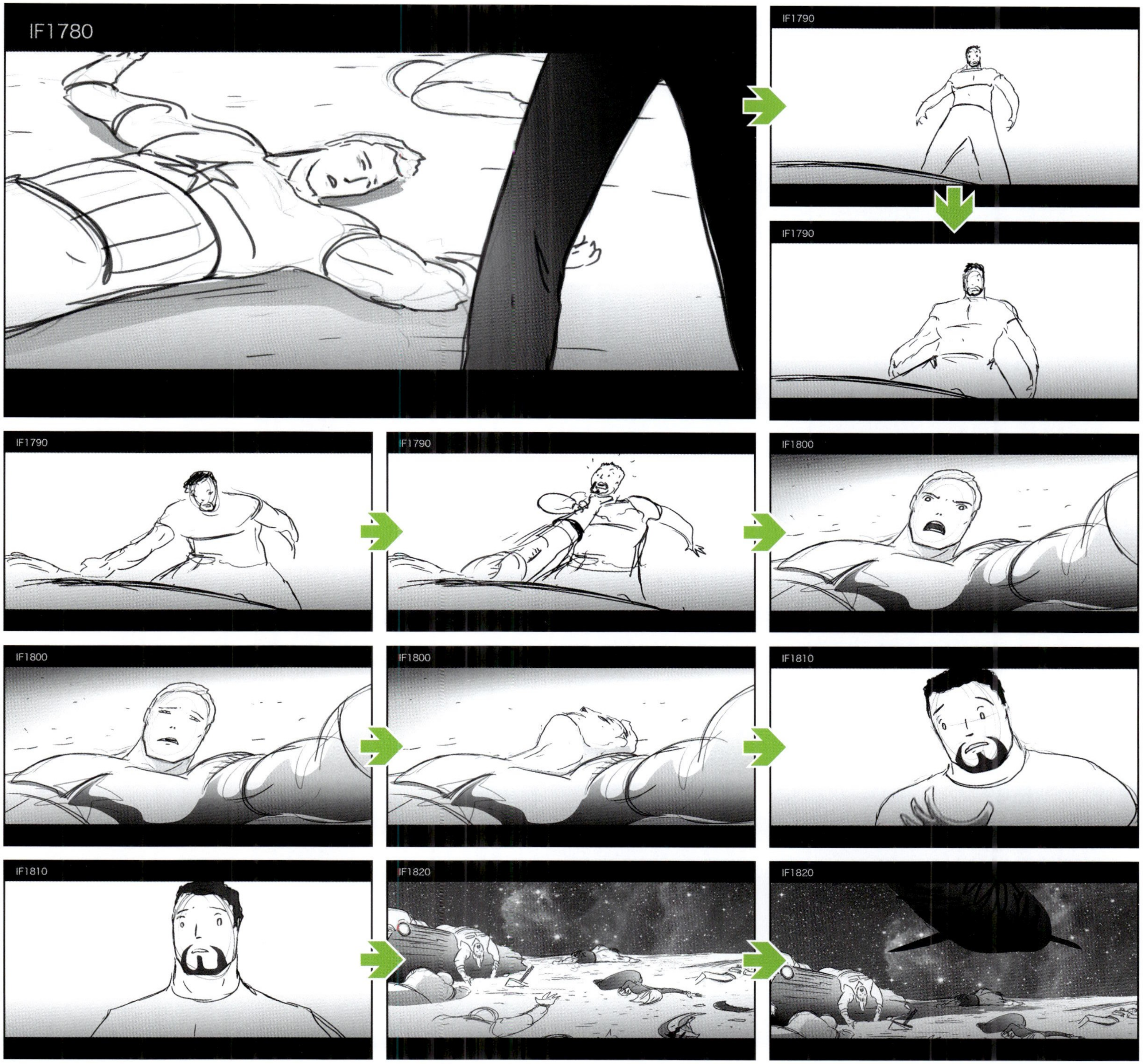
IF1780
IF1790
IF1790
IF1790
IF1790
IF1800
IF1800
IF1800
IF1810
IF1810
IF1820
IF1820

Bob Cheshire concept art.

"I wanted to get deeper into these characters. You need visual momentum, and these dream sequences are designed specifically to be as engaging as an action sequence. They are the fulcrum of the film because everybody reacts to them and acts from them, so for me they're visual exposition," Joss Whedon says. "Tony's dream is right up front, and it's: 'I failed, they invaded, they won, and I got everybody killed' and that makes his usual party intensity become almost messianic and desperate."

Stephen Wong
concept art.

CHAPTER TWO

AVENGERS HQ

The destruction of Stark Tower in the first Avengers film granted the opportunity for rebuilding and rebirth. Aptly renamed Avengers Tower, the structure acts as both a beacon of hope for the world and a home for our heroes between missions. Concept Artist Roberto Fernández Castro was one of the many illustrators working with Production Designer Charlie Wood to fabricate the tower's design. "As an architect, my main source of inspiration has been Frank Lloyd Wright, Le Corbusier and other main architects of the 20th century, but Avengers Tower takes inspiration from many different sources," Castro says. "The structure is around the perimeter, so the interior is free of structural elements. This is essential to distribute the spaces and articulate the different areas. It looks like a modern mansion, a luxury streamliner and a hi-tech laboratory. All of these ideas together are mixed and balanced to create a rich space with endless possibilities." Avengers Tower is more than just a decadent headquarters—it's a character in its own right, functioning as an extension of Tony Stark's personality. "Avengers Tower needed to be something that would befit the Tony Stark character, someone with that much engineering skill," Wood adds. "We looked at the whole engineering aspect of it and tried to add a lot of metal architectural elements and cantilevers that you would see in modern buildings. It's supposed to be an eco-tower. So it was many, many things. It wasn't just defining the look of it."

"From the beginning, Charlie Wood wanted a design where the Avengers' living and working areas could be blended architecturally rather than being isolated in separate sets, which they could have been. Doing so opened up a range of visual opportunities whereby we could make the set a much more dramatic and unique place," Concept Artist Stephen Wong says. "For inspiration, we looked at current trends in architectural thinking, as well as amazing penthouse apartments, since we wanted a style that was very high-tech and cutting-edge but also had the glamour and sense of style you associate with Tony Stark. We tried to make the apartment as sleek as possible and very dynamic: There are a lot of strong horizontal lines in the design, large diagonal columns that cut across them and sweeping curves that range around the room. There's always a sense of movement and tension through the space, which seemed appropriate for the Avengers' HQ."

Stephen Wong concept art.

Stephen Wong concept art.

QUINJET

Perched on the helipad of the newly upgraded Avengers Tower is the Avengers' vehicle of choice, the Quinjet, sporting a major overhaul that mirrors the film's edginess. "Originally, it was more in keeping with a commercial aircraft, and we played around with that a little bit and then actually moved away from that direction," Charlie Wood says. "Joss Whedon wanted to have something that had more of a military aspect to it. It needed to be something that could perform at extremely high speeds—something that was extremely versatile—which is why we built a lot of these sorts of vital systems into it. Joss wanted to be able to have a good look at the environment around you when you're flying it, so we sort of based the canopy on a helicopter cockpit. Meaning it's not just glass *here*—there's also glass below you. So hopefully in the film you get a tremendous sense of speed when you're flying through the cities, and it's a more exhilarating ride."

Roberto Fernández Castro concept art.

Realism in the design was our aim. I put in the drawing as much information as I could. Every shutline, device, sign and hinge is there to create a believable result," Roberto Fernández Castro explains. "I also wanted to put some of the Tony Stark personality into it. It looks like an advanced aircraft combined with a luxury plane and a space shuttle. The addition of two triangular VTOL engines provides an extraordinary amount of maneuverability."

Roberto Fernández Castro concept art.

Paul Catling concept art.

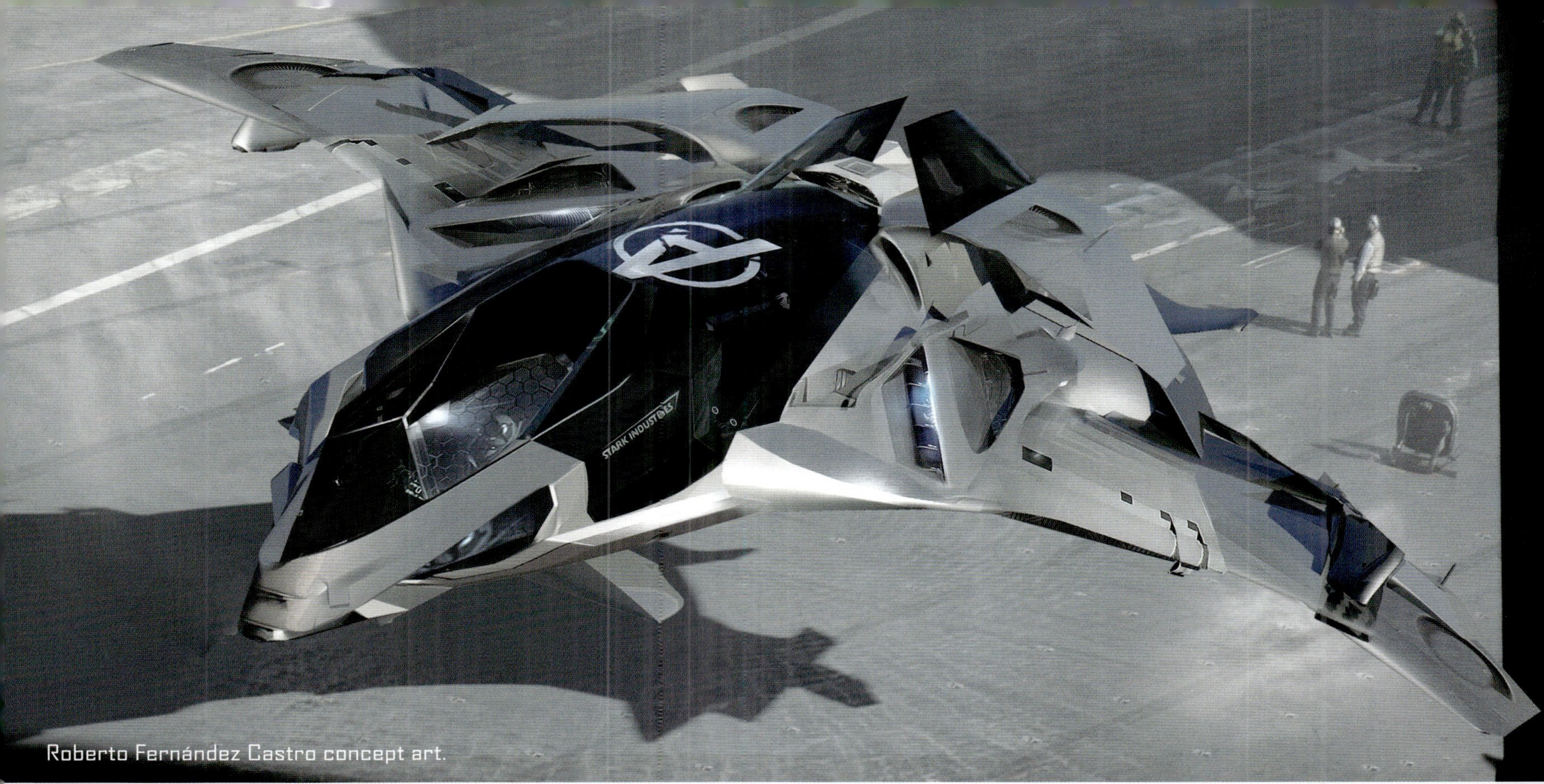

Roberto Fernández Castro concept art.

Paul Chandler concept art.

Making the Quinjet sleeker also came with the challenge of a minimized interior space. "In the end, we actually stripped it all down," Wood says. "There was a lot more padding, a lot more finished surfaces in it. And actually Joss Whedon wanted us to sort of tech it down in a way so the exterior is something more sleek, but with the interiors we sort of took some of those luxurious finishes away to strip it down a little bit and make it just slightly edgier."

Ivan Weightman concept art.

Ivan Weightman concept art.

INFIRMARY

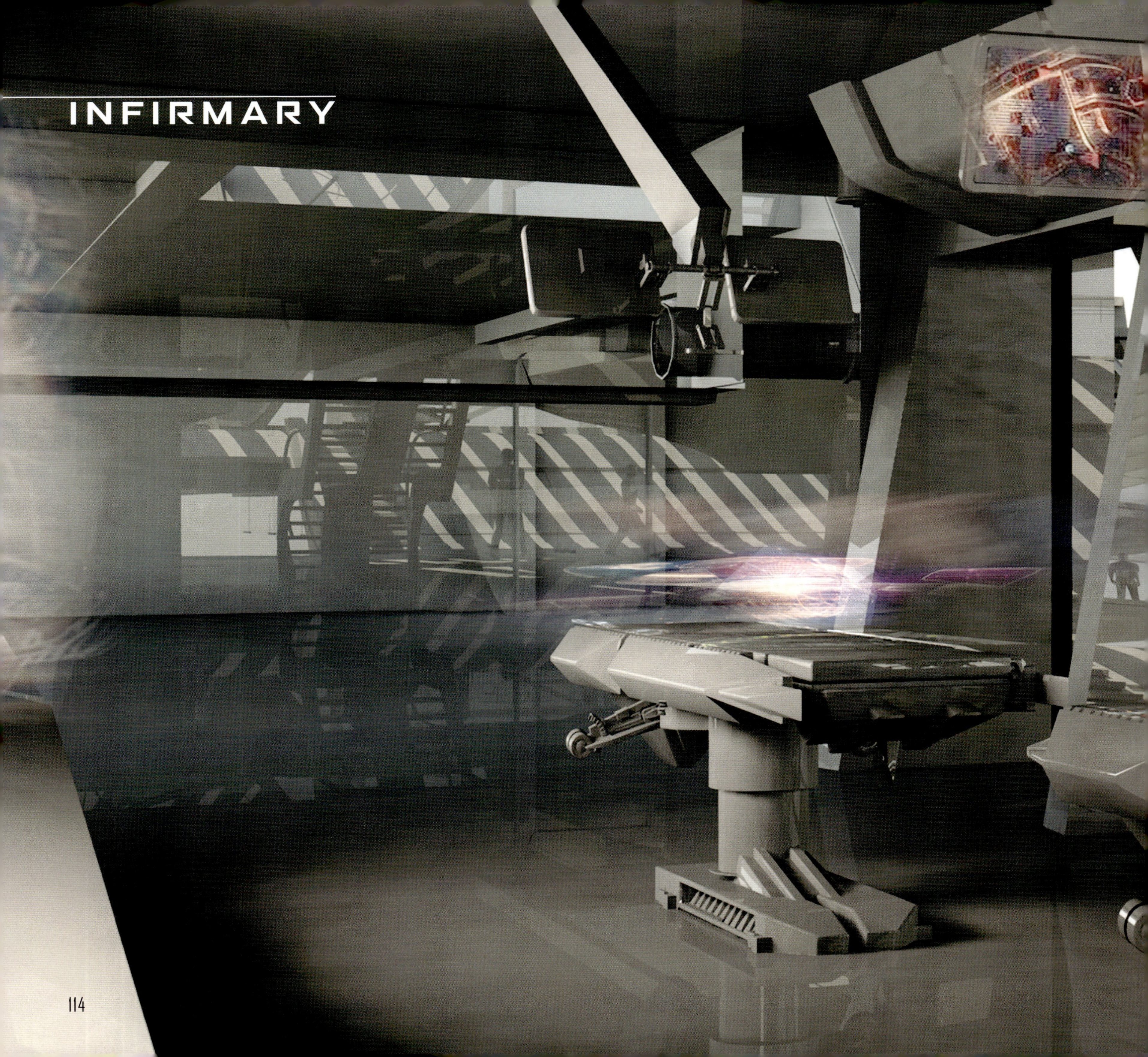

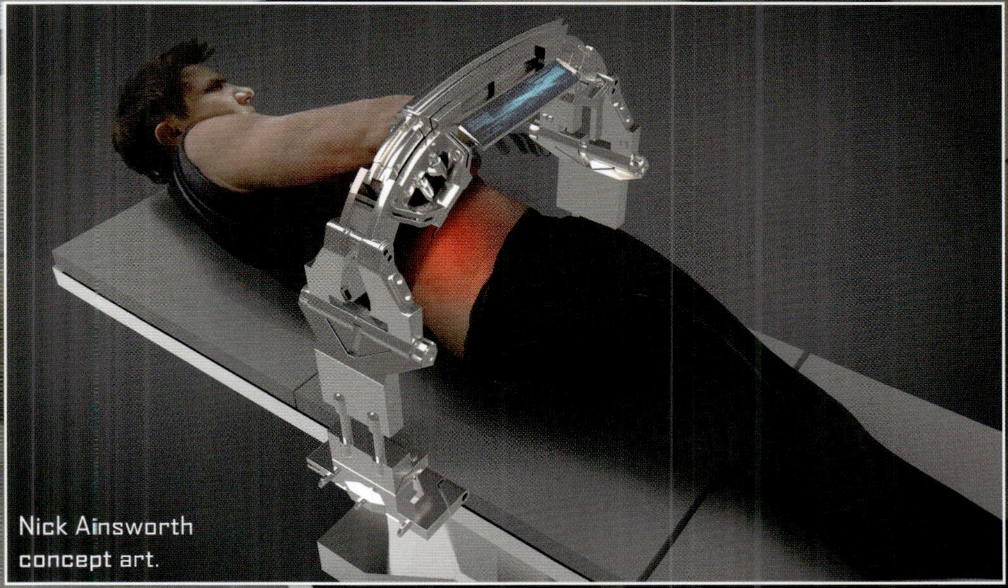

Nick Ainsworth concept art.

Stephen Wong concept art.

LIVING AREA

Stephan Martinière concept art.

Within Avengers Tower can be found living quarters, a lab, training grounds, locker rooms, bedrooms—essentially, the team's heart and soul: an expansive and refined interior that needed to mirror the impressive exterior aesthetic, as well as fulfill the demands of the script. "I think originally, really from the script, Joss Whedon wanted a big space because there was an awful lot we knew we were going to do in it," Charlie Wood explains. "We knew that there was a lot of screen time in there, and the problem with a small set is that may be fine for a few days—but if you're shooting twenty-something days in a set like that, you need to come up with something where you have multiple environments for the set. Joss wanted it all to be connected; he wanted to be able to move from downstairs to upstairs, and vice versa. He wanted to have lots of different fighting platforms, but also something beautiful—something with this beautiful view over the city of Manhattan. That's why we sort of built the big glass piece on the front of it—something very fluid, based on simple curves."

Pete Thompson concept art.

Stephen Wong concept art.

Pete Thompson concept art.

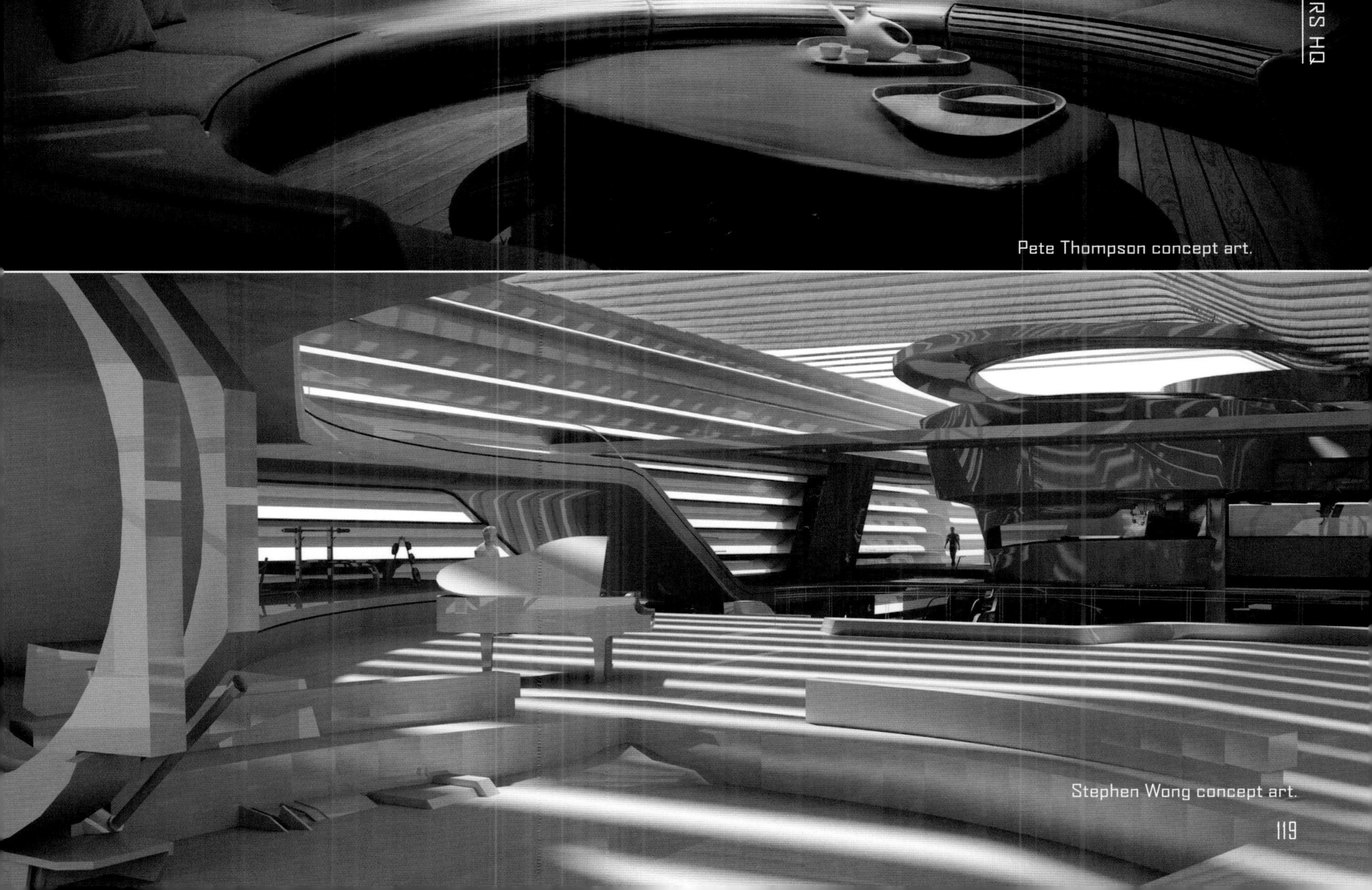
Stephen Wong concept art.

"The living room and the main space is very warm and welcoming. We used wood and polished tiles, and we decided to stay away from tech and metal surfaces," Roberto Fernández Castro says. "The decoration became a very important part of the set. The sofas, tables, musical instruments and art pieces give the space a domestic scale. I think Avengers Tower is a combination of different scales: It is a grand space containing small subspaces. The most challenging task is to move from the small detail to the big picture, and the opposite. That balance is the key for a successful design."

Roberto Fernández Castro concept art.

LOCKER ROOM

Pete Thompson concept art.

UNDER THE ARMOR

"There were going to be moments where, particularly on the Quinjet and within Avengers Tower, we don't want people in their full super hero looks, so they need to have something that feels practical. It still feels tactical, but it's not the full hero look," Costume Designer Alex Byrne says. "It was a very complicated tubular-net that we were working with, so you can't get back and change a bit—it's a whole garment that comes in one go, so getting the star-lines in the right places on the actor was a real challenge."

Jack Dudman concept art.

Jack Dudman concept art.

LAB

Roberto Fernández Castro concept art.

Geniuses Tony Stark and Bruce Banner come together in the Avengers' lab—a concoction of brilliance and skill that Charlie Wood approached with mindful experience. "We needed something rich, something that would befit Tony Stark's character as someone with extensive engineering skill."

Stephen Wong concept art.

MACHINE ROOM

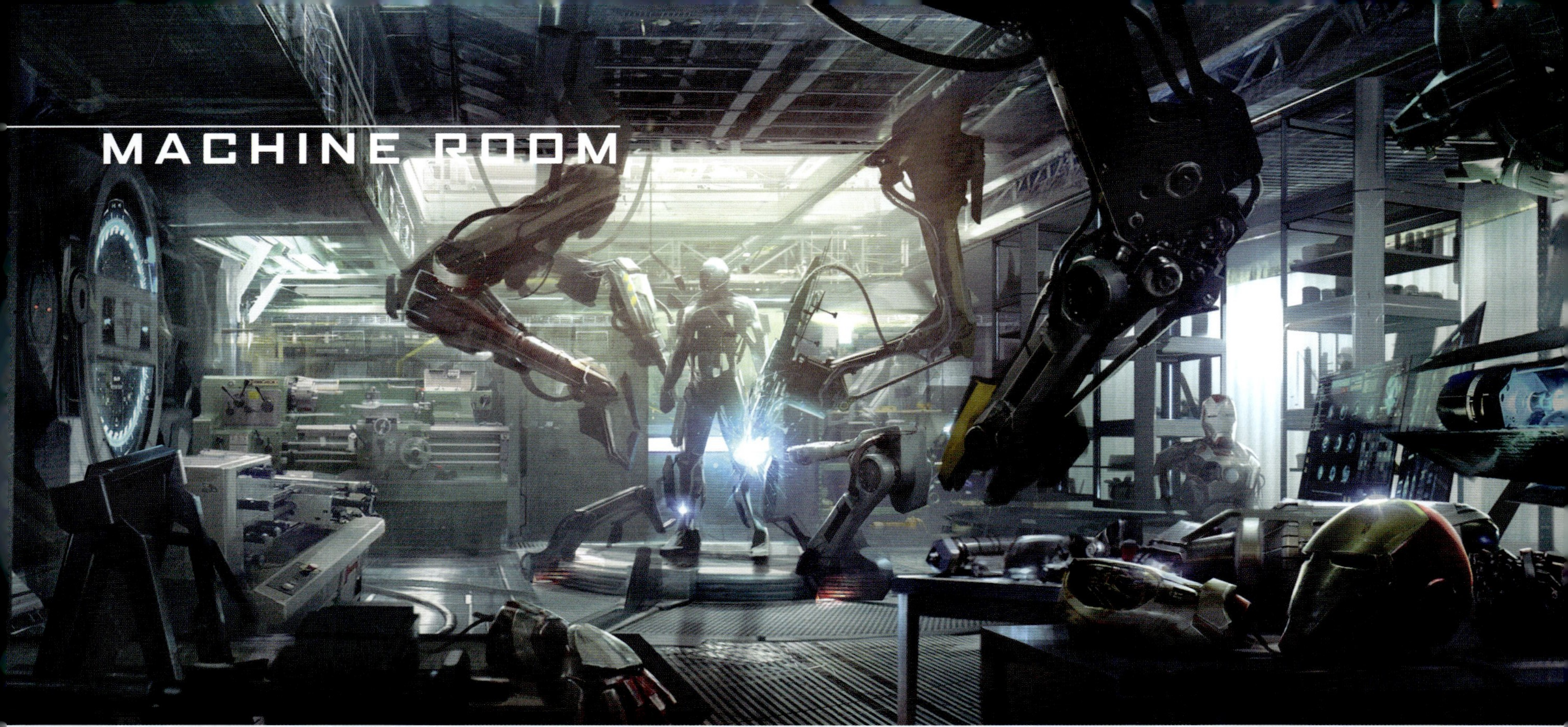

Among other areas of Avengers Tower, Roberto Fernández Castro was instrumental in creating the look of the machine room. "The space is designed as a small automated assembly line. Welding and drilling robotic arms, mounted on rails, hang from the ceiling. Everything is automated and controlled by computers. It's the perfect environment for the birth of Ultron," Castro says. "I feel the fact this space has just one window in the ceiling is also very important: The artificial light from the lab above falls into this space, creating a dramatic effect. There is no sunlight reaching this section of the tower, and this artificial environment frames the creation of Ultron."

Roberto Fernández Castro/concept art.

Stephen Wong concept art.

Andy Park keyframe.

CHAPTER THREE

RISE OF ULTRON

Bred from our heroes' folly and insatiable in his quest for domination, Ultron stands as the greatest threat any of the Avengers have faced thus far. Originally mentioned in 1968's *Avengers #54* before making his first full appearance in *Avengers #55*, Ultron's mission always has been to cleanse the world of humanity. "Ultron has been around 40, 50 years in the comic books, but is more relevant and more frightening than ever today when we all have in our pockets technology that tells people where we are and tells people what we're doing," Executive Producer Kevin Feige says. "Many people happily tell the whole world where they are and what they're doing and what they're thinking. We all know that there are people listening, there are people watching, and what if people could control that and what if that control went another few steps? At what point has humanity given over too much, and are they going to regret it? Ultron is able to exploit all of that in a very, very big way." Ultron's distinct yet unstable personality is also connected to his formidability. Writer/Director Joss Whedon was eager to highlight and explore this side of the villain. "He's doing math, like, emotionally that we don't see, and then suddenly he's angry about something, and then suddenly he's obsessed with something else because his mind is everywhere," Whedon says. "With Ultron I needed to know what kind of a person had that much rage, how it would be expressed, and also how could I have the fun that I needed to have with it? How could I make him, like Loki, somebody who is sympathetic and textured and not completely wrong in the way he views things?"

ULTRON MARK I

Creeping his way up from the machine room in Avengers Tower is the first iteration of Ultron, a monstrously deformed robotic shell that serves as a harbinger of what is to come. Concept Artist Andy Park was tasked with cracking the first version of this notorious villain. "Ultron has always had one of the most iconic designs, and capitalizing on what makes him stand out—his creepy eyes and smile—was the first step. Joss Whedon wanted the first Ultron you see to essentially be a piecemeal version made up of spare Iron Man parts. It's perfect because when you move his faceplate and open up his mouth area, he basically has the iconic smile. Joss also really wanted to play up the creepiness of Ultron's inaugural appearance, which was also a ton of fun to explore."

Andy Park concept art.

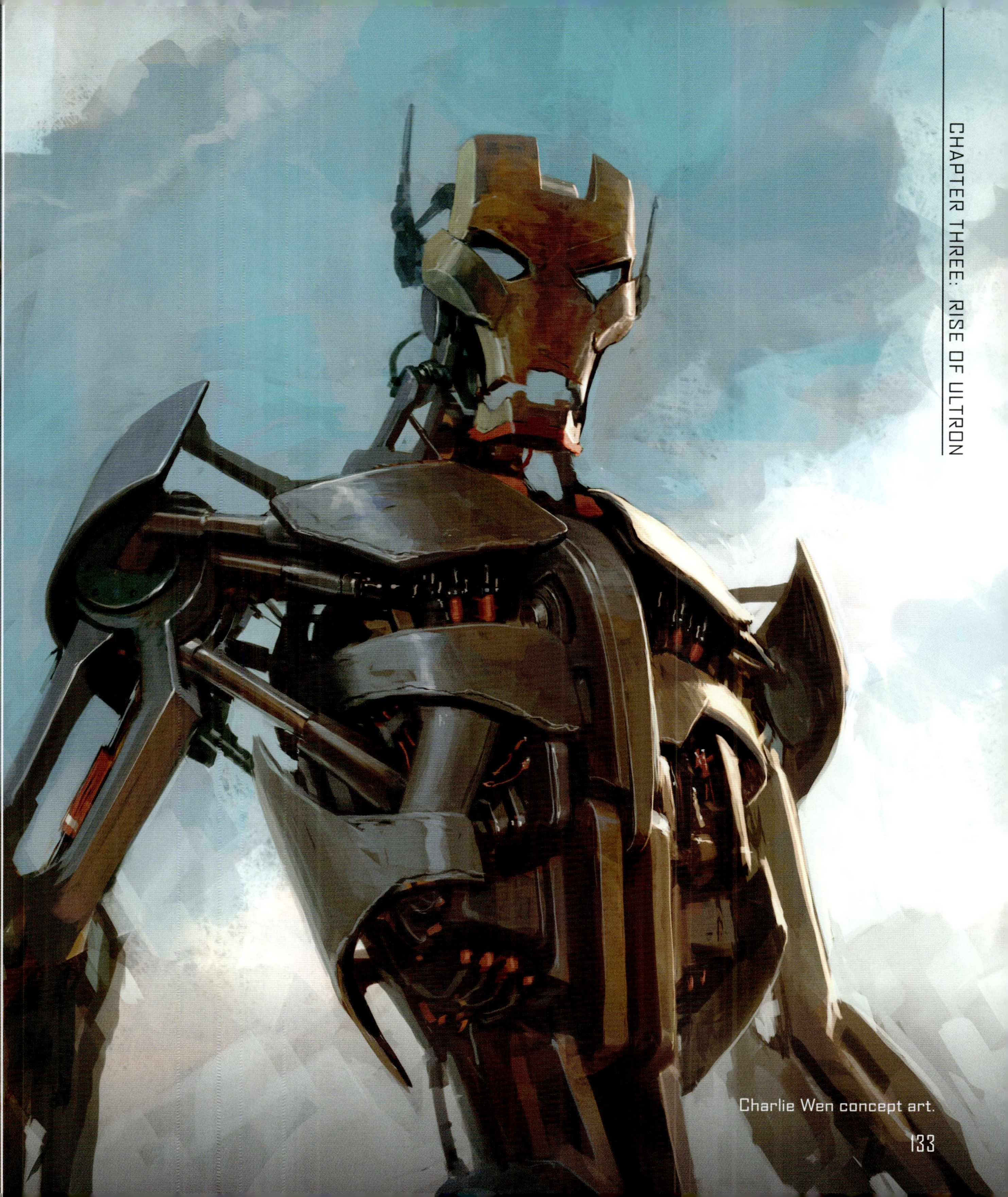

Charlie Wen concept art.

Andy Park concept art.

Andy Park concept art.

Charlie Wen concept art.

Charlie Wen concept art.

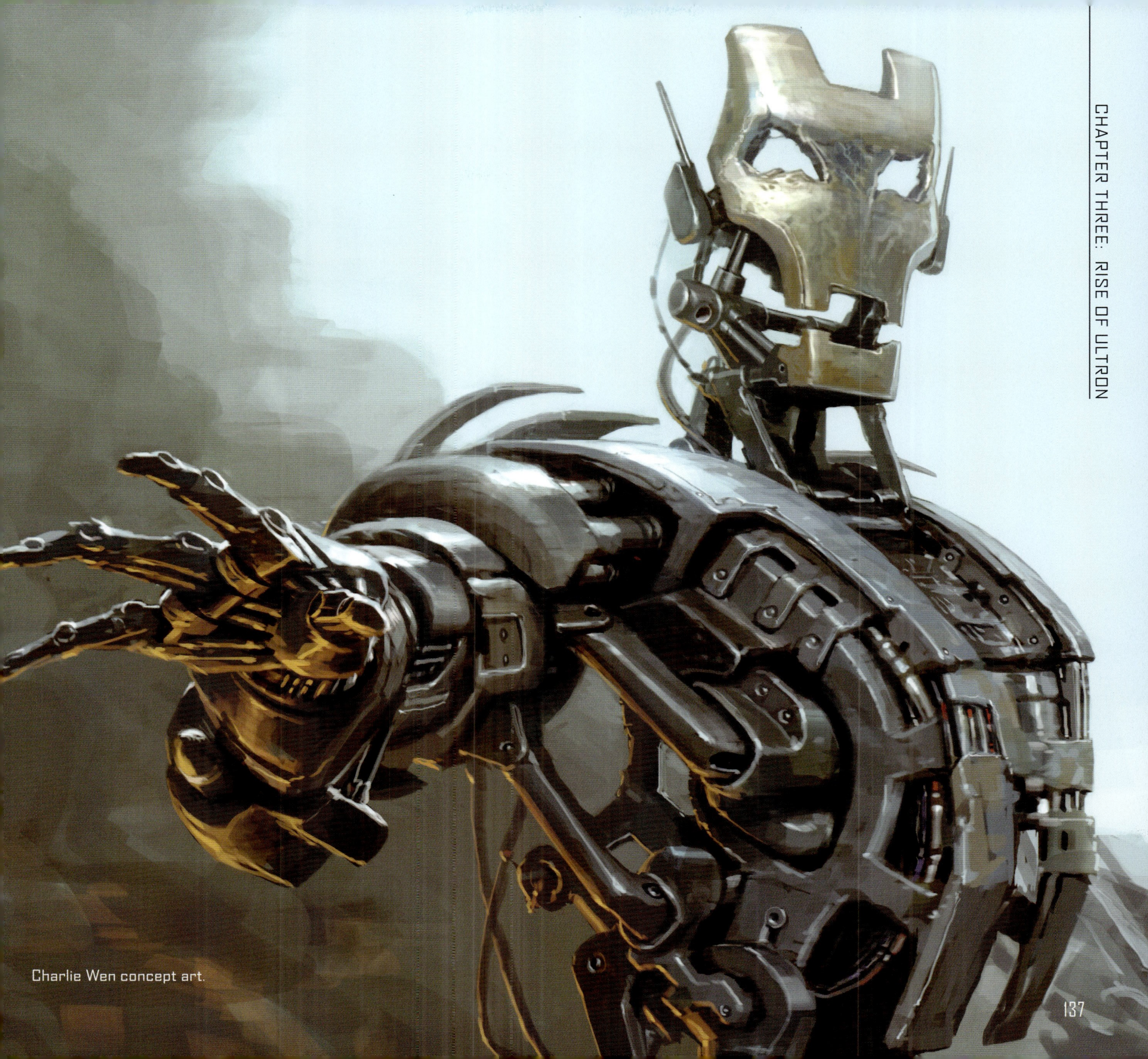

Charlie Wen concept art.

ULTRON PRIME

"I loved Ultron, reading about Ultron, but you go back and you see he makes the same face all the time," Joss Whedon says. "He's just constantly saying, 'I will destroy you! I really...I definitely will destroy you!' That's just meh. But artificial intelligence that has been created by an Avenger—that murderous-child aspect is fascinating to me."

"This image was inspired specifically by a day when Joss Whedon sat down and was describing this moment, and he sat just like this," Head of Visual Development Ryan Meinerding recalls. "He wanted to show the attitude, power and focus in Ultron's face, but it was sort of a casual power—at least that's how I interpreted the pose, and then I tried to reproduce it."

Ryan Meinerding concept art.

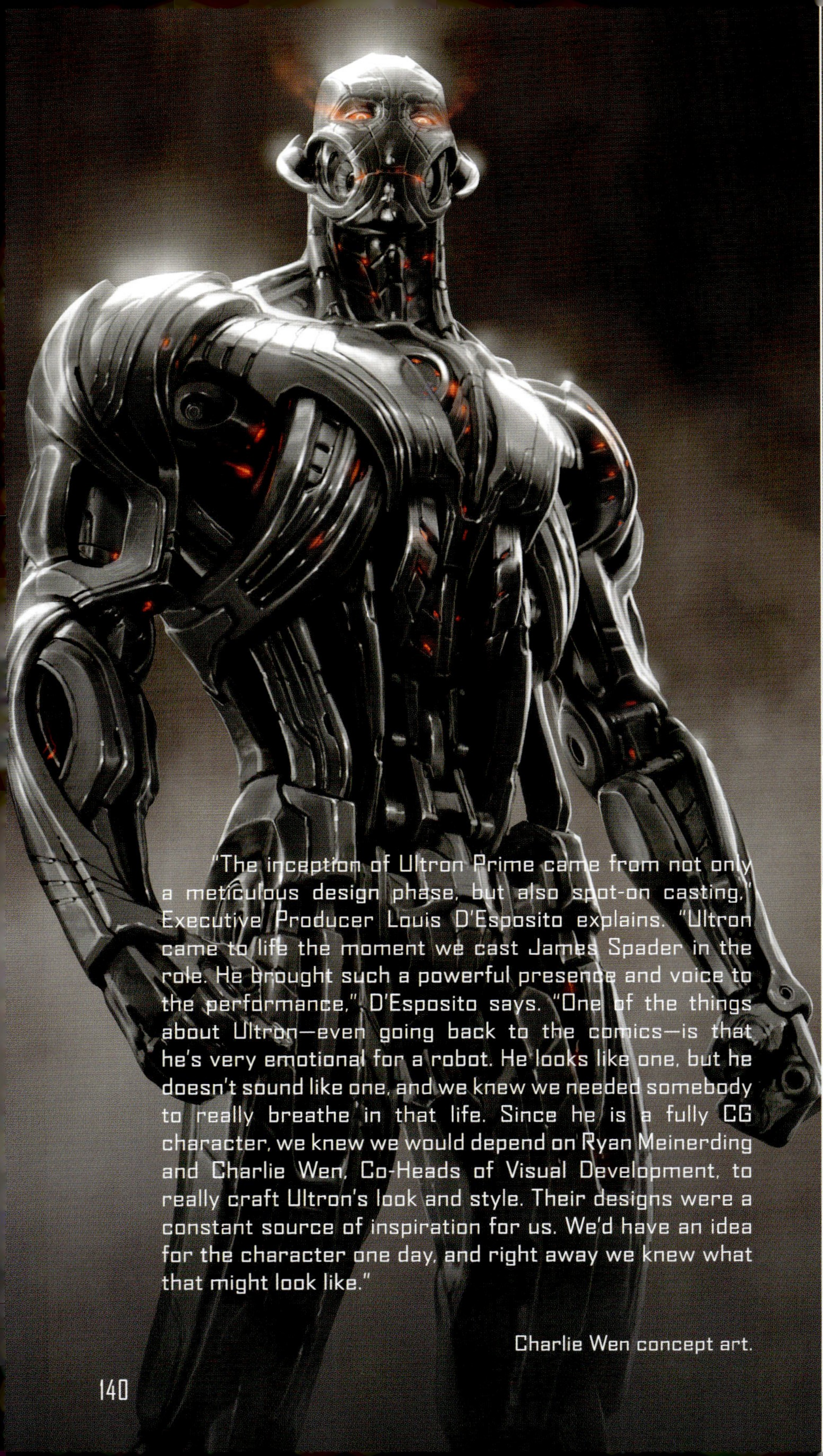

"The inception of Ultron Prime came from not only a meticulous design phase, but also spot-on casting," Executive Producer Louis D'Esposito explains. "Ultron came to life the moment we cast James Spader in the role. He brought such a powerful presence and voice to the performance," D'Esposito says. "One of the things about Ultron—even going back to the comics—is that he's very emotional for a robot. He looks like one, but he doesn't sound like one, and we knew we needed somebody to really breathe in that life. Since he is a fully CG character, we knew we would depend on Ryan Meinerding and Charlie Wen, Co-Heads of Visual Development, to really craft Ultron's look and style. Their designs were a constant source of inspiration for us. We'd have an idea for the character one day, and right away we knew what that might look like."

Charlie Wen concept art.

"I started by looking at a lot of metal work and scu pture and things that were done during the art-deco period; it was very inspiring," Meinerding says. "I also looked at hood ornaments and the fine details of engraving—I always saw Ultron's face having a jewelry-level refinement to it. t was meant to be the most sophisticated piece of machinery you've ever seen, and beautiful at the same time."

Ryan Meinerding concept art.

Phil Saunders concept art.

Phil Saunders concept art.

Phil Saunders concept art.

Charlie Wen concept art.

Charlie Wen concept art.

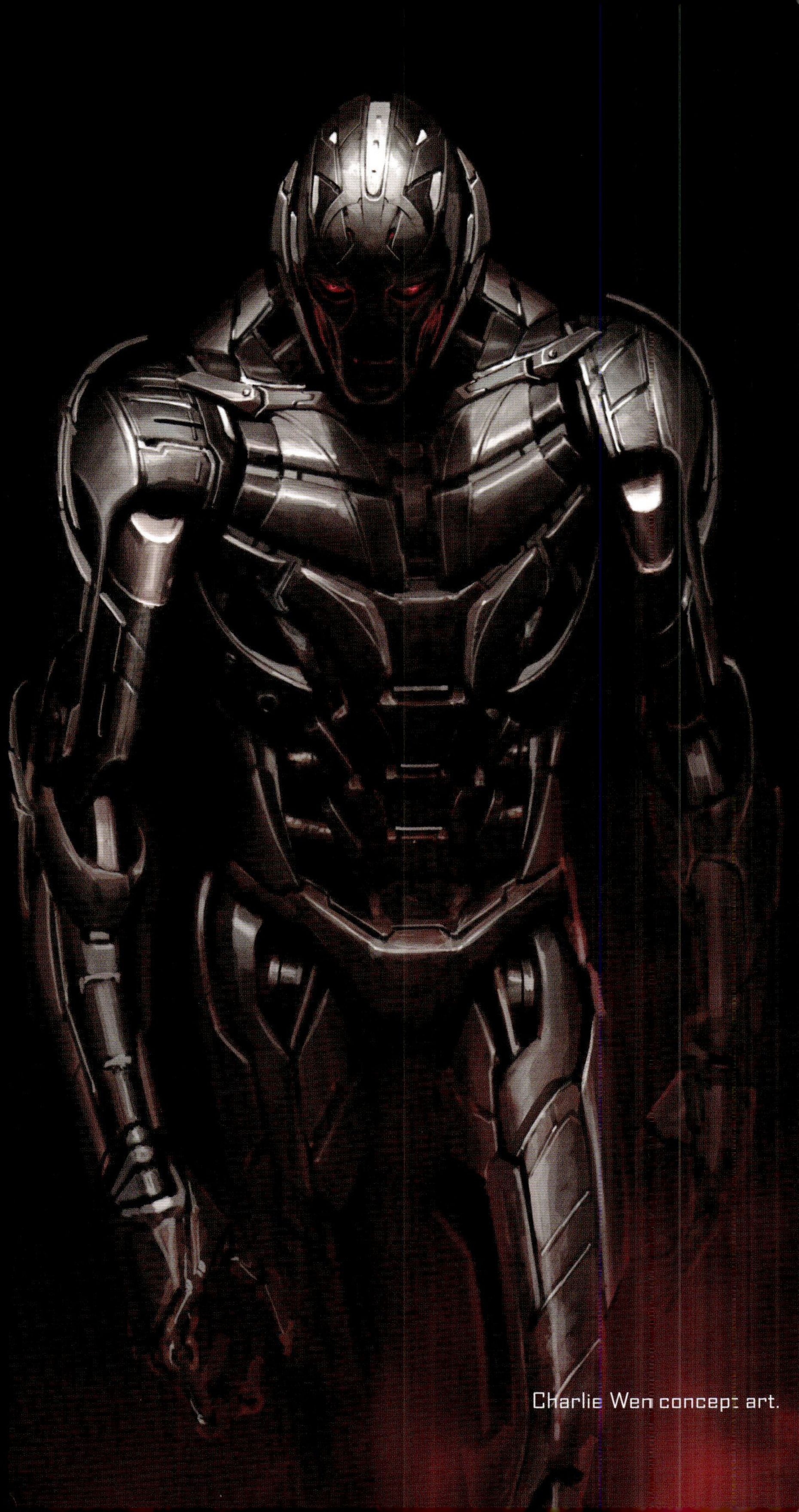

Charlie Wen concept art.

Phil Saunders concept art.

"Joss Whedon, as always, had a very clear idea of what he wanted for Ultron. A key direction was to develop a design that was clearly understandable mechanically, and so for the bulk of the development we were pursuing a very industrial-looking body," Concept Artist Phil Saunders says. "Ultimately, we recognized that the design was lacking the majesty of a super villain, so at the eleventh hour Charlie Wen came up with the beautiful, sculptural and imposing design that became the movie's Ultron."

Phil Saunders concept art.

"Initially our approach to Ultron was to develop something far more sophisticated than Iron Man, mechanically. Cut lines would be finer and tighter-fitting, joint articulation should be broken up at a far more granular level," Saunders says. "I had done an early design that cut into the torso, legs and arms, which immediately differentiated it from a man in a suit. That idea carried through all the way to the final design."

Phil Saunders concept art.

Concept Artist Rodney Fuentebella ventured toward concepts that were far different—based less on structure and more on Ultron's distinctive comic-book characteristics. "I came from the perspective of his powers and what makes him unique. I focused on the ideas for how he is put together not by mechanical joints and structural bits, but by a force foreign to any technology we are familiar with," Fuentebella says.

Rodney Fuentebella concept art.

"As opposed to being sleek and modern, Ultron can be more industrial, rough and even alien," Andy Park says.

Andy Park concept art.

Phil Saunders concept art.

Ryan Meinerding concept art.

Josh Herman concept art.

Andy Park concept art.

Ryan Meinerding concept art.

Ryan Meinerding concept art.

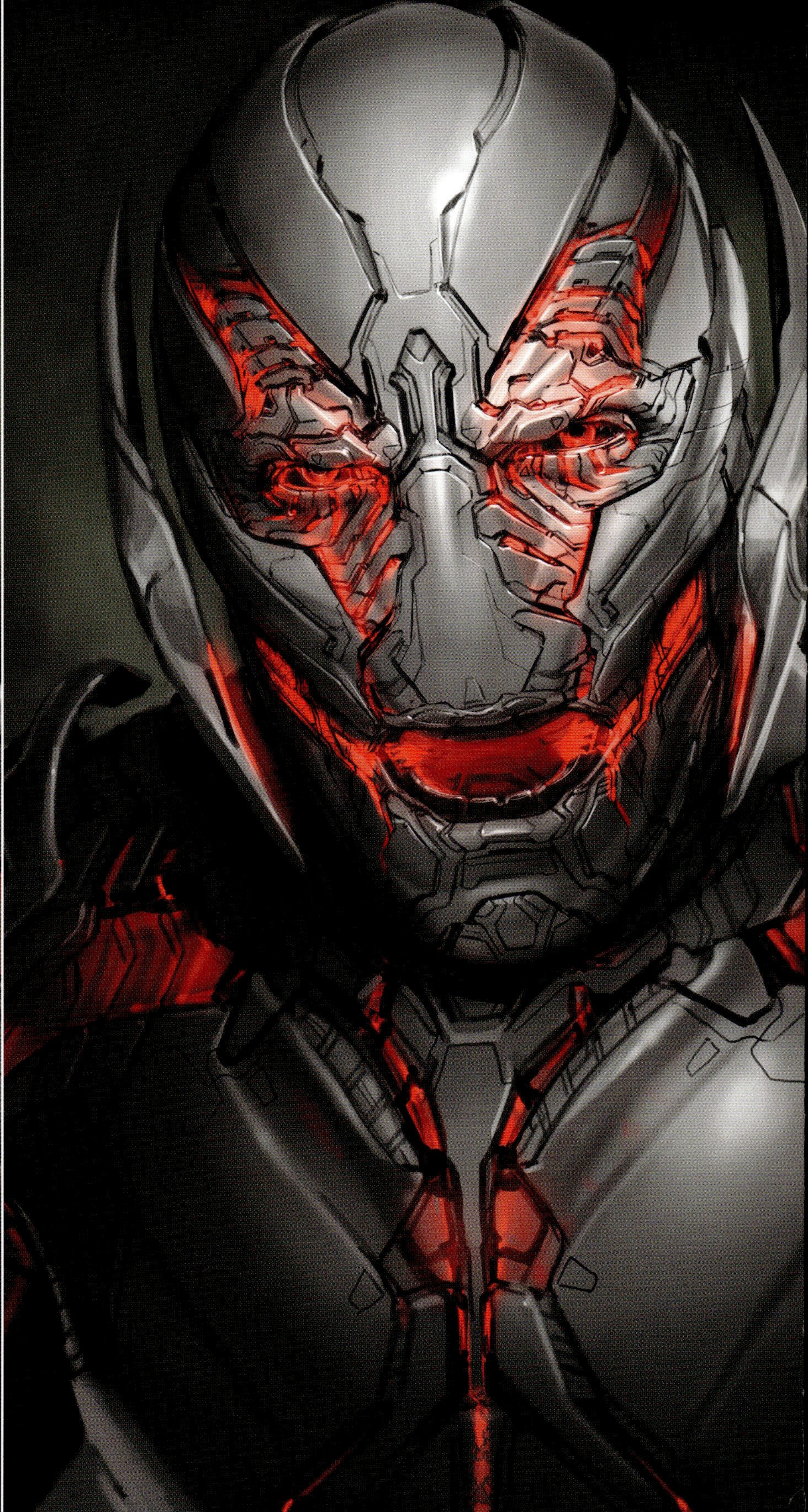

Before the design process began to detail Ultron's full body, Wen, Meinerding, Saunders and the other members of the Visual Development team explored methods of creating an expressive, but equally iconic, head design. "Ultron, in the comics, is a really great design. The one issue with it, cinematically, is that he only has one expression: this manic, screaming face," Meinerding says. "The first issue when we started with the design was how to make his face able to emote a full range of expressions. It was one of the things Joss Whedon was most adamant about with the character—that even though he was digital, he was actually able to be a full character with a full range of emotions. I started with a range of more comic-book-inspired Ultrons to ones that were a little more human. In the end, Joss gravitated toward the one that was the most human."

Ryan Meinerding concept art.

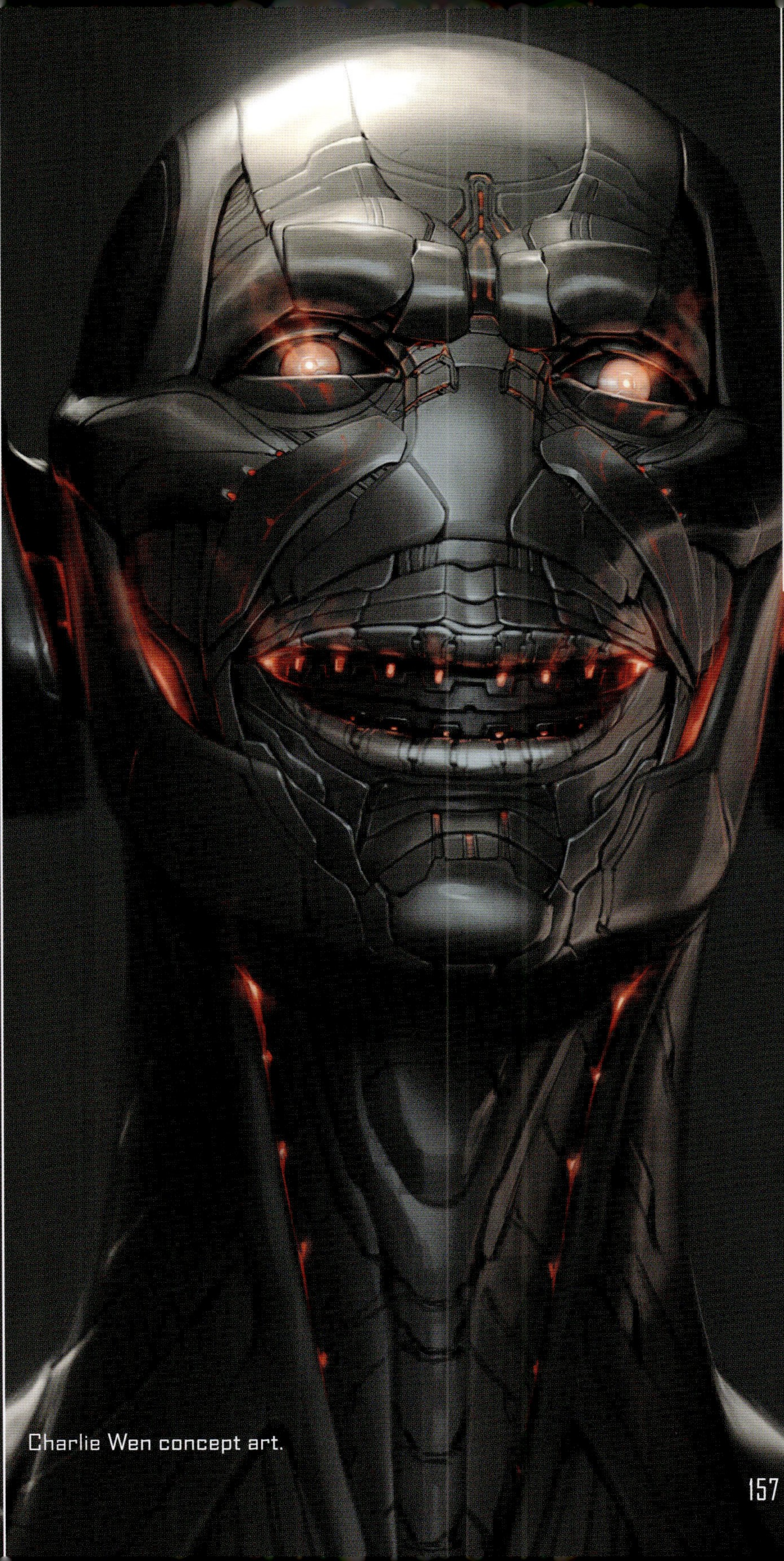

Charlie Wen concept art.

"Ultron is subdued, yet coy and off the cuff—almost the alter ego of Tony Stark," Executive Producer Victoria Alonso says. "The mouth was a huge challenge—trying to find a way to do it so that he didn't look like a puppet. There is a lot of intricacy with the metal teeth and the hollow head—we added this red light, this glow, to give him life so the interior of his mouth wasn't a black hole. James Spader was so on the nose with this character. Sometimes he did things that we didn't think we could translate—but somehow the genius of Industrial Light & Magic and Visual Effects Supervisor Chris Townsend made it work out beautifully."

Ryan Meinerding concept art.

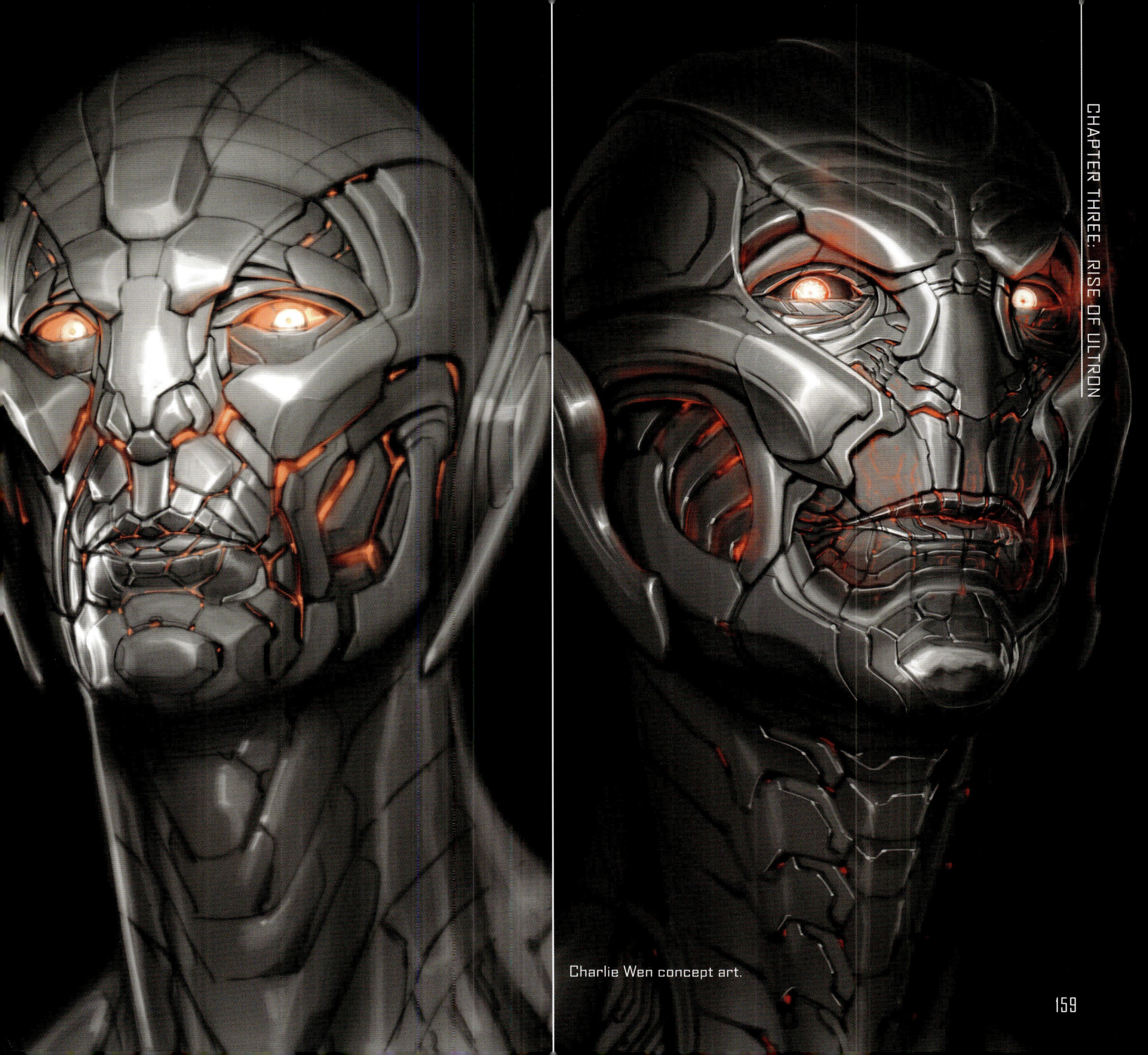

Charlie Wen concept art.

Charlie Wen concept art.

Charlie Wen concept art.

Phil Saunders concept art.

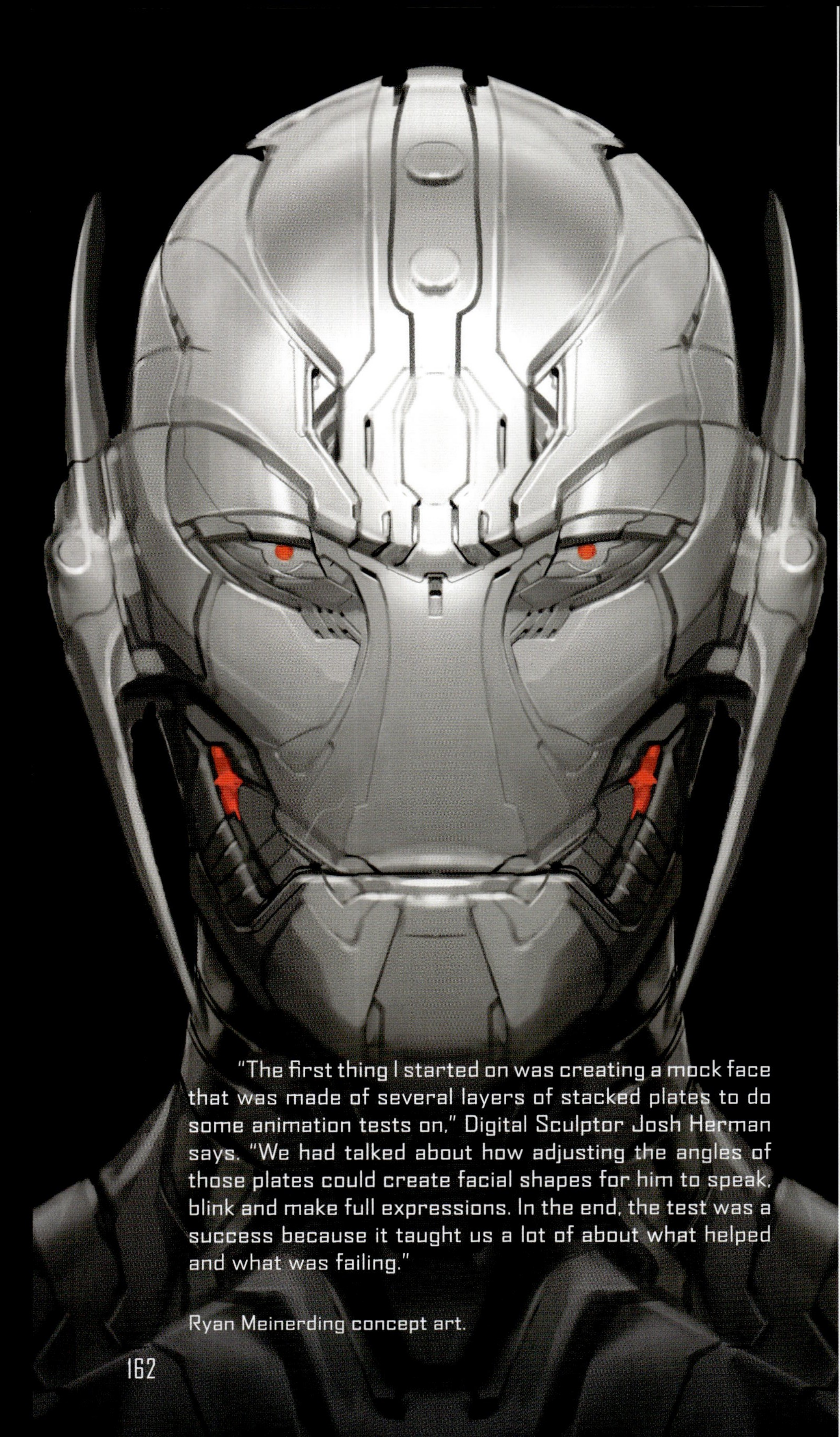

"The first thing I started on was creating a mock face that was made of several layers of stacked plates to do some animation tests on," Digital Sculptor Josh Herman says. "We had talked about how adjusting the angles of those plates could create facial shapes for him to speak, blink and make full expressions. In the end, the test was a success because it taught us a lot of about what helped and what was failing."

Ryan Meinerding concept art.

"We learned that you can create a graphic shape to represent facial phonemes, but certain shapes didn't work from three-quarter and side views, such as the 'o' shape that requires you to purse your lips," Meinerding continues. "From a side view, it was hard to tell what he was trying to say. We also learned that using ideas from camera lenses and irises, we could exaggerate shapes far beyond the neutral state. The entire eye and mouth area could iris back to create the classic Ultron icon, but could still maintain all the movement and naturalness of a human face."

Phil Saunders concept art.

"When we started on Ultron, I knew right away that he was going to be incredibly difficult to model and would also require a lot of R&D," Herman says. "He needed to have the range of expression and movement of a person, but would also have to feel purely mechanical—no bending metal, nothing that would give away the illusion of him feeling constructed from thousands of small pieces."

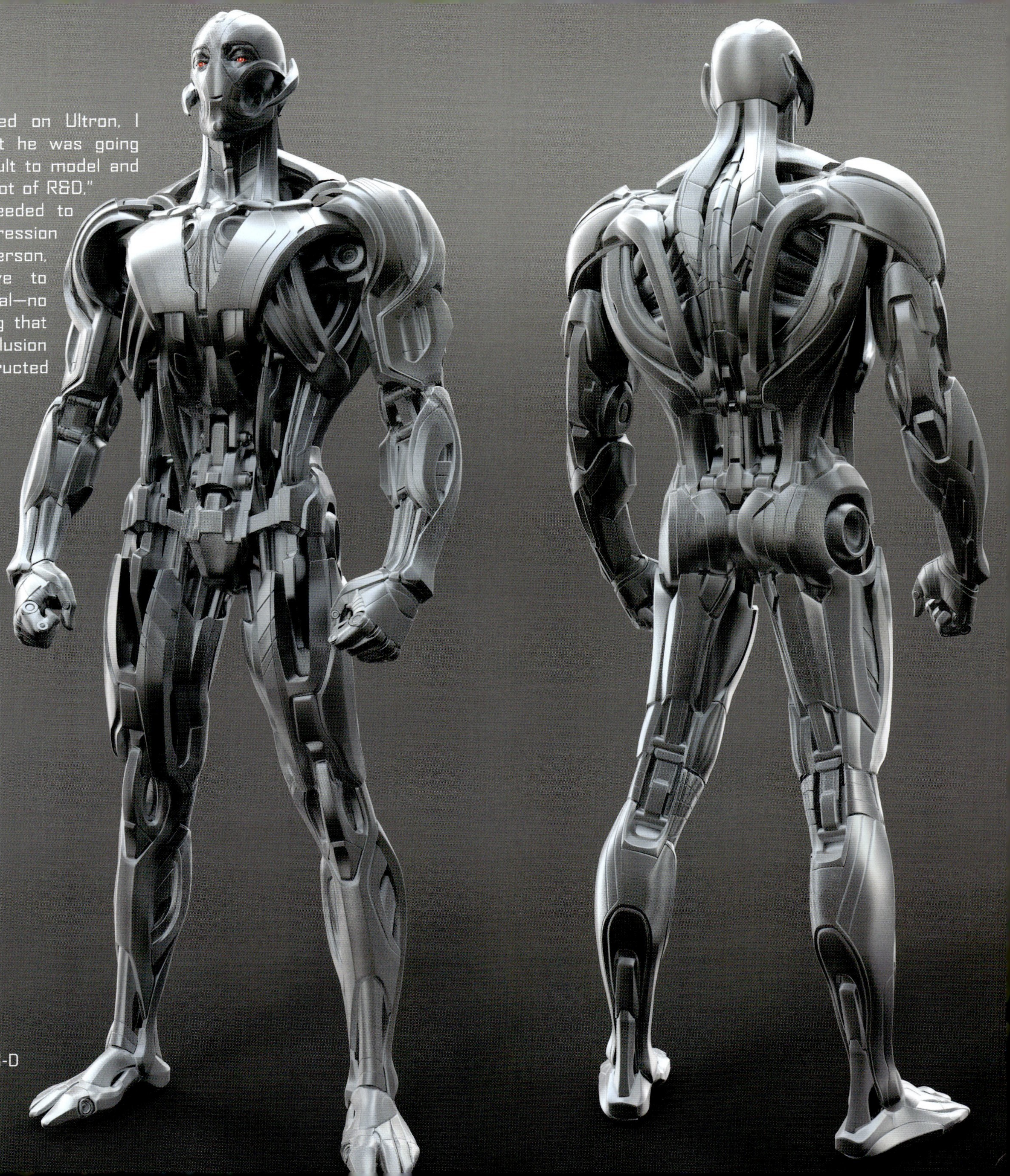

Design by Charlie Wen, 3-D sculpt by Josh Herman.

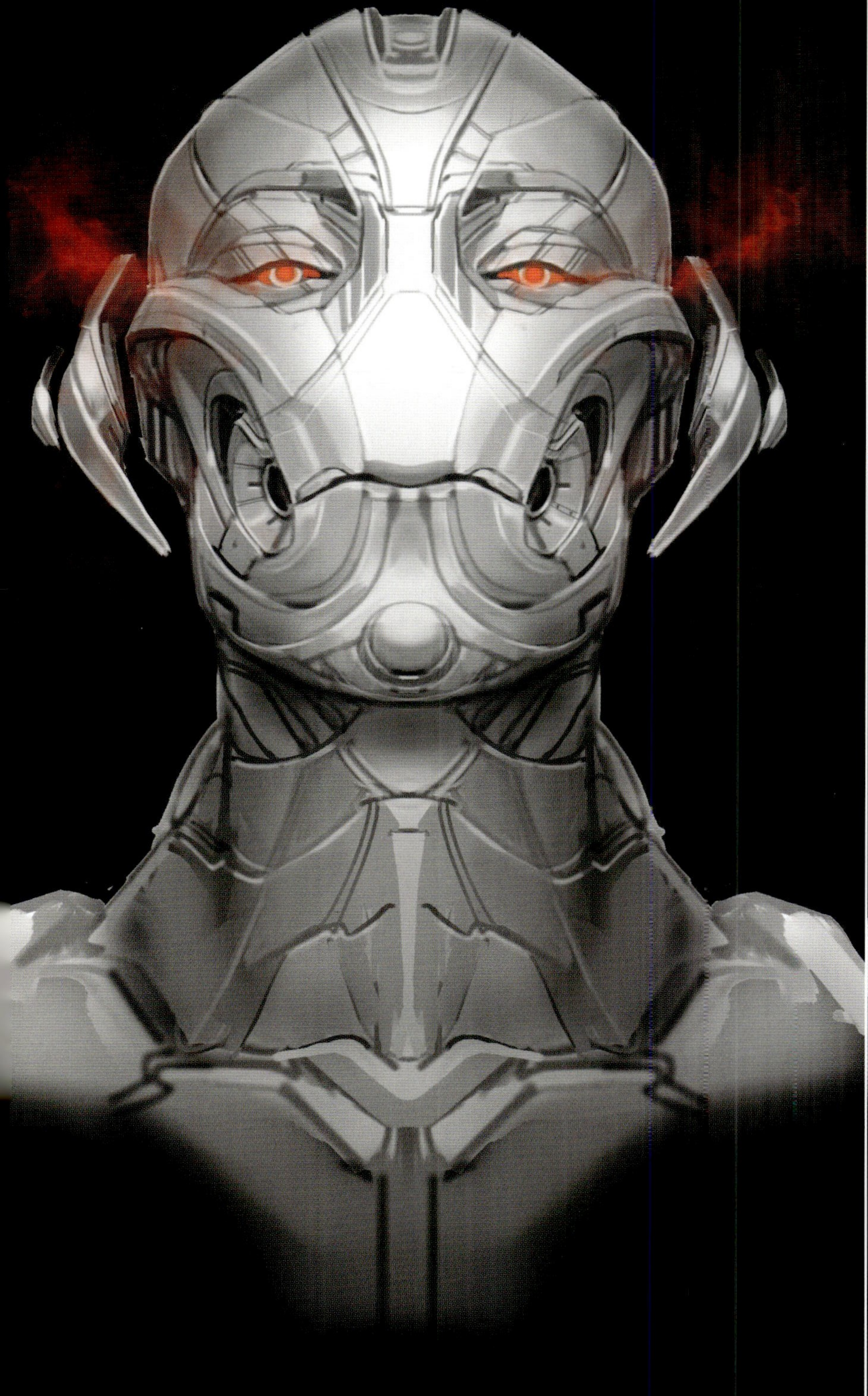

Ryan Meinerding concept art.

ULTRON SENTRIES

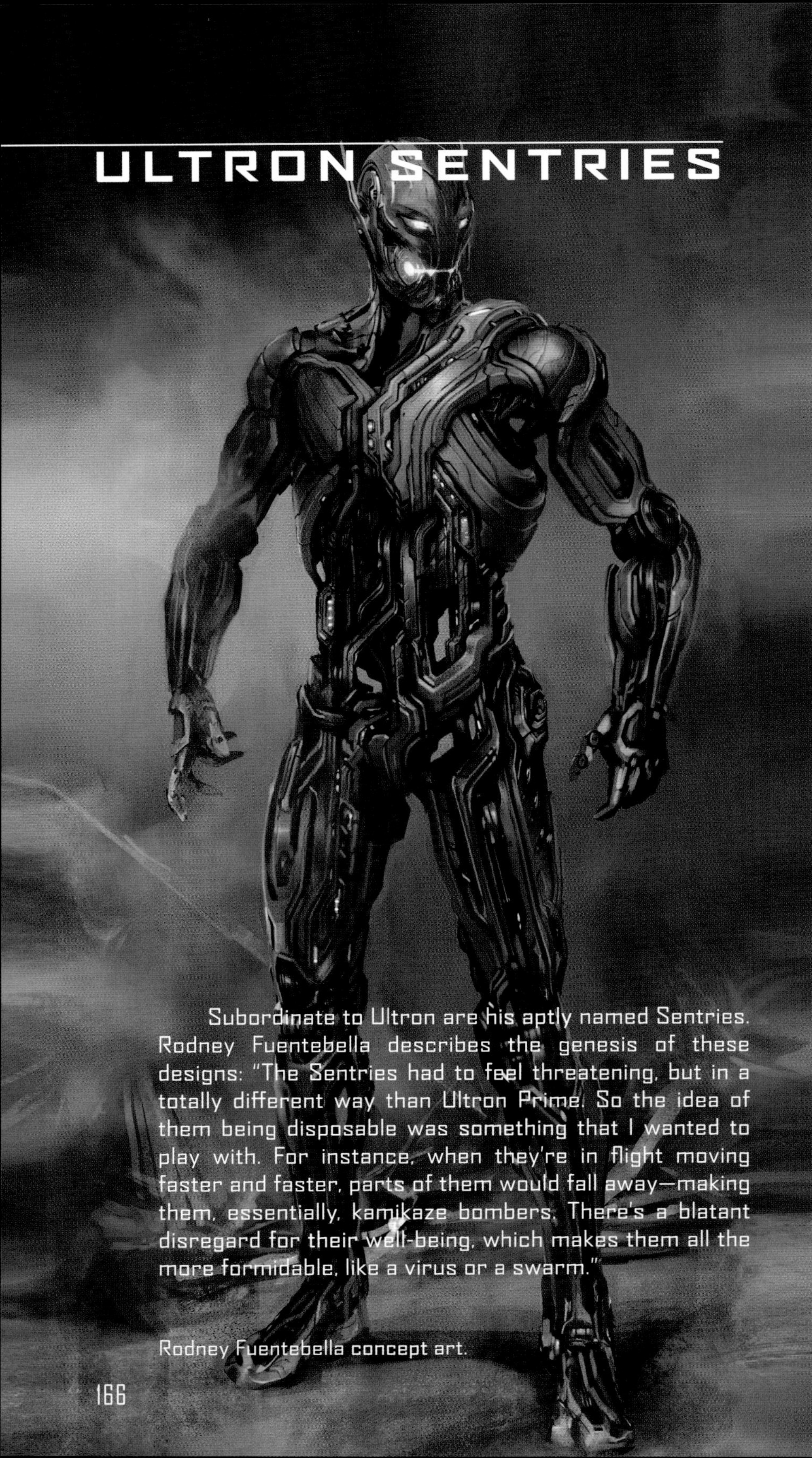

Subordinate to Ultron are his aptly named Sentries. Rodney Fuentebella describes the genesis of these designs: "The Sentries had to feel threatening, but in a totally different way than Ultron Prime. So the idea of them being disposable was something that I wanted to play with. For instance, when they're in flight moving faster and faster, parts of them would fall away—making them, essentially, kamikaze bombers. There's a blatant disregard for their well-being, which makes them all the more formidable, like a virus or a swarm."

Rodney Fuentebella concept art.

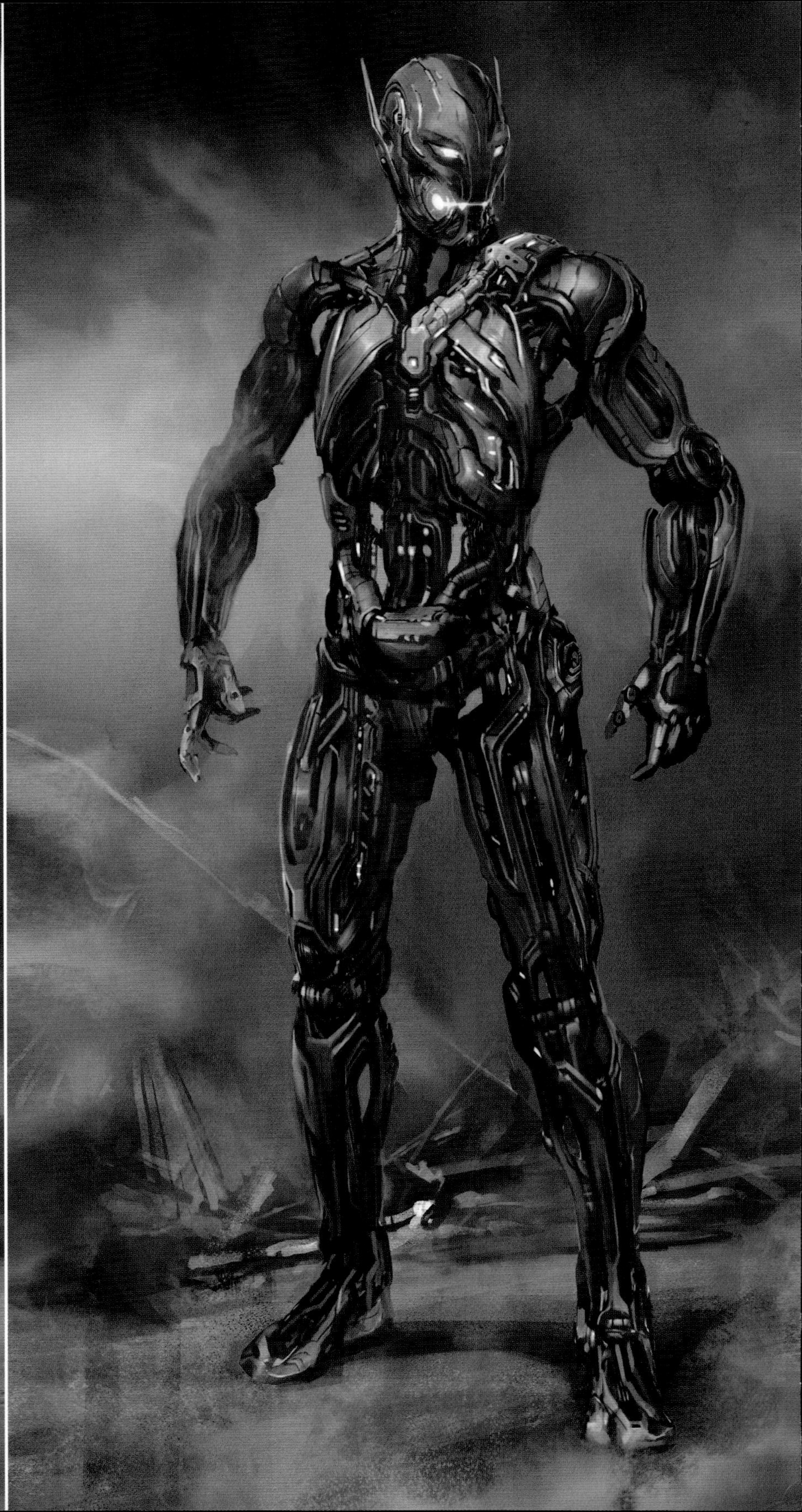

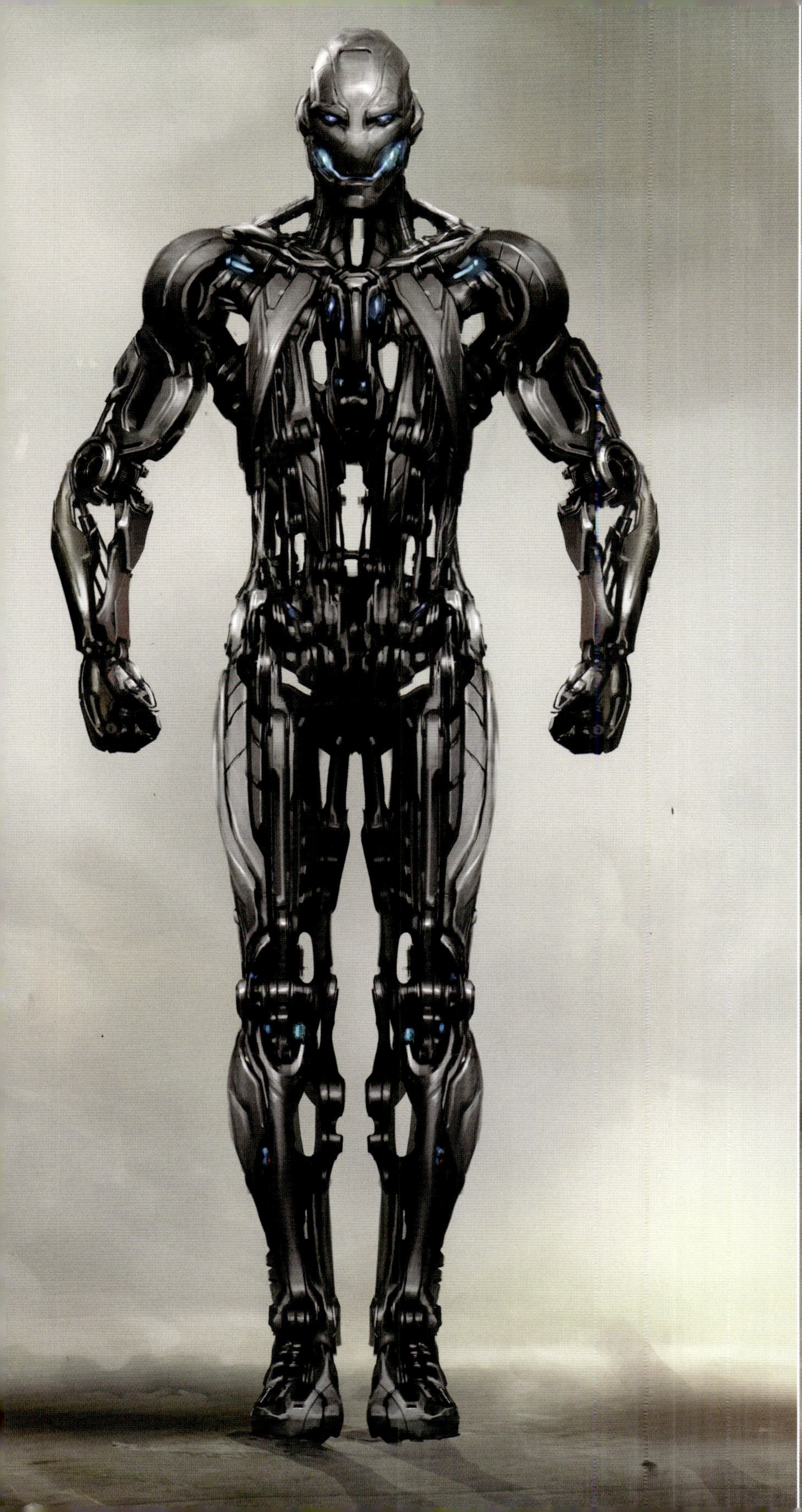

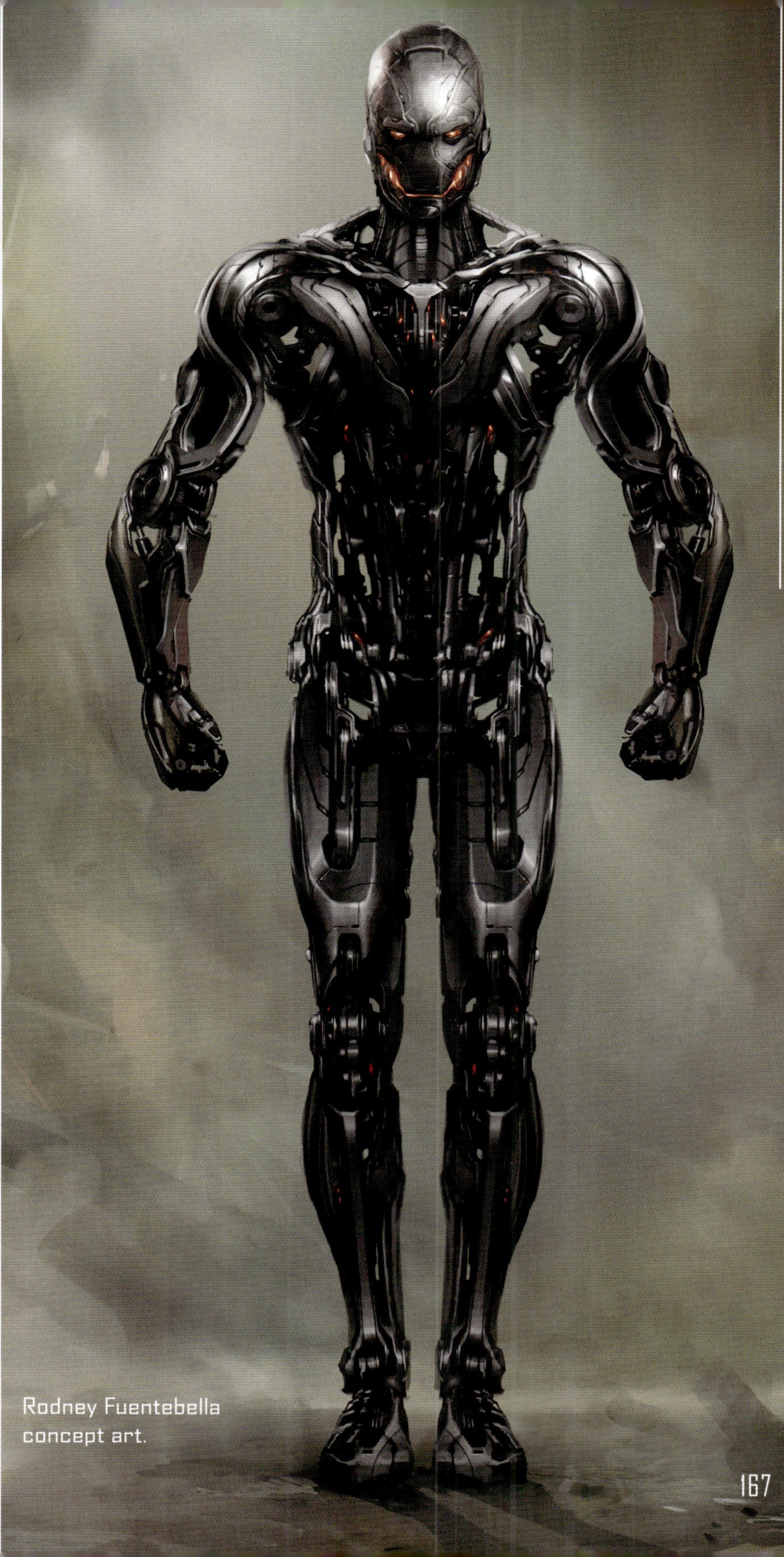

Rodney Fuentebella concept art.

Andy Park also helped create the Ultron Sentries' look. "Ultron Prime went through several design stages before his final form was approved by Joss Whedon," Park explains. "Earlier on, he had a more industrial look made up of actual human industrial parts. So my take on the Sentries was a very rudimentary version of Ultron Prime. It was a primitive, not-so-sophisticated look I was going for. They would also be able to transition their form from humanoid to a flying mode—and to a gunner mode, as well."

Charlie Wen concept art.

Andy Park concept art.

Andy Park concept art.

Rodney Fuentebella concept art.

Another unique challenge was trying to create various concepts for the Ultron Sentries' flight and fire abilities to visually differentiate them from Iron Man. "When crafting the ideas for the Ultron Sentry power studies, it was a sandbox of possibilities," Fuentebella says. "The one driving question was: How can we create powers that are frightening and can also emulate the unstable personality of Ultron? I wanted whatever they did to feel a bit otherworldly, but mostly carnal."

Rodney Fuentebella concept art.

ULTRON TECH

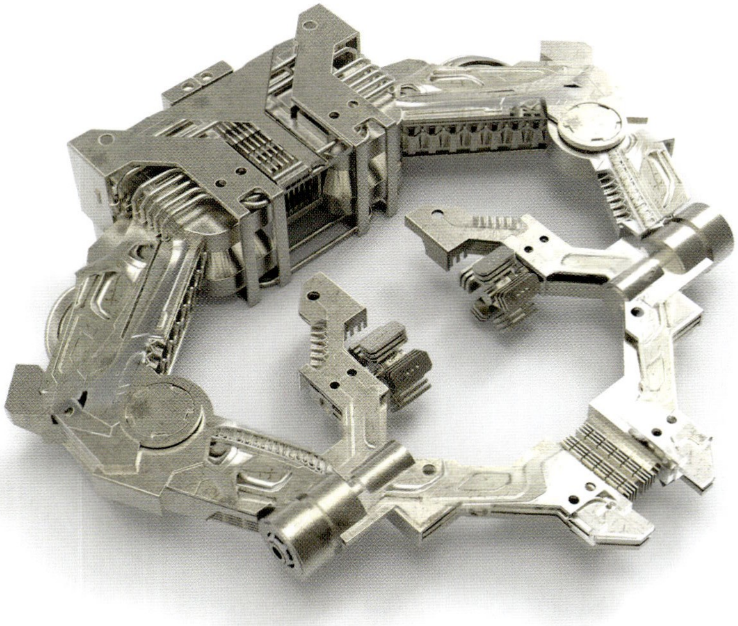

Ultron's hands contain antigravity devices based on technology lodged within the Chitauri leviathan strung up in Baron Strucker's lab. Ultron repurposed the tech that allowed the leviathans to fly as smaller mechanisms in his palms to use the environment around him as a weapon.

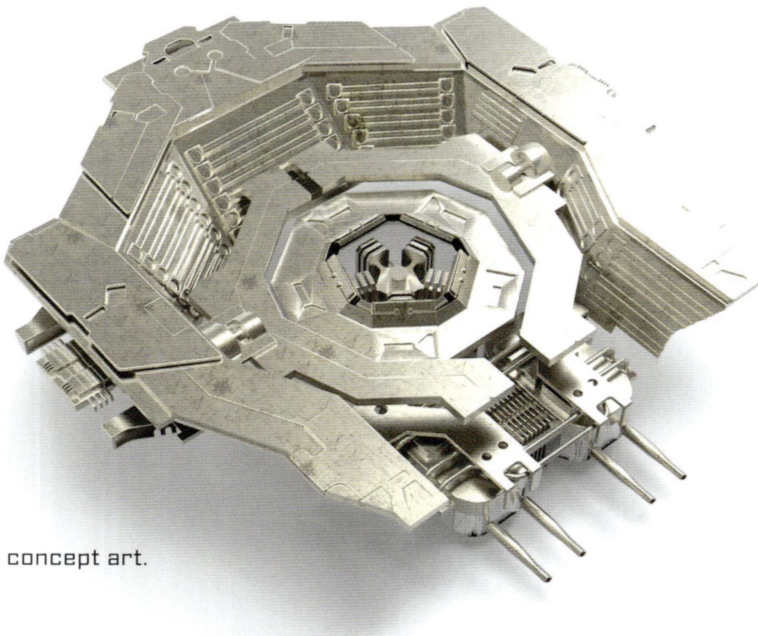

Nick Ainsworth concept art.

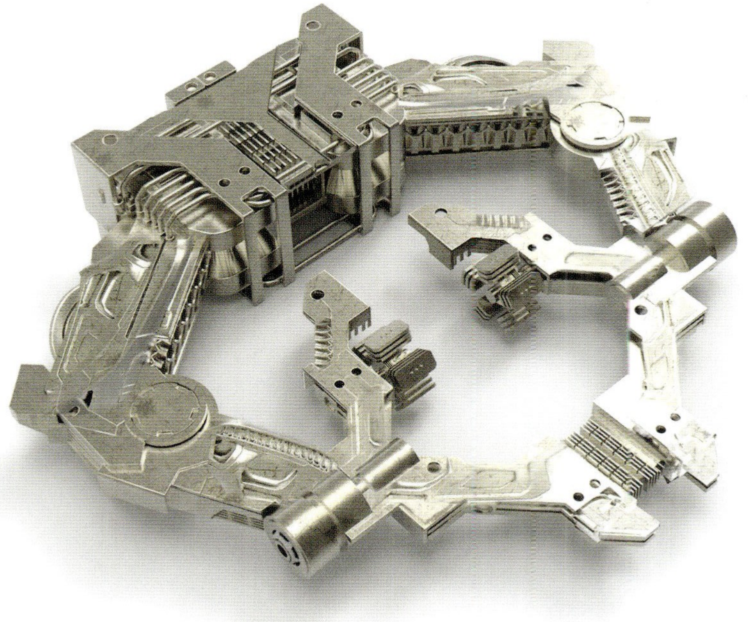

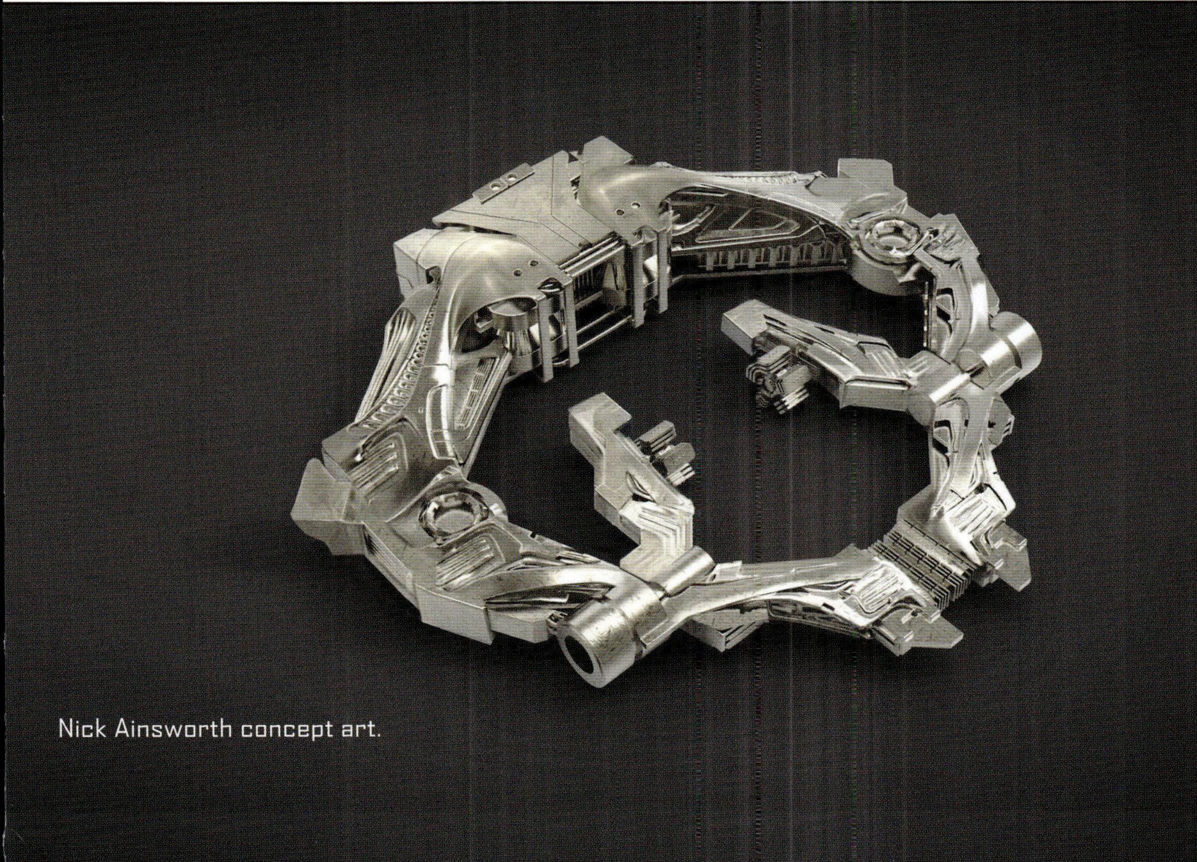

Nick Ainsworth concept art.

Ryan Meinerding concept art.

Ryan Meinerding concept art.

Ryan Meinerding concept art.

CHAPTER FOUR
VISION QUEST

Rodney Fuentebella keyframe.

As the threat of Ultron intensifies, the Avengers embark on a worldwide adventure to uncover his master plan—and, more important, figure out how to stop it. "The Avengers are not just a New York super hero team—they do not just belong to New York. So sure, Avengers Tower is in the middle of Manhattan right above Grand Central, but the Avengers themselves are a global peacekeeping force," Executive Producer Jeremy Latcham says. "They're there for everybody. So when we set out to make this film one of the things Joss Whedon and Kevin Feige and I really talked about early on was the question: How do we give it the scope and scale that it deserves? How do we really break it open?" It was a question for Production Designer Charlie Wood, as well: The Marvel veteran was enthusiastic about creating a world that felt more like a natural environment than a soundstage. "Joss wanted a very varied palette, and the beauty about this film is that we've been able to go all over the world," Wood says. "I think that adds so much to the experience, to the film, that you could never possibly achieve out of a purely studio-based film."

President of Marvel Studios and Executive Producer Kevin Feige also was keen to bring the signature Marvel Cinematic Universe authenticity to the table. "When you have computer-generated characters and so many sequences that need to rely on visual effects as you do in our kinds of films, that shot of your actors coming out onto a real street in a real country on a real location just adds that much more to it, grounding a film as outrageous and as fantastical as a Marvel film in some kind of reality," Feige explains.

ULYSSES KLAUE

Jack Dudman concept art.

Concept art by Renata Gilbert and Laura Lilley.

"Ulysses Klaue has quite the outlandish look in the comics, and it really wouldn't work within the current environment in the film," Costume Illustrator Jack Dudman recalls. "He is definitely a character we went in more of a real-world direction with." An arms dealer well-versed in the ways of the world, Klaue carries a shroud of tattoos that further accentuates his personality and history. "His backstory being a man-for-hire meant that his tattoos could be quite eclectic and varied in style," Dudman continues. "For instance, in the comics, Klaue ends up with this mechanical arm/claw, and I wanted to hint at this possible future in a very unsubtle way: a massive scorpion claw reaching down onto the back of his hand. 'The Murderous Master of Sound' is his name from the books, and the bold, jagged shapes from his original costume also influenced some of the tattoos."

Jack Dudman concept art.

KLAUE'S FREIGHTER

Ultron's quest for the precious metal Vibranium brings him to the realm of Ulysses Klaue, a pirate-like arms dealer whose base of operations is a massive freighter in South Africa. That kind of location wasn't easy to find, so it was up to Charlie Wood to bring this set to life. "The idea started with an old printing press. The building just happened to follow exactly the same proportions as the interior of a ship. We knew it straightaway. We had one look at it, and that was it. It's a wonderful place because really we didn't have to change much. From a construction aspect, we just heightened it. We put a lot of our money into the set dressing, the armaments and all of that, and again it was a massive building so it gave both the main unit and the second unit an awful lot of opportunities. Cinematographer Ben Davis did a lovely job of lighting it—he kept it very shadowed and very hot—and that was a part of the film where Joss Whedon really wanted to feel a lot of heat, sweat, darkness and worry."

Roberto Fernández Castro keyframe.

VIBRANIUM

Industrial Light & Magic concept art.

While aboard Klaue's freighter, the Avengers discover he's been wheeling and dealing the precious metal Vibranium, a rare substance that originates from the African nation of Wakanda. "The Vibranium ingots were a design that Joss Whedon wanted very clean, as if it was a valuable commodity like gold," Property Master Barry Gibbs says.

Industrial Light & Magic concept art.

Andy Park keyframe.

Jackson Sze keyframe.

SOUTH AFRICA

While aboard Ulysses Klaue's freighter, Scarlet Witch taps into our heroes' psyches, tearing through their fears and insecurities. She spurs something within each of them, but no one could have expected the effect her tampering would have on Bruce Banner. As he transforms into the Hulk, his skin takes on a paler shade of green, his veins throb with ferocity, and he begins a rampage through Johannesburg, South Africa. "The idea is he's more of the Hulk than the Hulk normally is. So we set out to see what that means," Head of Visual Development Ryan Meinerding recalls. "The first images I did Joss Whedon felt he was a little too green and wanted to add some red to the eyes. And he wanted to add sweat, like a flop sweat, just all over the place. His teeth are more messed up, his veins are thicker and more exposed, and there's spittle coming out. He just can't control himself at all—he's more feral and animalistic."

Ryan Meinerding concept art.

VERONIKA SATELLITE

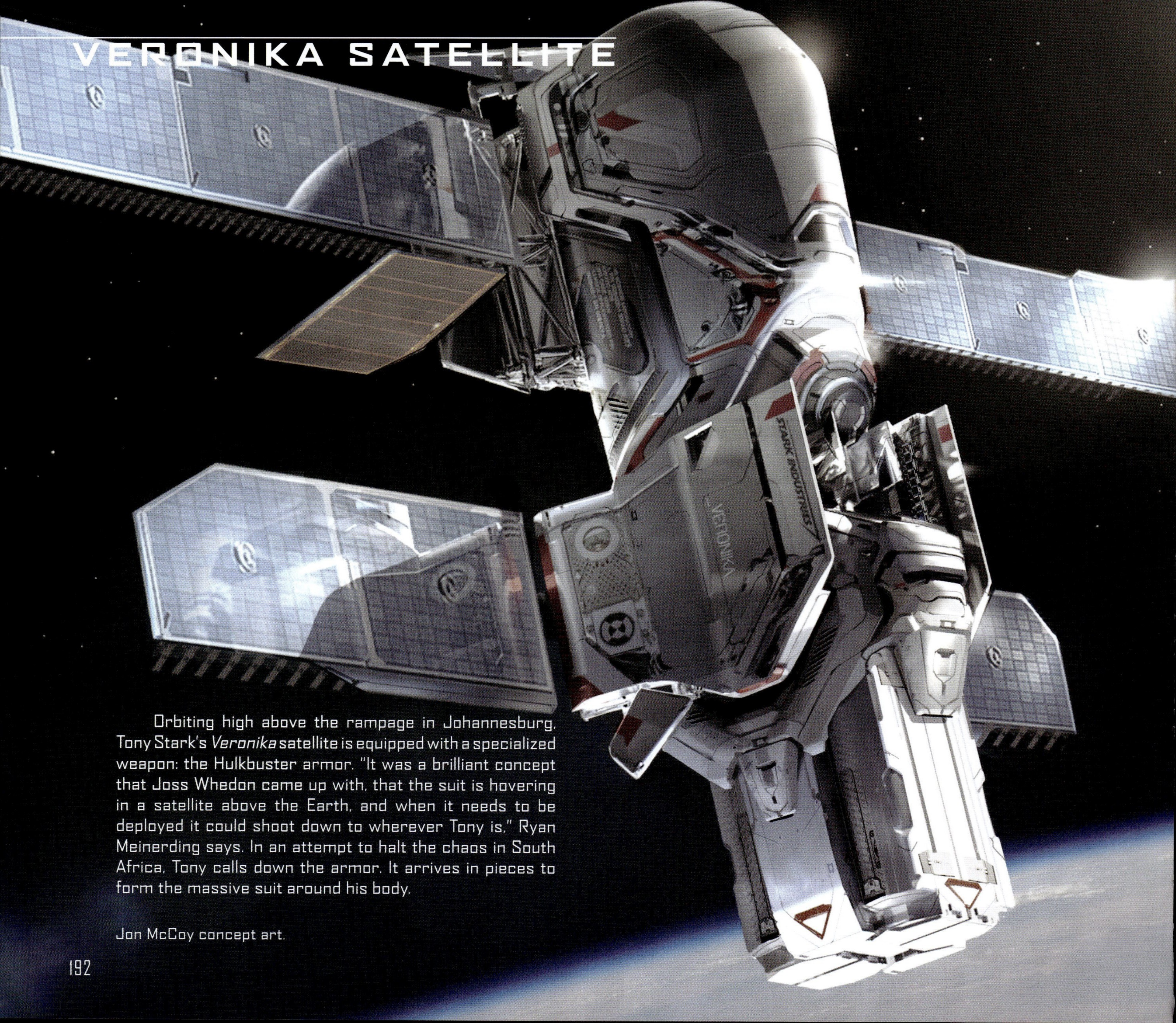

Orbiting high above the rampage in Johannesburg, Tony Stark's *Veronika* satellite is equipped with a specialized weapon: the Hulkbuster armor. "It was a brilliant concept that Joss Whedon came up with, that the suit is hovering in a satellite above the Earth, and when it needs to be deployed it could shoot down to wherever Tony is," Ryan Meinerding says. In an attempt to halt the chaos in South Africa, Tony calls down the armor. It arrives in pieces to form the massive suit around his body.

Jon McCoy concept art.

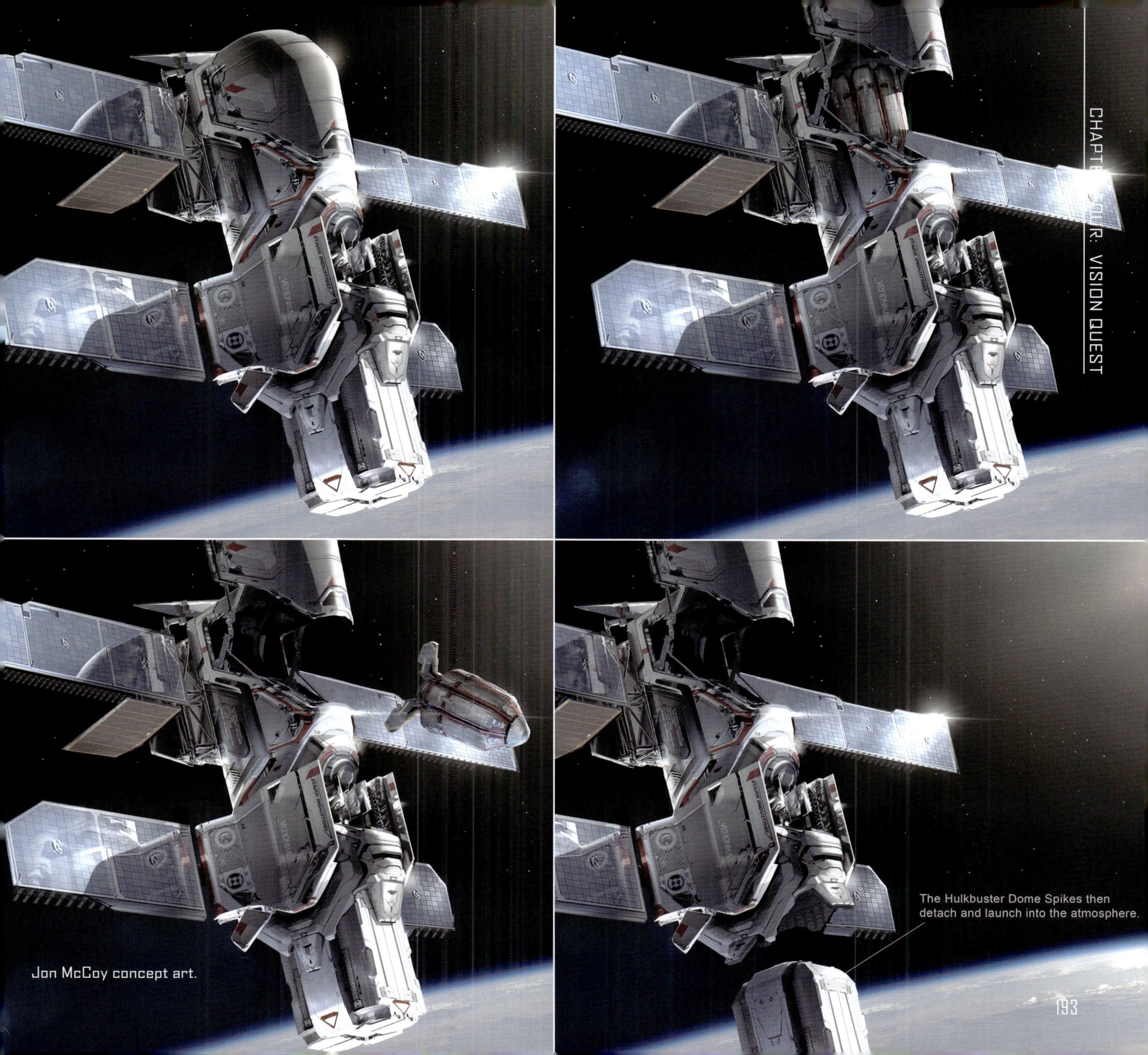

The Hulkbuster Dome Spikes then detach and launch into the atmosphere.

Jon McCoy concept art.

Chris Rosewarne concept art.

Pete Thompson concept art.

Pete Thompson concept art.

Jon McCoy concept art.

HULKBUSTER POD

Josh Nizzi concept art.

Josh Nizzi concept art.

Jon McCoy concept art.

Jon McCoy concept art.

Ryan Meinerding was eager to see an idea from an earlier film finally make its debut in *Avengers: Age of Ultron*. "Something we had talked about on *Marvel's The Avengers* with the Mark 7 armor was the idea of a hovering replacement-part system so that if some part of the suit was damaged, the suit could immediately call down a replacement arm or leg or something. It was great to bring that back and make use of it this time around."

Industrial Light & Magic concept art.

The Hulkbuster, originally called Model 14, made its first appearance in 1994 in *Iron Man #304*. The suit almost immediately became iconic as one of the few weapons capable of bringing down the unstoppable Hulk—the comic-book showdown was one of epic proportions. "We knew it was going to be in the movie. It was always going to be in the movie. Every iteration of *Avengers: Age of Ultron* had a Hulk vs. Hulkbuster fight in it. It's something fans want; it's something we want. It's a story you want to tell," Jeremy Latcham says.

Ryan Meinerding keyframe.

HULKBUSTER

"The Hulkbuster was specifically designed by Tony Stark to subdue the Hulk if he lost control. In order to combat the Hulk, the suit needed to be large, heavily armored and very strong. The weaponry on the Hulkbuster was geared toward facing and repelling the Hulk's preferred method of combat, hand-to-hand," Concept Artist Josh Nizzi explains. "I explored different ideas around this, such as electrical discharge on the exterior of the suit, shock-absorbing materials, synthetic muscle and replaceable body parts. The comic-book design for the Hulkbuster has such an interesting head-and-neck area. That was something I really wanted to preserve, but for dynamic poses and range of motion I knew that would be a challenge. Range of motion was also a challenge when it came to the thick armor—I tried to design the armor so that it allowed the suit to move, but also conveyed the strength and mass it needed to fight the Hulk. I didn't want it to look like an all-around athlete like the Iron Man suit—rather a power lifter."

Josh Nizzi concept art.

Josh Nizzi concept art.

"Since the Hulk would be demolishing and removing the armor plating on the Hulkbuster, I had to design the inner workings of the suit, as well. Ryan Meinerding had the idea that under the armor there should be sharp gear-like parts in constant motion, which would be a deterrent for the Hulk grabbing it. I also had to take into consideration how the suit assembled around Iron Man when it was activated," Nizzi says.

Josh Nizzi concept art

Josh Nizzi concept art.

"For being as loved as Hulkbuster is, there really aren't than many versions of it in the comics—he doesn't appear that often. So as far as comic-book inspiration, Adi Granov did a really beautiful cover that we were referencing, but it was more about trying to capture what Joss Whedon wanted out of the character," Ryan Meinerding says. "The previous Iron Man suits were about creating a wearable aircraft, and this suit is distinctly not that. The bigger, beefier shapes that don't necessarily fit together as gracefully seemed to be what Joss really responded to."

Ryan Meinerding concept art.

Ryan Meinerding concept art.

Concept Artist Phil Saunders, who had already designed his fair share of Iron Man suits for previous films, did a number of early passes at the Hulkbuster design. "The gold 'Y' shape in Iron Man's face is key to making a suit feel like Iron Man. Besides that, and the gold-and-red color breakup and the obvious RT in the center of the chest, there is in fact a lot of freedom in what you can do with the forms and still keep it recognizable as ol' metal-head," he explains. "The opportunity to create a completely different silhouette for Iron Man, since all of his traditional suits are effectively human proportioned, is also very exciting."

Phil Saunders concept art.

Phil Saunders concept art.

Charlie Wen concept art.

Ryan Meinerding concept art.

Josh Nizzi concept art.

"For the design I did, I wanted to create something that is more defensive, a counter-puncher suit. So I looked at modern armor like football pads and heavy-duty military padding," Concept Artist Rodney Fuentebella says.

Rodney Fuentebella concept art.

Phil Saunders concept art.

"It was important to not make it so chunky that you don't believe that it moves. We didn't want it to seem like he's just a giant boulder—it doesn't offer the dynamism that you need to have for the fight," Executive Producer Victoria Alonso says. "We also needed it to keep from becoming too slick, as we risk it becoming something that doesn't feel big enough to take on the Hulk."

Josh Nizzi concept art.

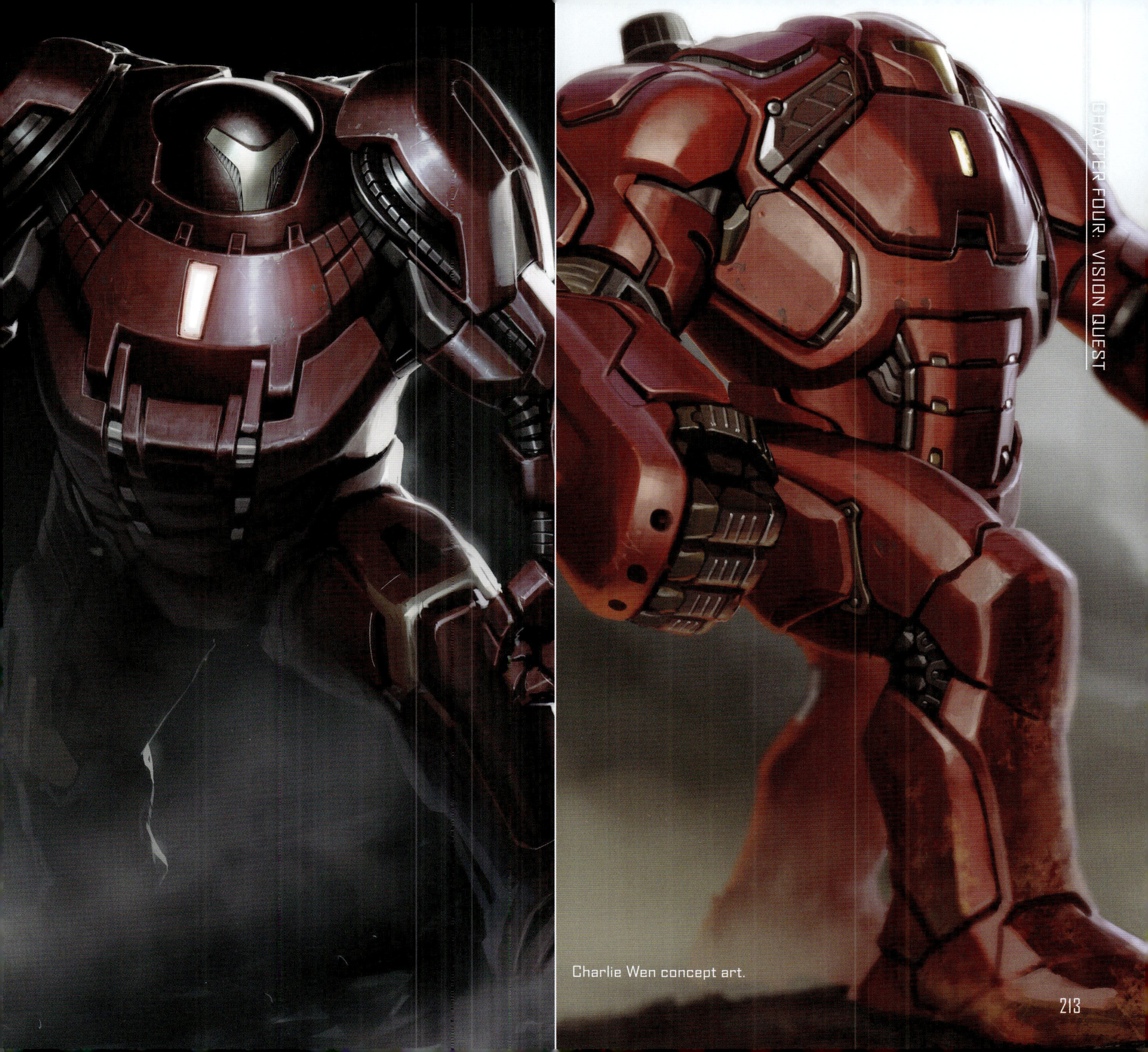

Charlie Wen concept art.

Andy Park concept art.

Phil Saunders concept art.

“Joss had talked about Banner and Tony working together to develop this suit—that it was as much Banner’s design as it was Tony’s. The idea being that Banner was always worried about the fact he could become the Hulk and destroy a bunch of stuff, so he wanted to have a failsafe. This led to the idea of Tony and Banner coming up with various ways to bring down the Hulk—for instance, calculating how many pounds per square inch on Hulk’s jaw it would take to knock him out, and then creating a specific arm for that,” Meinerding explains.

Design by Josh Nizzi, 3-D sculpt by Josh Herman.

Josh Nizzi concept art.

Blow after blow, the Hulk and Hulkbuster tear their way through Johannesburg in an all-out, splash-page-worthy brawl. "I think this sequence is dynamic and fun and different. And considering that we've done a lot of robot/Iron Man models before, we always have to find new ways to make it different," Alonso says. "I think one of the funniest moments in the movie is given to the Hulkbuster when it's punching Hulk, trying to keep him down—it's really cool to see that happen with very few words."

Ryan Meinerding keyframe.

HULK VS. HULKBUSTER FIGHT GAGS

BY RODNEY FUENTEBELLA

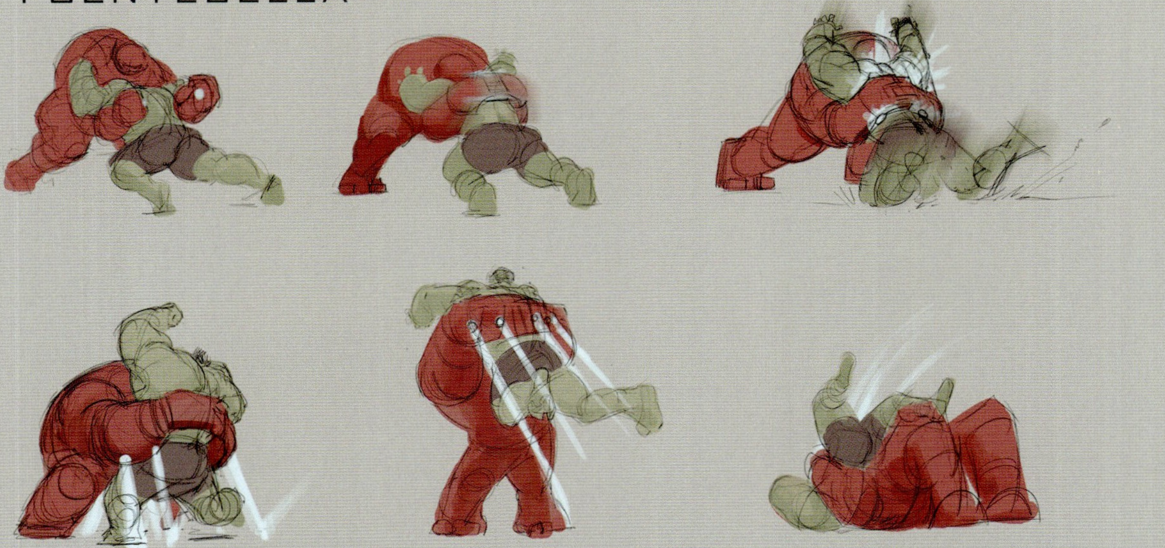

TARGETING...

Charlie Wen concept art.

Ryan Meinerding concept art.

Charlie Wen concept art.

BARTON'S HOMESTEAD

The events in South Africa paint a dark picture for the Avengers, particularly the Hulk—the real, uncontrollable and mercilessly destructive Hulk. In the aftermath, the Avengers search for a place to call home in a world slowly turning against them. Hawkeye speaks up, revealing he knows of a location that Nick Fury kept out of S.H.I.E.L.D.'s files. The stronghold turns out to be his country home, in the middle of nowhere—where the team will be safe, for now. The idea for making Hawkeye's secret haven a farmhouse was inspired by Writer/Director Joss Whedon's own upbringing. Charlie Wood explains, "It all sprang from Joss: He was brought up on a farm, I think on the Eastern Seaboard somewhere, and from day one he wanted something that was very, very natural—unnoticeably natural. He wanted to create an environment that was actually slightly edgy, because there's a lot of stress there—they're all starting to fight."

Paul Chandler concept art.

Bob Cheshire concept art.

Ryan Meinerding concept art.

Ryan Meinerding concept art.

THOR'S NIGHTMARE

During the confrontation, some of the Avengers fall under the Scarlet Witch's spell, forcing them to face their greatest fears. For Thor's sequence, Concept Artist Bob Cheshire was tasked with creating a piece that placed Thor in the resting place for his fallen comrades. "This space had to feel both reverential and fittingly grand, as it was the mausoleum of Bor, Odin's father/Thor's grandfather," Cheshire explains. "So tonally and architecturally, it needed to be proud, stately and grand—but also sober, respectful and peaceful."

Bob Cheshire concept art.

PEOPLES OF HEL

Jack Dudman concept art.

Jack Dudman concept art.

SOUTH KOREA

The next stop on the Avengers' globetrotting mission brings them to the bustling streets of South Korea. "South Korea is a visually dynamic place, but a lot of specific photo reference had been provided by Locations, art directors and so on," Bob Cheshire says. "The concepts we did within the Art Department were an example of taking a number of existing real-world spaces and sets, and visually combining them to achieve a cohesive look and general direction—but the visuals are only the tiniest of beginnings for hundreds of people doing far more complicated work. You have scenes shot in South Korea; a train that is bought and delivered to the UK to be smashed up; sets designed, built and dressed to replicate South Korea in London. Concept visuals support the visual thinking of the production designer and art directors. That's what, why and whom we are there for."

Bob Cheshire concept art.

横浜
42
5
横浜
静岡
横浜
厚木
4
3

DR. CHO'S LAB

South Korea is also the home of the brilliant Dr. Cho, whose lab needed to rival the sprawling genius of Tony Stark. "It was necessary to visually distinguish Dr. Cho's lab from Stark's. So for example, the lighting became much cooler, more ambivalent and brooding in Dr. Cho's lab, which contrasts against the silvery optimism and swagger of Tony Stark's lab," Bob Cheshire explains.

Jack Dudman concept art.

Bob Cheshire concept art.

Bob Cheshire concept art.

THE CRADLE

Introducing Dr. Cho and her lab in South Korea were all ways, as Jeremy Latcham says, of "enriching the Marvel Cinematic Universe." "She's working in regenerative medicine and making all kind of strides," Latcham explains. "She's got a Marvel Universe tie-in, a son that some people might have heard of—maybe we'll get to that one day. But she's definitely connected to the Universe. You want to keep broadening the Universe, you want to keep telling new stories and introducing new characters. But if there's someone who can answer the question that already exists, let's seek 'em out. Let's go talk to 'em."

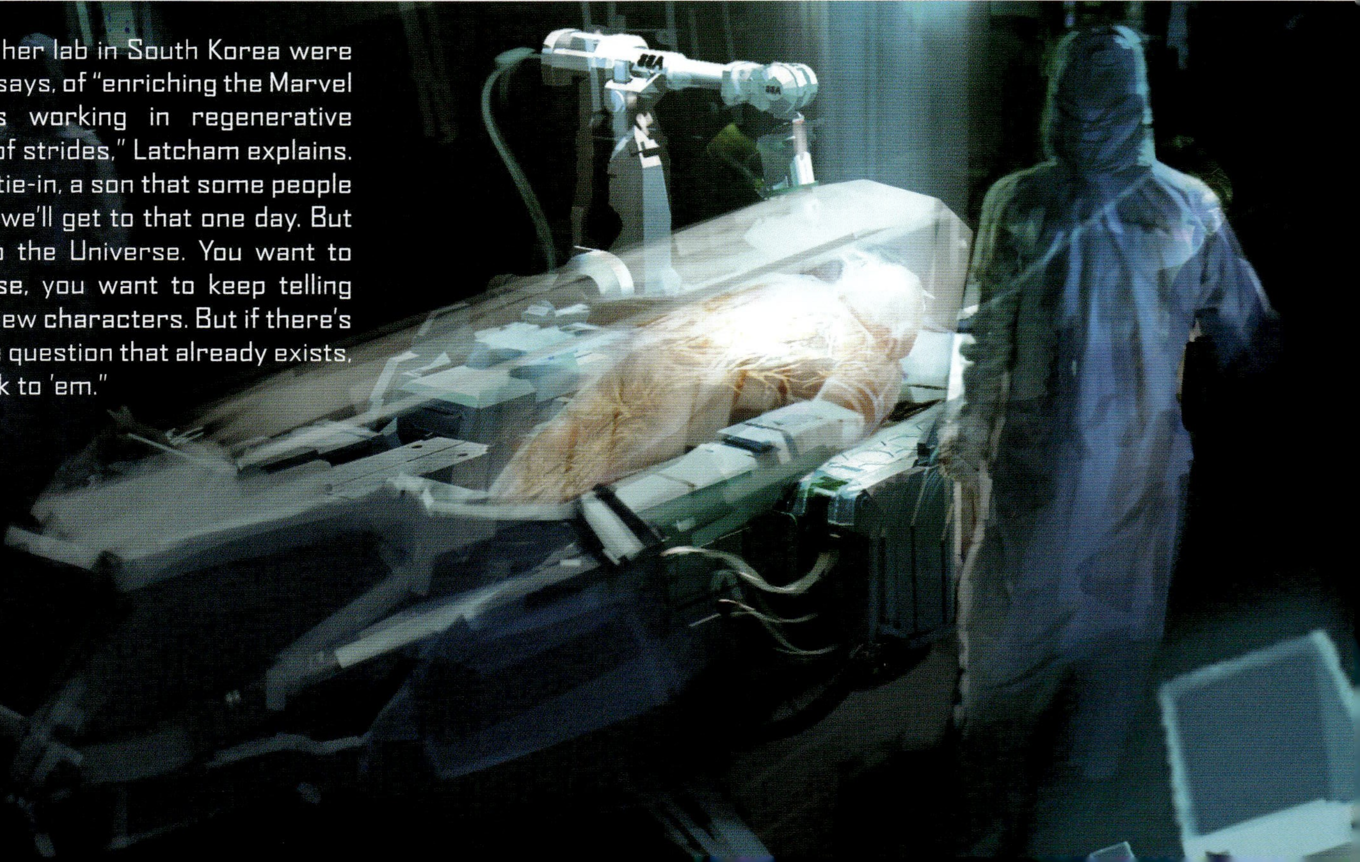

Tim Hill concept art.

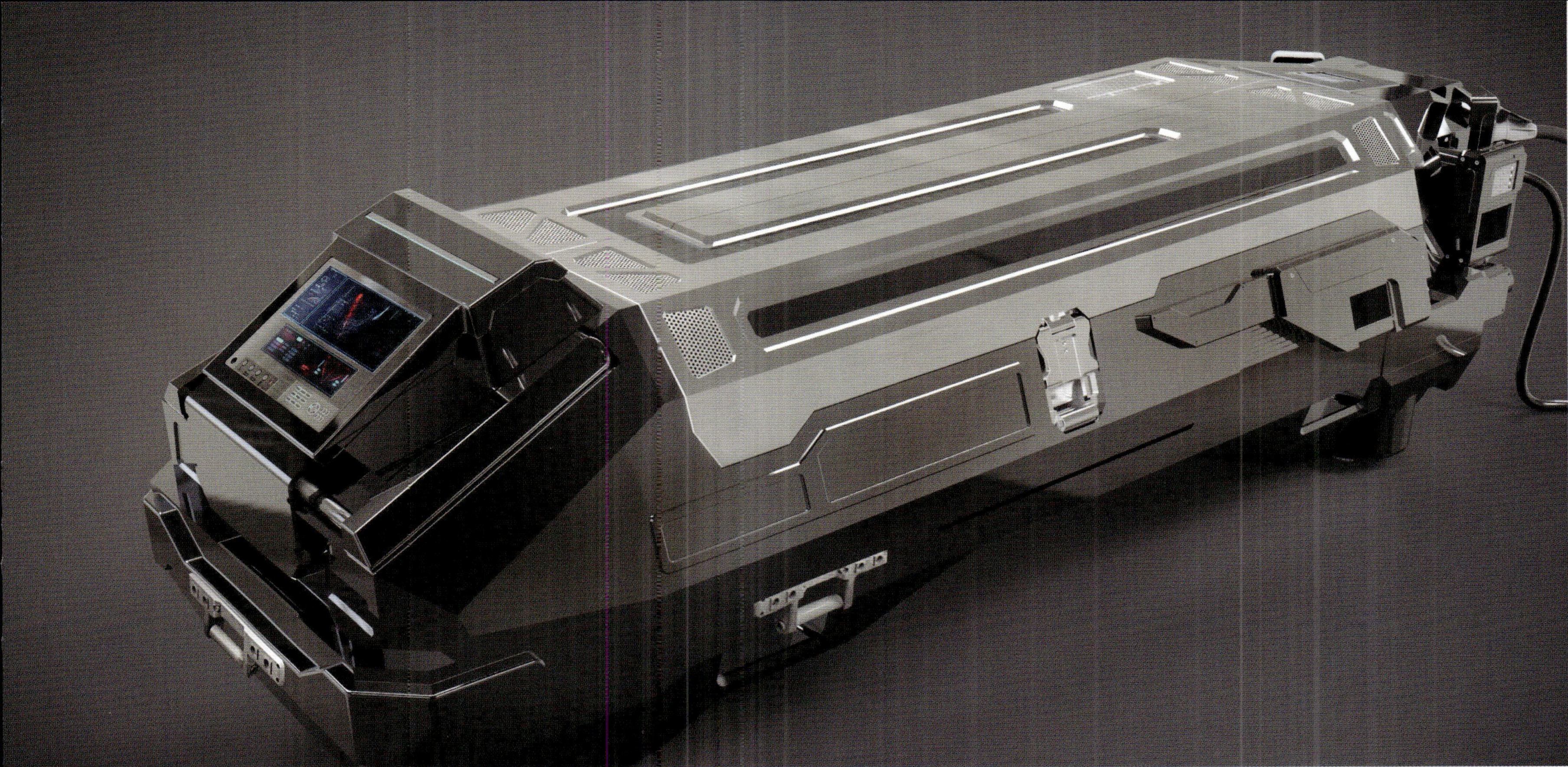

Paul Catling concept art.

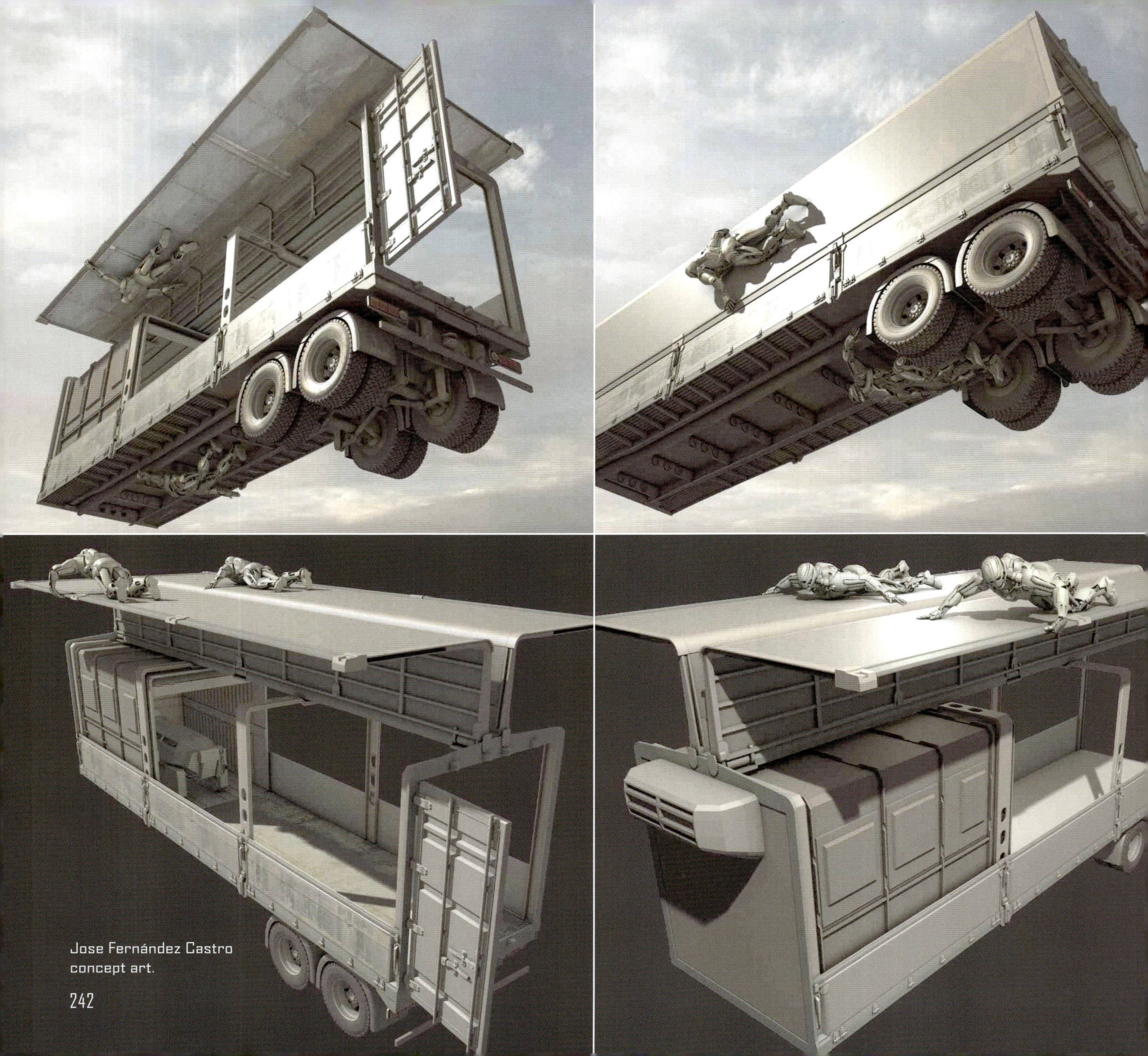

Jose Fernández Castro concept art.

Ivan Weightman concept art.

"Black Widow, though just a human amongst gods, is just as skilled and powerful as her comrades," Concept Artist Andy Park says.

Andy Park keyframe.

"I love creating moments with frenetic action and fun poses," Rodney Fuentebella says. "I created a bunch of thumbnails first to find the best way to have the sense of speed and the dire consequences if they do not succeed. Eventually, I created two illustrations: one depicting an overall look of the scene as Iron Man flies in, and another more intimate scene of both Iron Man and Quicksilver keeping time with the out-of-control train."

Rodney Fuentebella keyframe.

Bob Cheshire concept art.

THE VISION

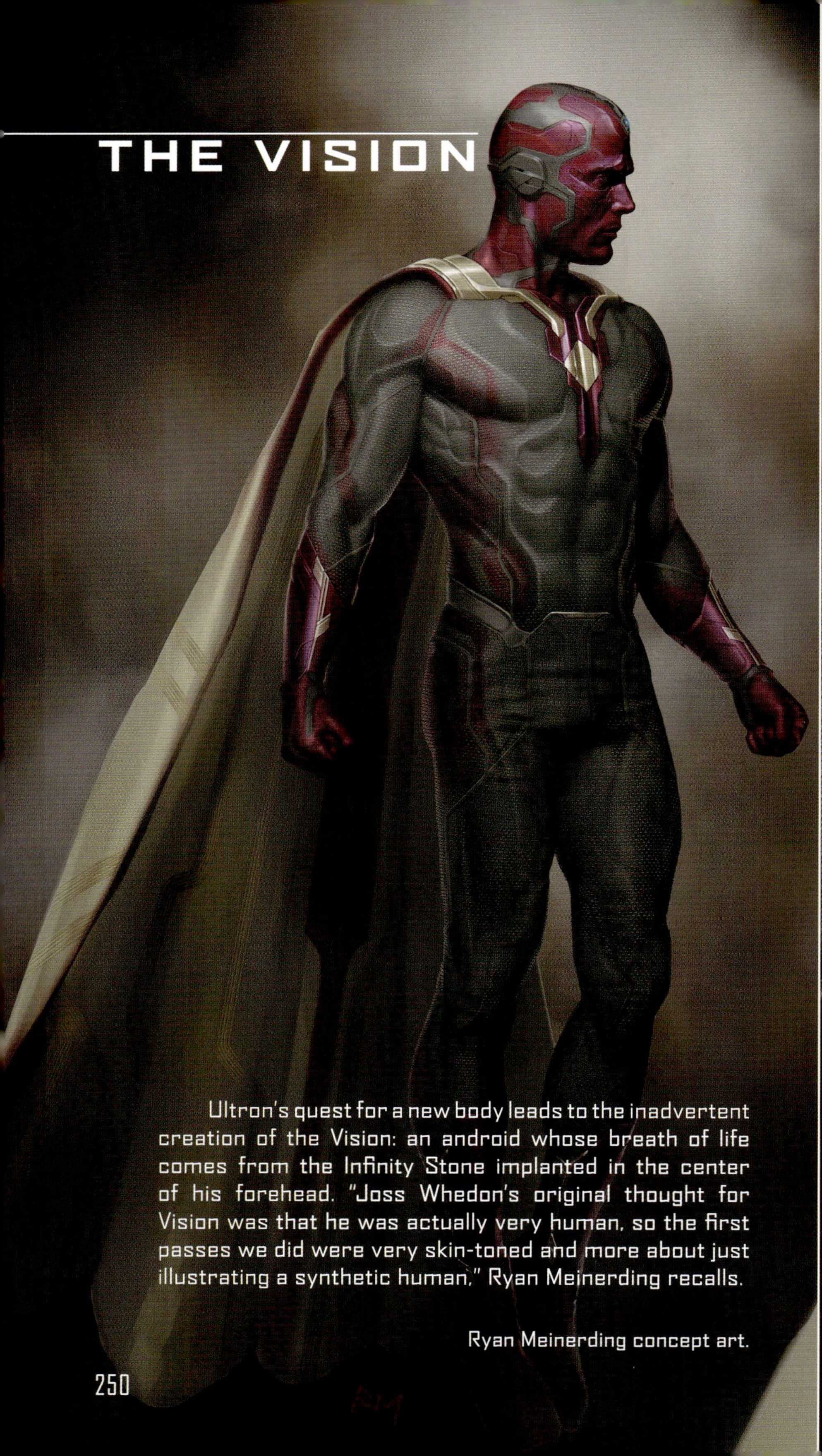

Ultron's quest for a new body leads to the inadvertent creation of the Vision: an android whose breath of life comes from the Infinity Stone implanted in the center of his forehead. "Joss Whedon's original thought for Vision was that he was actually very human, so the first passes we did were very skin-toned and more about just illustrating a synthetic human," Ryan Meinerding recalls.

Ryan Meinerding concept art.

"We also threw in some very comic-book-heavy designs, some that were the classic red and green, some that had a touch of maroon and red and green, and even some that used the all-white design from the comics. The one that Joss ended up responding to was actually more based on his red-and-green look, I think because the human versions ended up looking a little too creepy—it goes to a strange place when you're trying to make a synthetic human, and it still reads as very human. I think Joss saw the potential in being able to do the classic comic version and try to get it as correct as possible."

Ryan Meinerding concept art.

"In the mythology in our comic books, you see two things: You see the creation of Ultron, who is one of the scariest, deadliest villains we have based purely on technology's evil. But the genius of the comic creators is that they had another A.I. come about in Vision. And he sort of spun out of the origins of Ultron and became one of the primary members of the Avengers," Kevin Feige says. "We've loved Vision for many, many years, but we needed to find the right way to do that. And the right way to bring him about was obviously as part of an Ultron origin story."

Ryan Meinerding concept art.

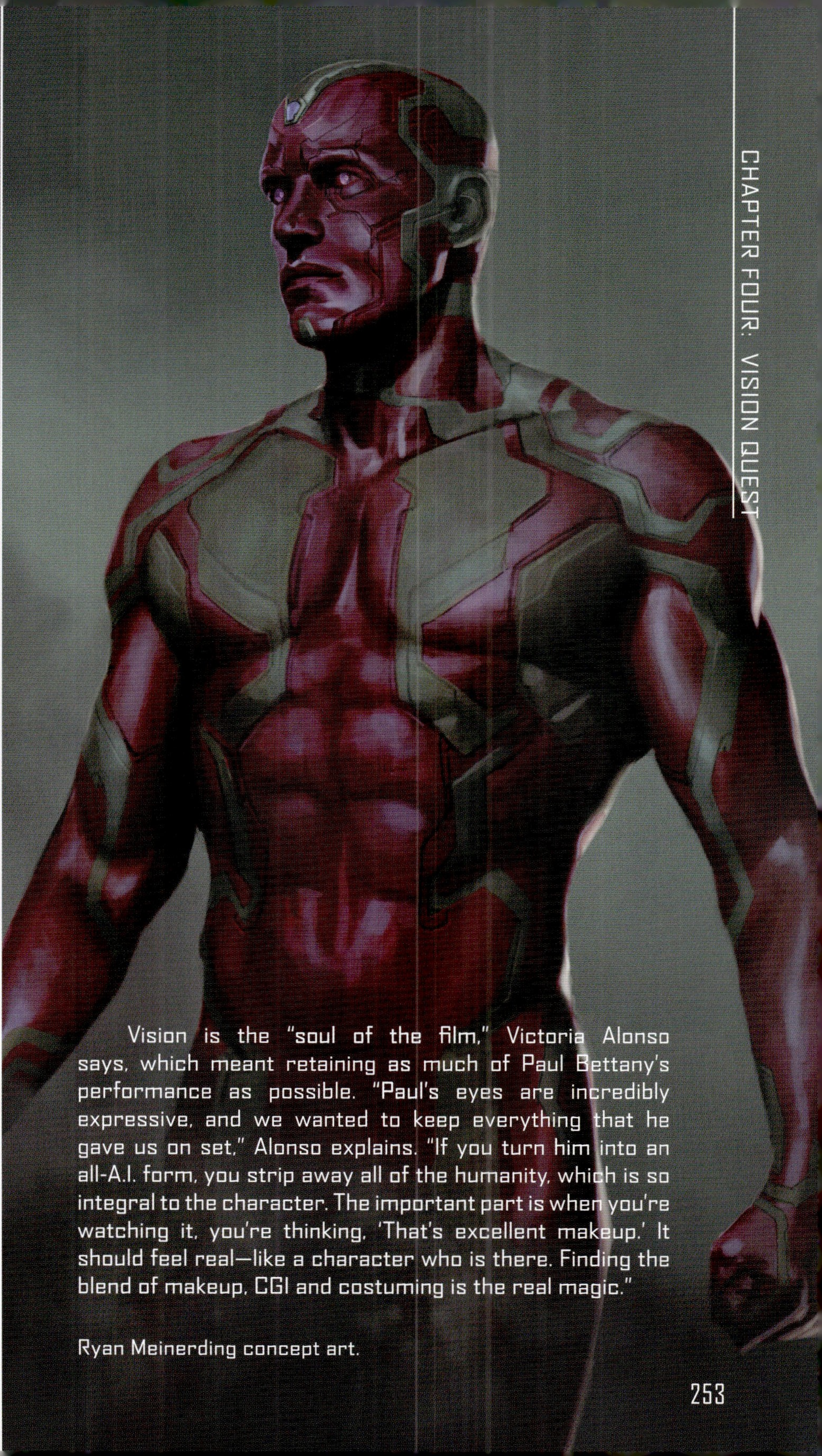

Vision is the "soul of the film," Victoria Alonso says, which meant retaining as much of Paul Bettany's performance as possible. "Paul's eyes are incredibly expressive, and we wanted to keep everything that he gave us on set," Alonso explains. "If you turn him into an all-A.I. form, you strip away all of the humanity, which is so integral to the character. The important part is when you're watching it, you're thinking, 'That's excellent makeup.' It should feel real—like a character who is there. Finding the blend of makeup, CGI and costuming is the real magic."

Ryan Meinerding concept art.

Ryan Meinerding concept art.

Ryan Meinerding concept art.

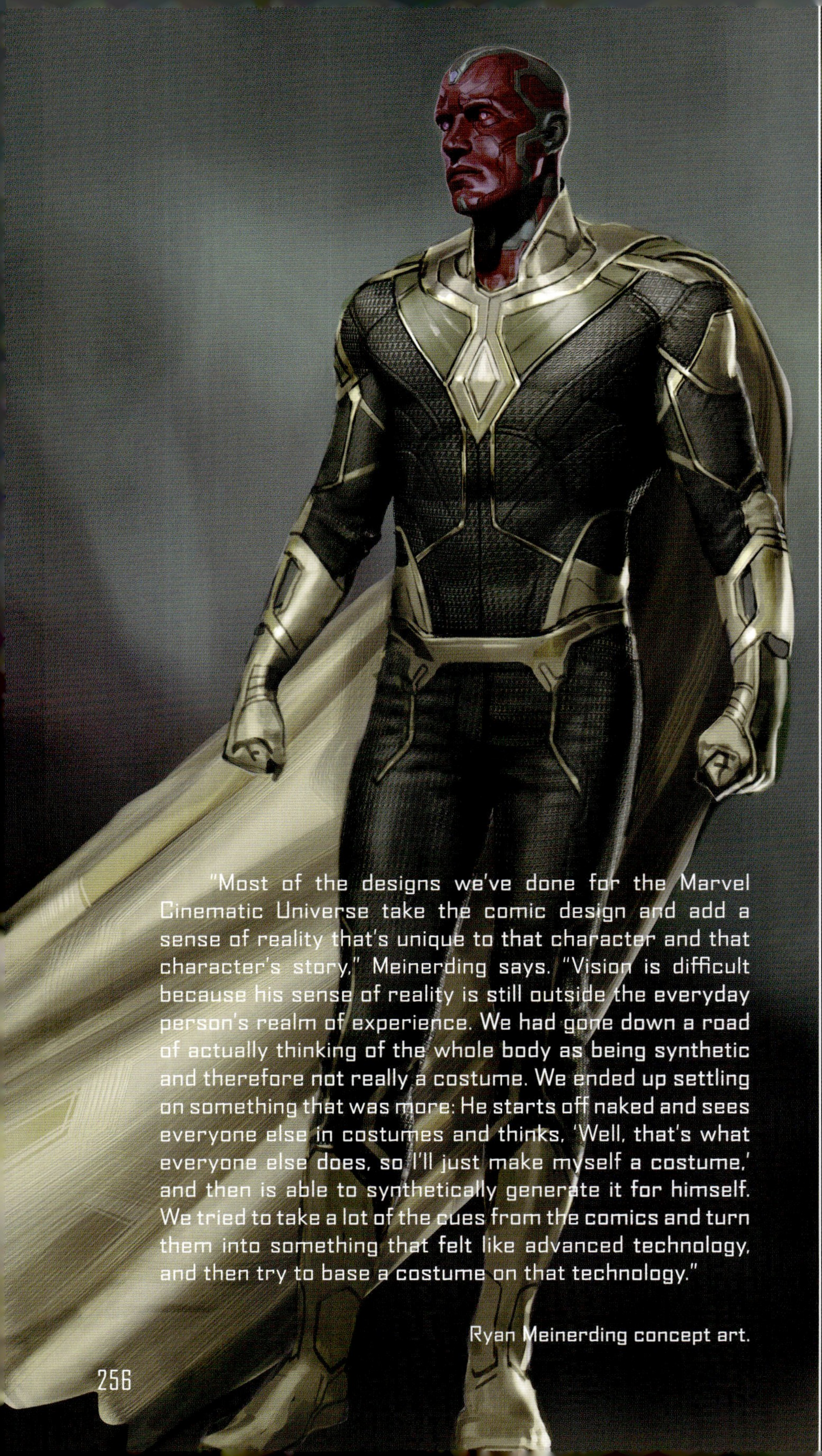

"Most of the designs we've done for the Marvel Cinematic Universe take the comic design and add a sense of reality that's unique to that character and that character's story," Meinerding says. "Vision is difficult because his sense of reality is still outside the everyday person's realm of experience. We had gone down a road of actually thinking of the whole body as being synthetic and therefore not really a costume. We ended up settling on something that was more: He starts off naked and sees everyone else in costumes and thinks, 'Well, that's what everyone else does, so I'll just make myself a costume,' and then is able to synthetically generate it for himself. We tried to take a lot of the cues from the comics and turn them into something that felt like advanced technology, and then try to base a costume on that technology."

Ryan Meinerding concept art.

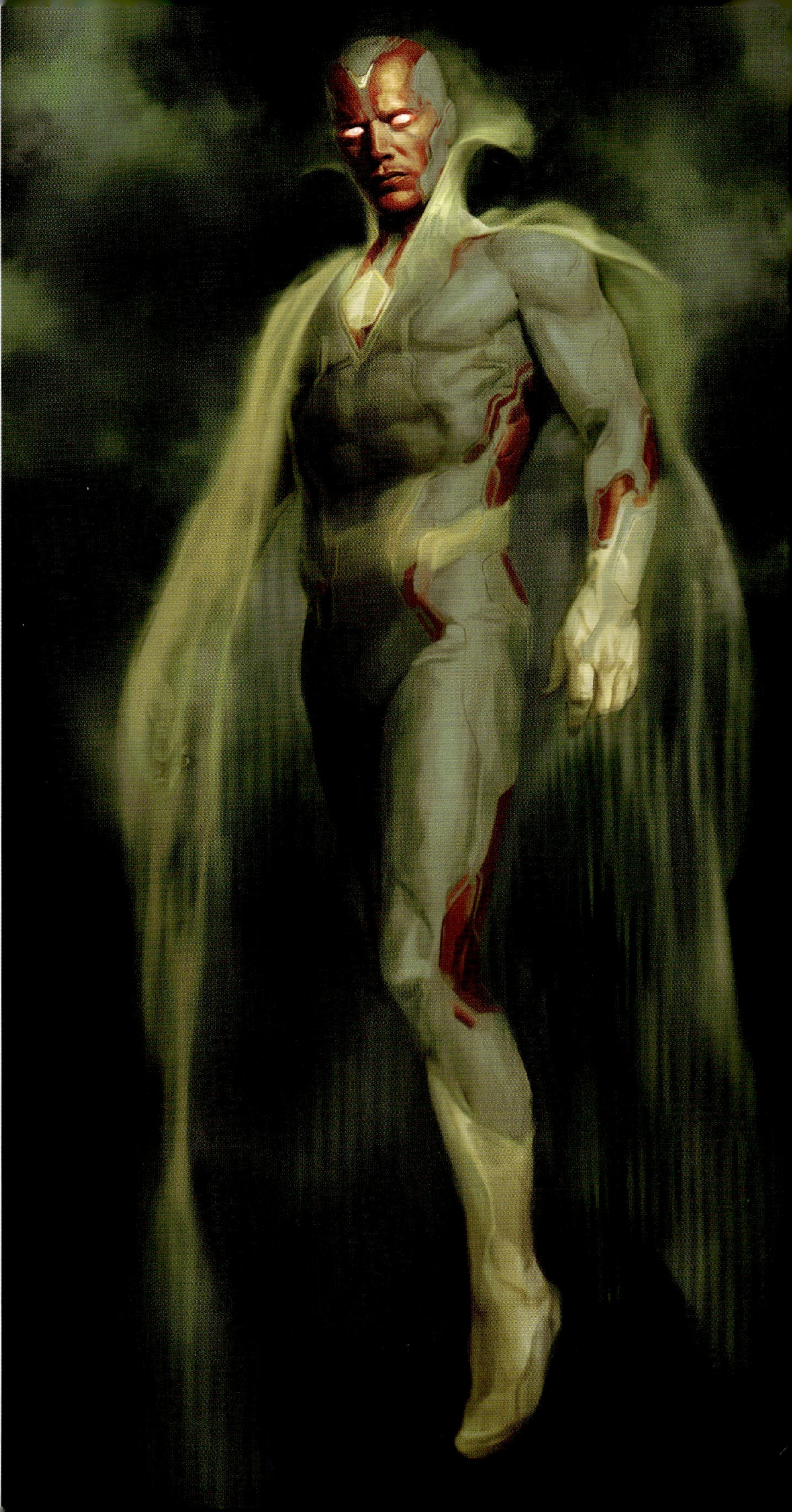

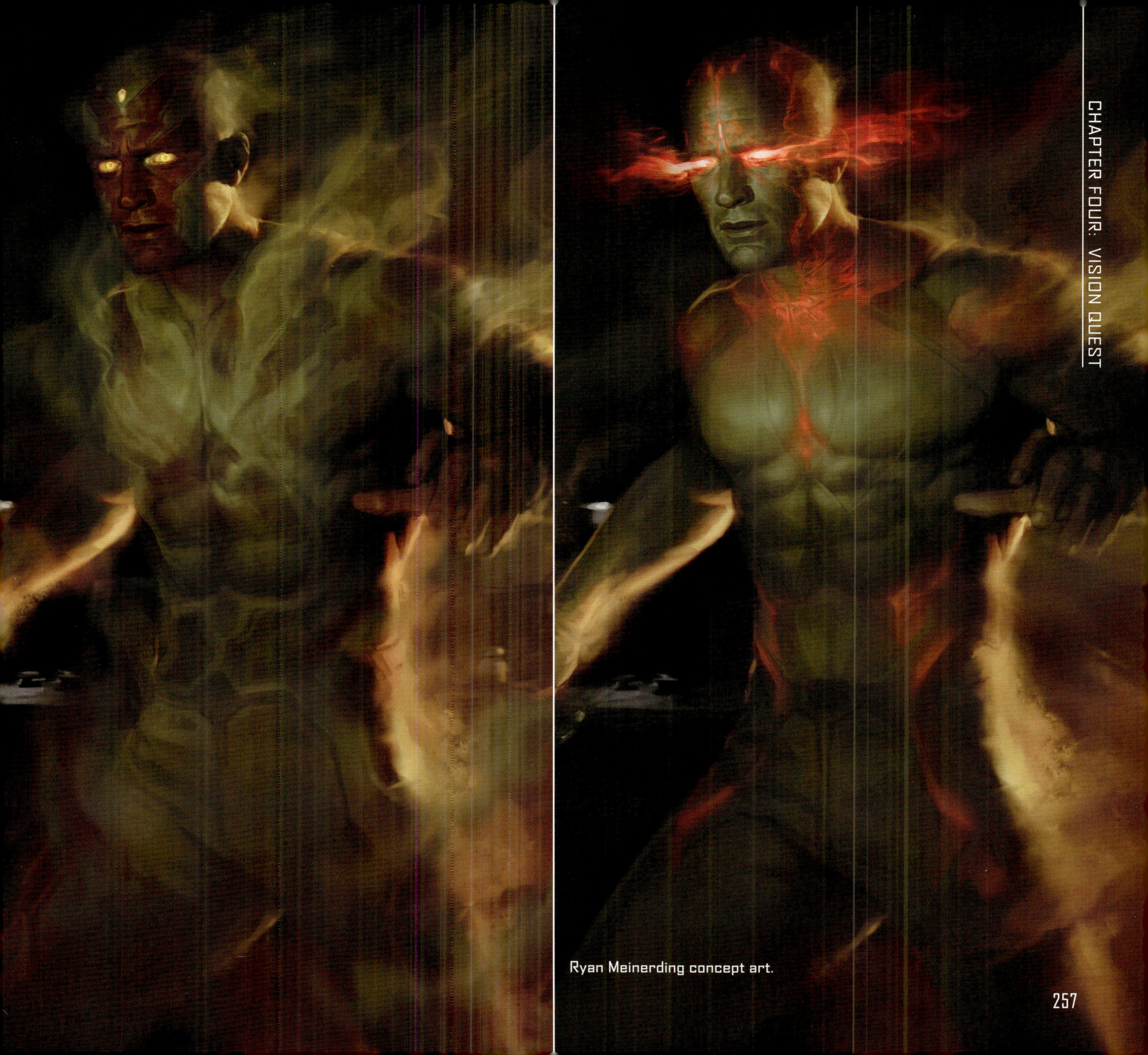

Ryan Meinerding concept art.

"Our first passes on Vision were also a lot about the face, trying to find a way for the character to have emotion and to read as human, as Joss saw the character," Meinerding says.

Ryan Meinerding concept art.

Ryan Meinerding concept art.

Andy Park concept art.

Andy Park concept art.

CHAPTER FIVE
SHOWDOWN IN SOKOVIA

Ryan Meinerding concept art.

The Age of Ultron dawns as the sun rises over the city of Sokovia, and the final confrontation begins to unfold. Our heroes, still reeling from the damage Scarlet Witch has done to their minds, find themselves back in the very place their mission began. A swarm of Ultron Sentries descends on the Avengers as Ultron enters the frame, horrifically upgraded and primed to execute his catastrophic master plan. "We always had the idea that the only way the Avengers could beat Ultron was—as Captain America says to Tony early in the film, and as Tony recounts during the finale—together. They're so different in their powers and strategies, so the question became: How do you get them to do it together?" Executive Producer Victoria Alonso says. "Balancing their powers in the finale is like a well-choreographed dance with different styles of dance, but each character is given their moment to shine."

As with any Marvel film, the finale is not only about spectacle, but also focuses on the characters and emotional beats. "Early on, Joss Whedon said, 'Listen, it's not about going bigger.' Joss is smart enough, as we are, to know that bigger doesn't necessarily mean better," Executive Producer Kevin Feige says. "We want it to hit the same emotional beats that the first one hit, to go even further with the character interactions and the relationships between those characters."

WORLD HUB

Roberto Fernández Castro keyframe.

ULTIMATE ULTRON

Industrial Light & Magic concept.

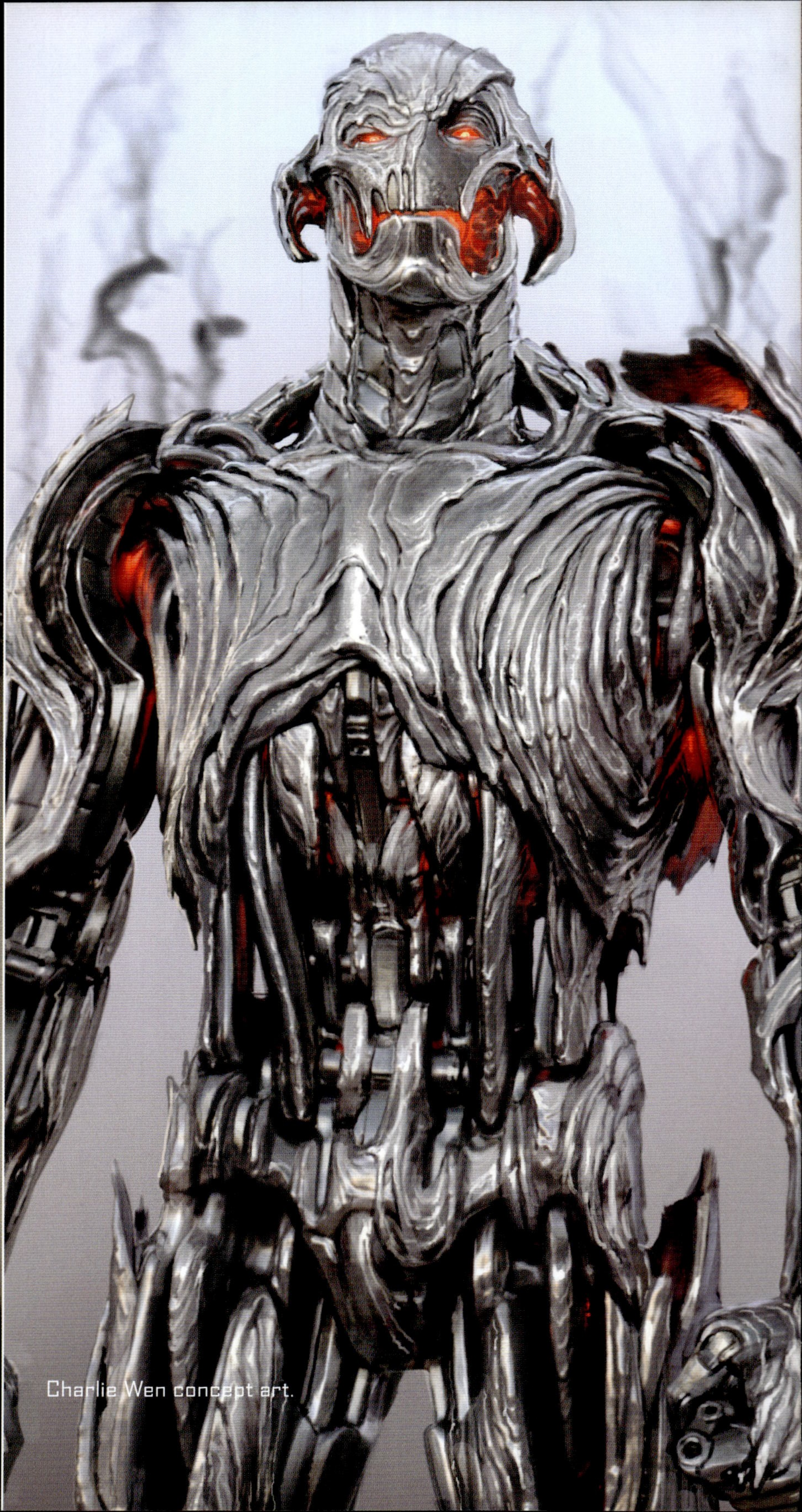

Charlie Wen concept art.

Charlie Wen concept art.

ULTRON'S HEART

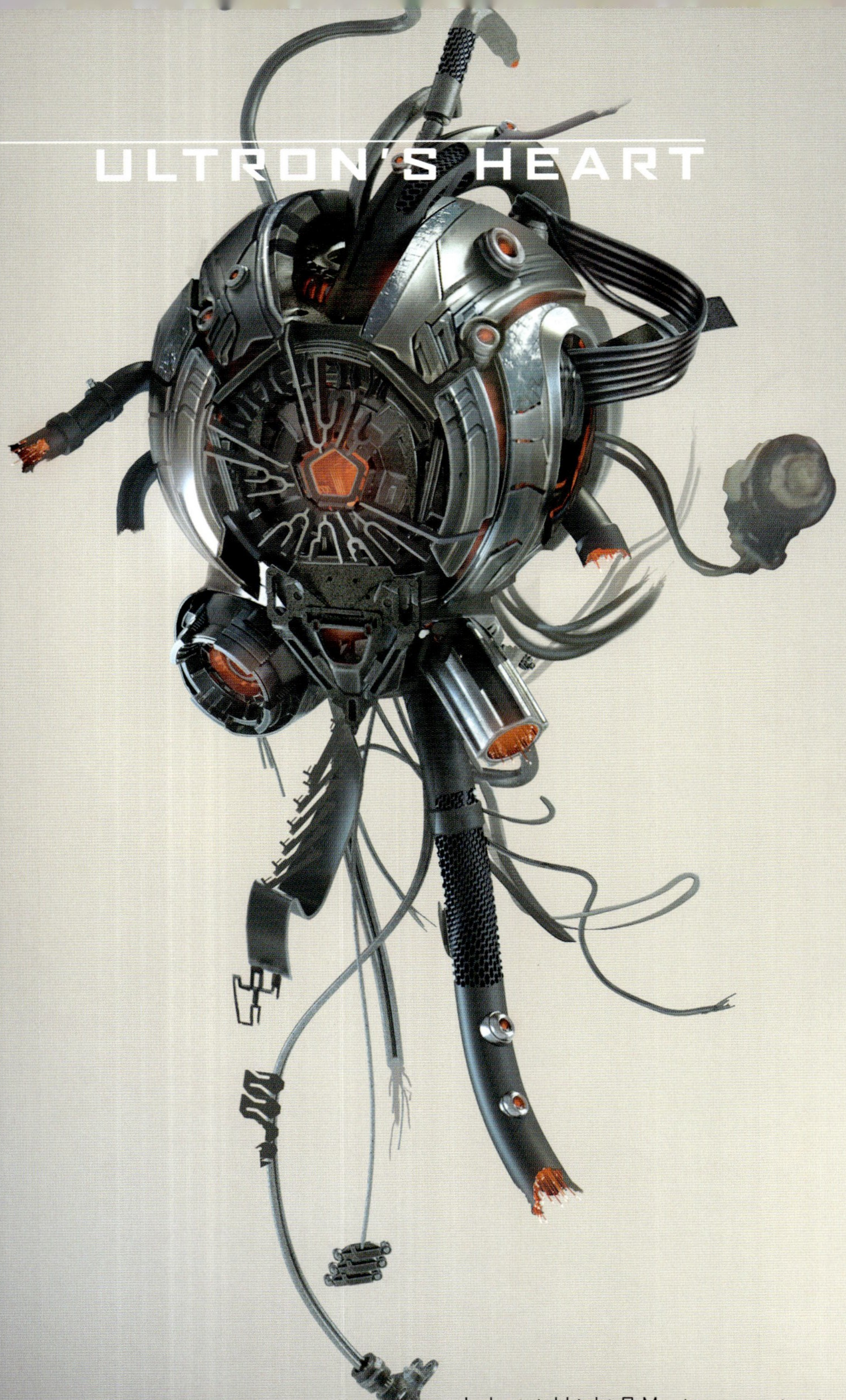

Industrial Light & Magic concept art.

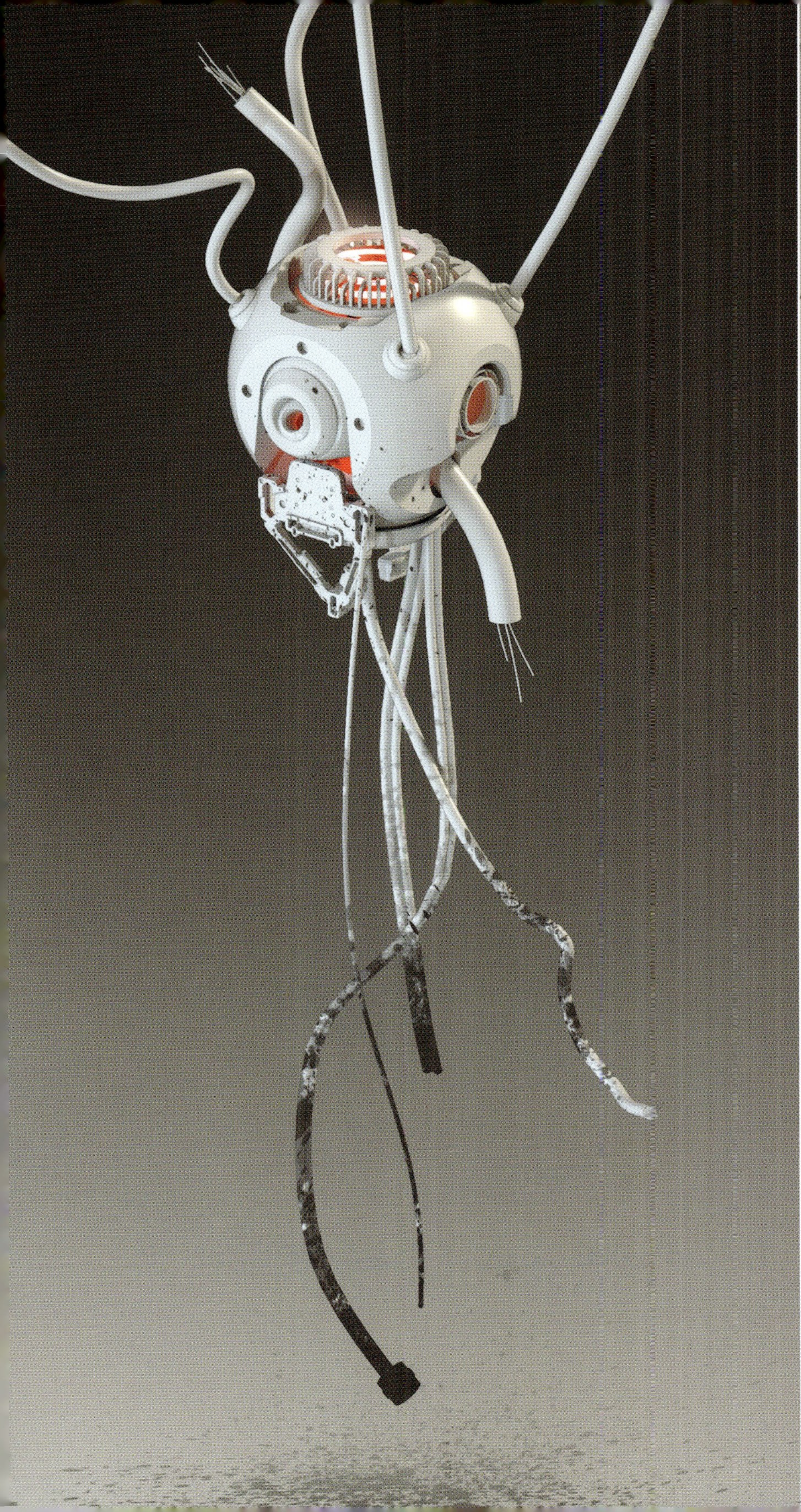

Industrial Light & Magic concept art.

Andy Park keyframe.

IRON MAN MARK 45

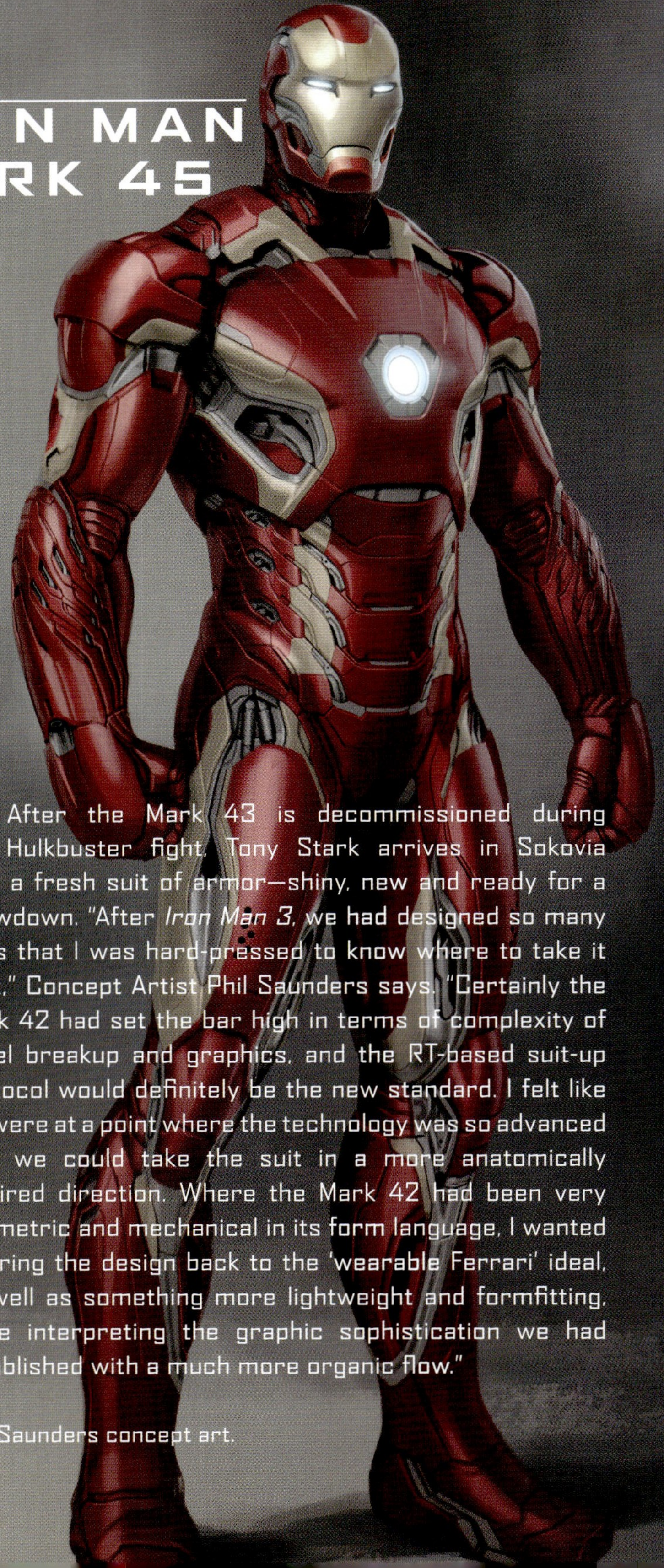

After the Mark 43 is decommissioned during the Hulkbuster fight, Tony Stark arrives in Sokovia with a fresh suit of armor—shiny, new and ready for a showdown. "After *Iron Man 3*, we had designed so many suits that I was hard-pressed to know where to take it next," Concept Artist Phil Saunders says. "Certainly the Mark 42 had set the bar high in terms of complexity of panel breakup and graphics, and the RT-based suit-up protocol would definitely be the new standard. I felt like we were at a point where the technology was so advanced that we could take the suit in a more anatomically inspired direction. Where the Mark 42 had been very geometric and mechanical in its form language, I wanted to bring the design back to the 'wearable Ferrari' ideal, as well as something more lightweight and formfitting, while interpreting the graphic sophistication we had established with a much more organic flow."

Phil Saunders concept art.

Design by Phil Saunders,
3-D sculpt by Josh Herman.

Phil Saunders concept art.

Ryan Meinerding concept art.

Phil Saunders concept art.

SOKOVIA CITY

Bob Cheshire concept art.

The film's finale encompasses the entire fictional core of the city of Sokovia, all of which had to be constructed outside of London. "It fit it extremely well into that sort of slightly post-Communist-type look that we had found in certain areas in Italy," Production Designer Charlie Wood says. "We then set forth to design around this area. We knew we needed certain elements—a bridge environment, a church and a market square—and we very quickly realized this location worked incredibly well. It gave us a lot more stuff that added to the action beats in the film."

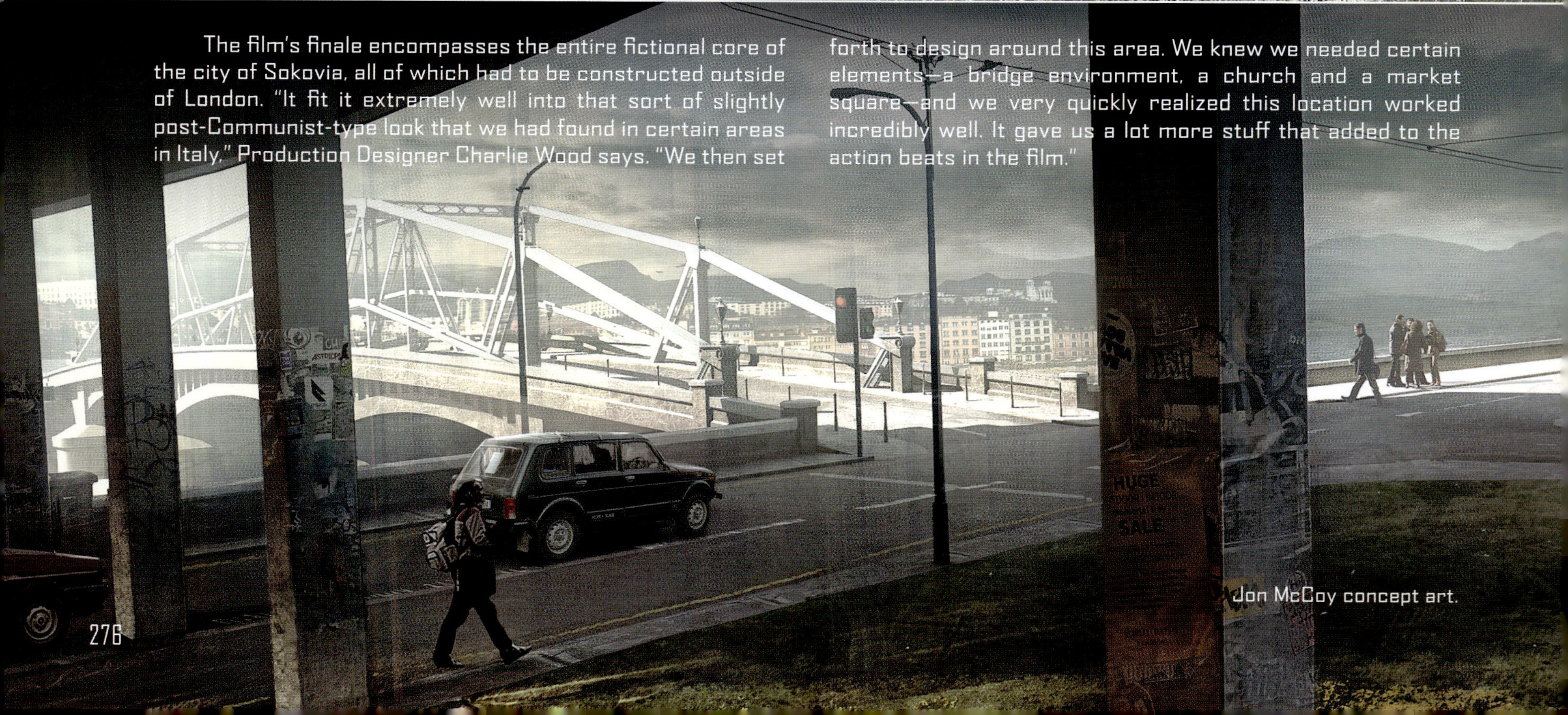

Jon McCoy concept art.

Bob Cheshire concept art.

Bob Cheshire concept art.

Paul Chandler concept art.

Hope begins to diminish as the surrounding environment starts to act against the Avengers and they find themselves wildly outnumbered. Executive Producer Louis D'Esposito explains the creation of the high-stakes finale: "Joss Whedon pitched that idea, and I think he was surprised when we loved it as much as we did. We began developing it, and thinking how it could relate to Ultron's objective and how it relates to his pathos. It actually wasn't until we started seeing concept art that it really dawned on us how spectacular it could be."

Bob Cheshire concept art.

"I think the fact that Joss had it be almost an homage to Hayao Miyazaki's *Laputa: Castle in the Sky* is one thing that made the final sequence so unique," Storyboard Artist Bryan Andrews says. "Super-fun idea: Raise the city they're fighting in like a castle in the sky. The battlefield itself is constantly changing, falling off, rising through the clouds; the air is getting thinner—all sorts of visual texture to play with."

Paul Chandler concept art with Rodney Fuentebella keyframe roughs (insets).

VIBRANIUM DETONATOR

Within the center of Sokovia, in the middle of the church, is a distinct metallic structure, both beautiful and dangerous. This is Ultron's plan, his final resort: to turn Sokovia into a floating, city-sized missile whose detonator is a mechanism made of the precious metal Vibranium. "The design came from working together with Charlie Wood, Set Decorator Richard Roberts and one of our concept artists, Chris Rosewarne. It was treated as a drill that responds to a Vibranium-spike key and plunges into the ground—turning the entire city into, basically, a meteorite," Property Master Barry Gibbs says.

Tim Hill concept art.

HELICARRIER RESCUE

To the Avengers' surprise, Sokovia itself isn't the only thing flying high in the finale. Nick Fury, Maria Hill and War Machine ascend in the last remaining Helicarrier and begin helping the Avengers on their rescue mission. Even though S.H.I.E.L.D. has been decimated, Executive Producer Jeremy Latcham asserts that Fury "is always five steps ahead, and he always wants to do the right thing. The moment when he shows up at the end of the movie and that Helicarrier swoops into view, you go, 'That is what S.H.I.E.L.D. was always supposed to be; that's the S.H.I.E.L.D. that we care about!'"

Paul Chandler concept art.

THE RESCUE SHIPS

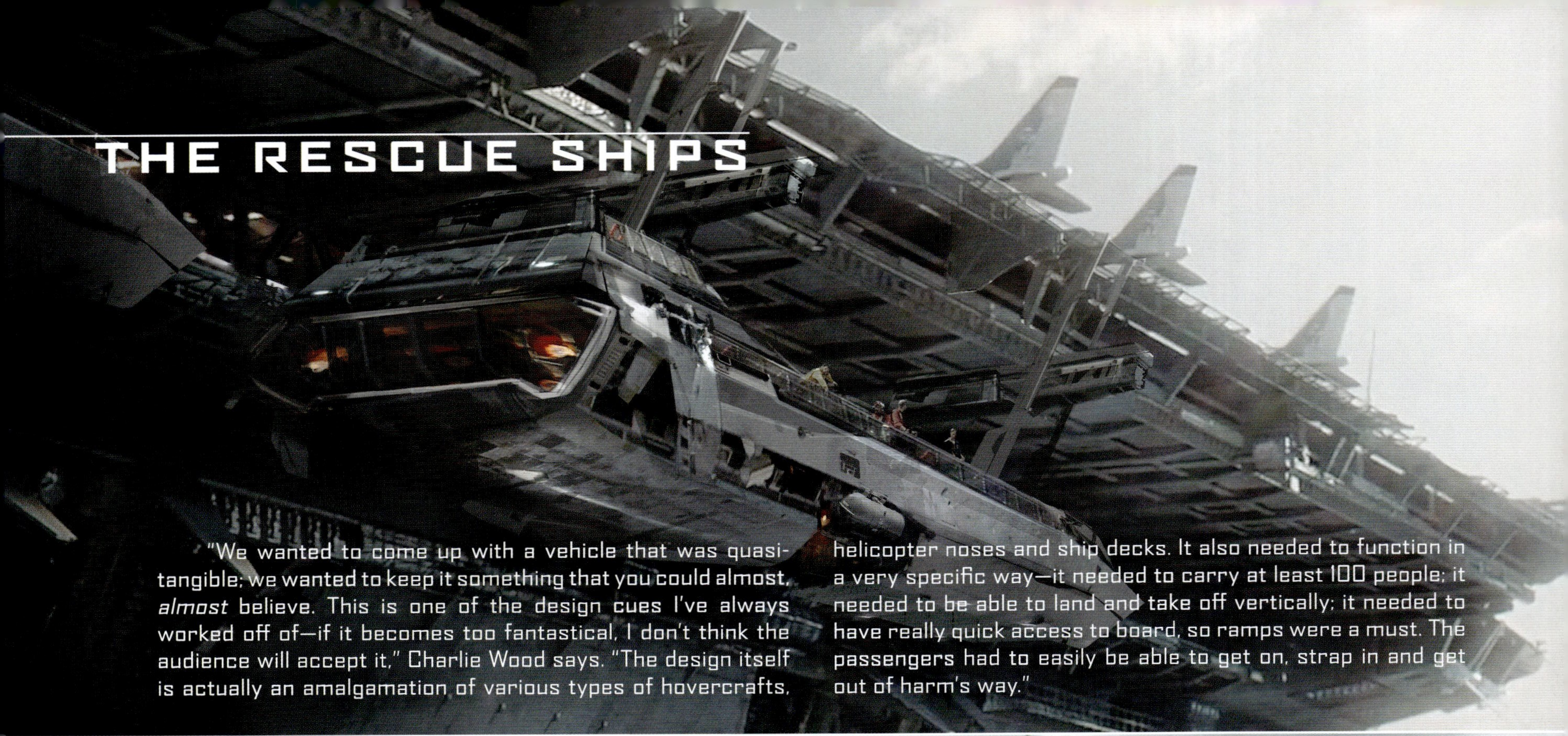

"We wanted to come up with a vehicle that was quasi-tangible; we wanted to keep it something that you could almost, *almost* believe. This is one of the design cues I've always worked off of—if it becomes too fantastical, I don't think the audience will accept it," Charlie Wood says. "The design itself is actually an amalgamation of various types of hovercrafts, helicopter noses and ship decks. It also needed to function in a very specific way—it needed to carry at least 100 people; it needed to be able to land and take off vertically; it needed to have really quick access to board, so ramps were a must. The passengers had to easily be able to get on, strap in and get out of harm's way."

Pete Thompson concept art.

Jon McCoy concept art.

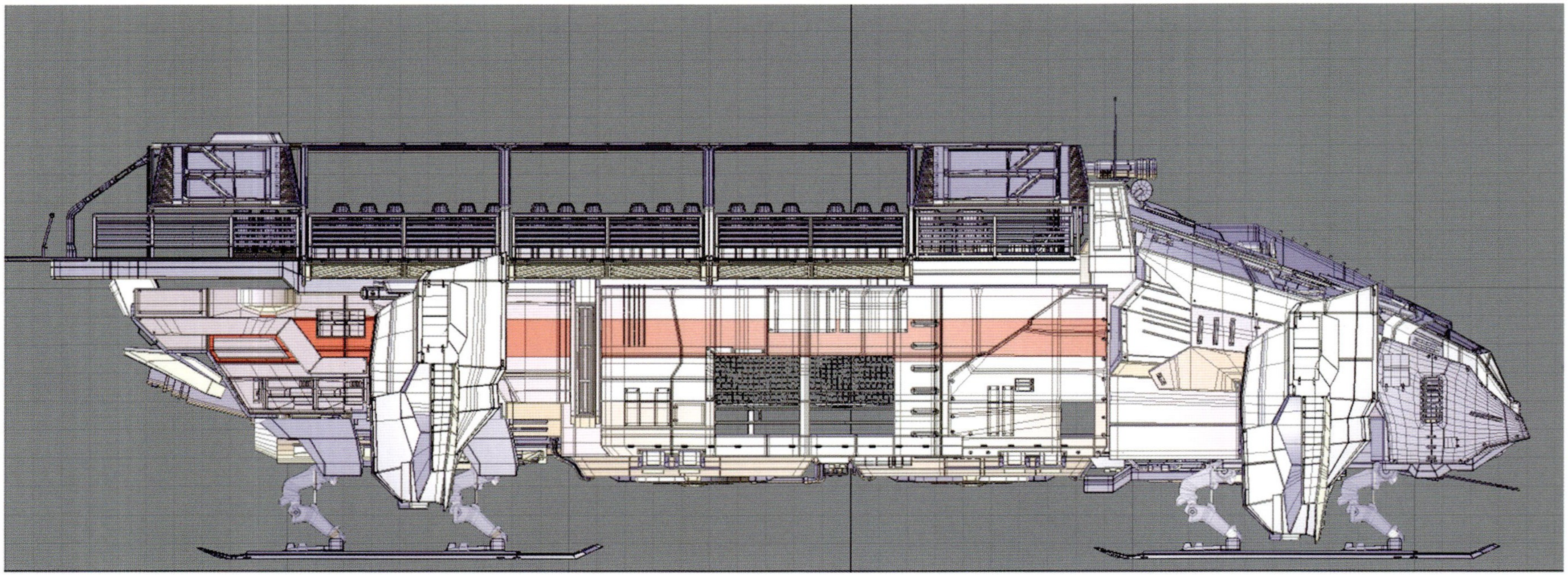

Liferaft Side Concept (landing gear deployed)

Pete Thompson concept art.

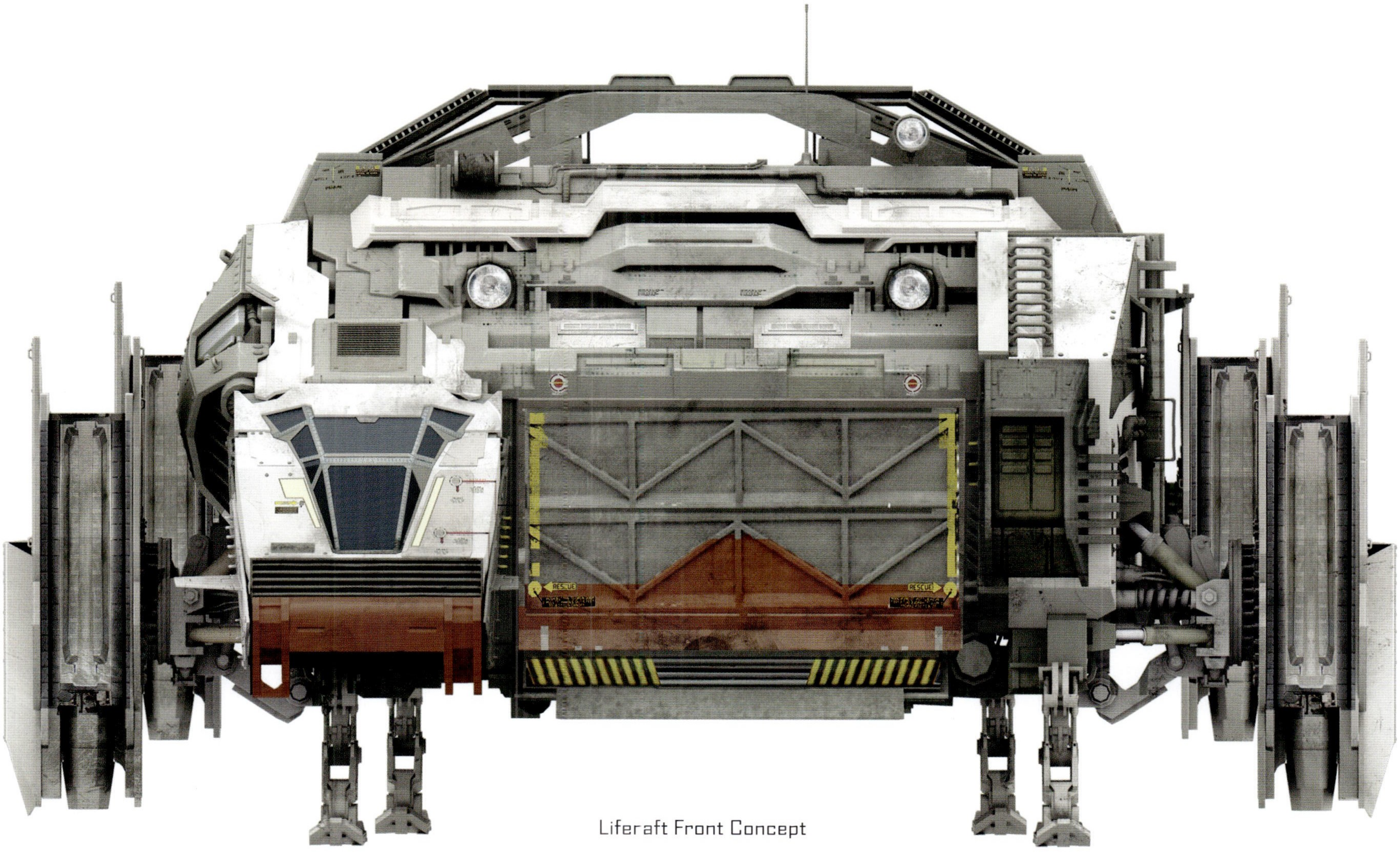

Liferaft Front Concept

Pete Thompson concept art.

ULTRON SENTRY FORMATION

"With these series of moments, I was trying to find a creepy way for the Ultron Sentries to emerge from the river," Concept Artist Jackson Sze says. "The gestures, poses and head-tilts were important in trying to convey that feeling of evil and dread."

Jackson Sze concept art.

Jackson Sze concept art.

Andy Park keyframe.

"What makes Quicksilver so scary, so unique, is that our eyes are not fast enough to perceive him. You can't anticipate his attacks. While in motion, he is only visible through the interaction or consequence of his presence in the environment," Victoria Alonso says.

Andy Park keyframe.

Rodney Fuentebella keyframe.

FINAL BATTLE
STORYBOARDS BY BRYAN ANDREWS

"Thankfully, the template Joss Whedon provided in the script really set the plan up for staging the final battle, and as usual it inspires so many other ideas. He'll nerd out over some of the concepts while others inspire a new idea of his own," Bryan Andrews says. "It was a matter of getting it visualized so you can really see it. That's when the new ideas come, as well as problems. Like, 'Oh, we haven't seen Cap in a bit—we have to intercut more,' or 'Let's move that bit over there to make room for this new Wanda moment or Vision moment.' It really starts to coalesce. I'll also come in armed with as many cool action ideas for all of them as I can—a grab bag of cool ideas both small and large. Giving Widow her powered-up Escrima sticks so she'll stand a chance, new stuff for Hawkeye to do, working with the team to figure out some fun Vision stuff. Thor vs. Ultron in the church was a fun moment, as well. Basically, I was trying to make sure all of the characters have shine moments and struggle moments."

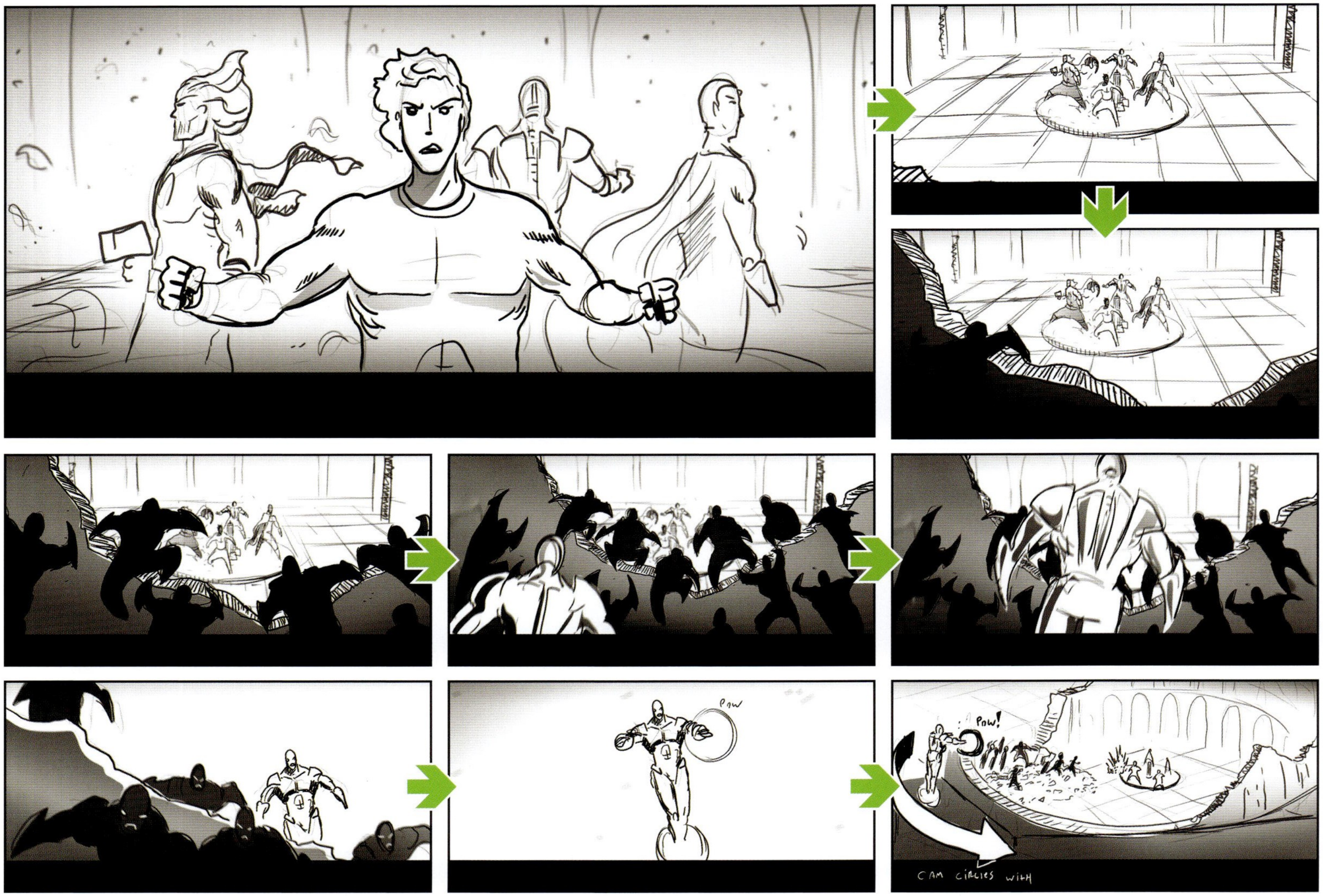

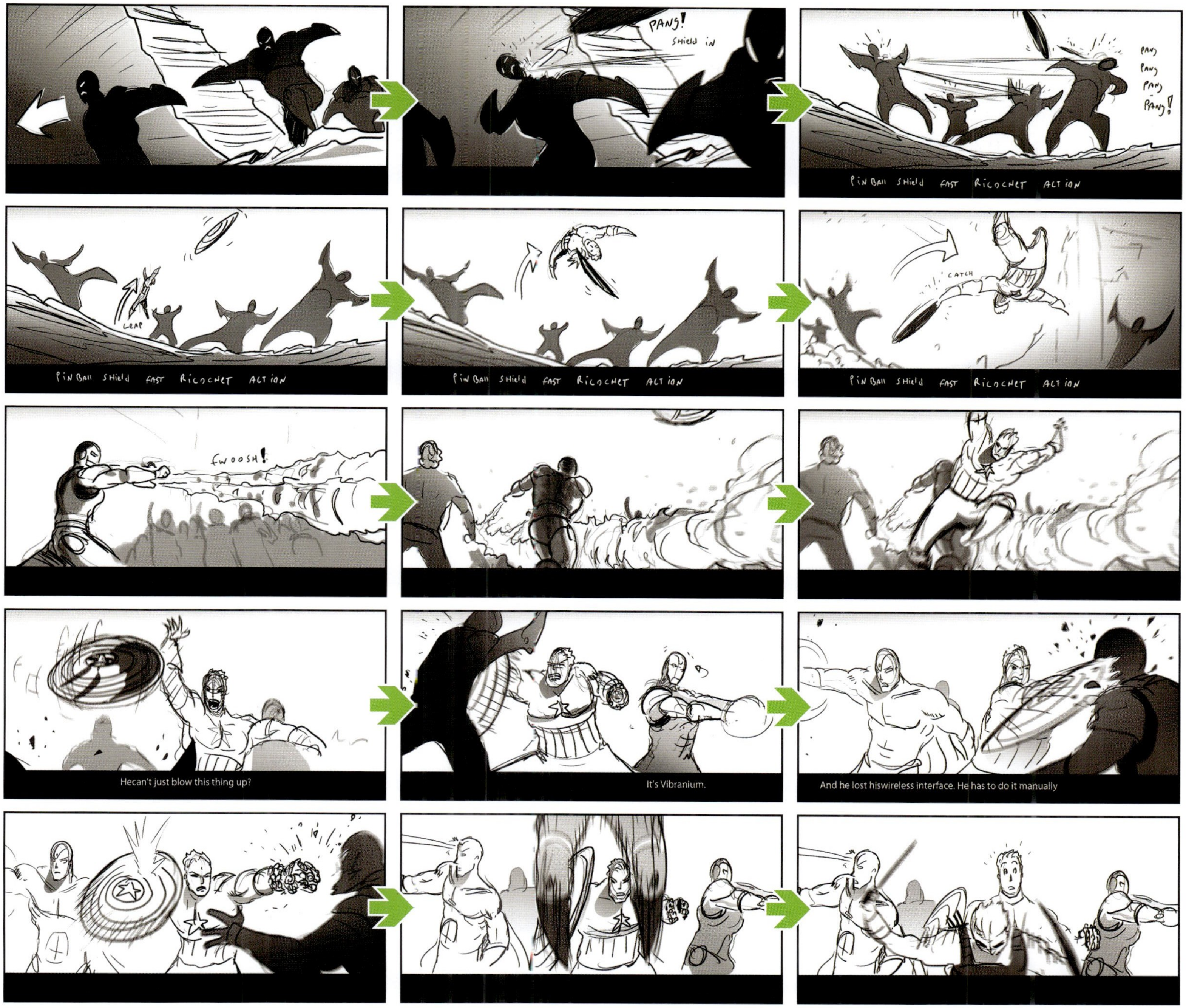
PANG!
SHIELD IN
PANG PANG PANG PANG!
PINBALL SHIELD FAST RICOCHET ACTION
LEAP
PINBALL SHIELD FAST RICOCHET ACTION
PINBALL SHIELD FAST RICOCHET ACTION
CATCH
PINBALL SHIELD FAST RICOCHET ACTION
FWOOSH!
Hecan't just blow this thing up?
It's Vibranium.
And he lost hiswireless interface. He has to do it manually

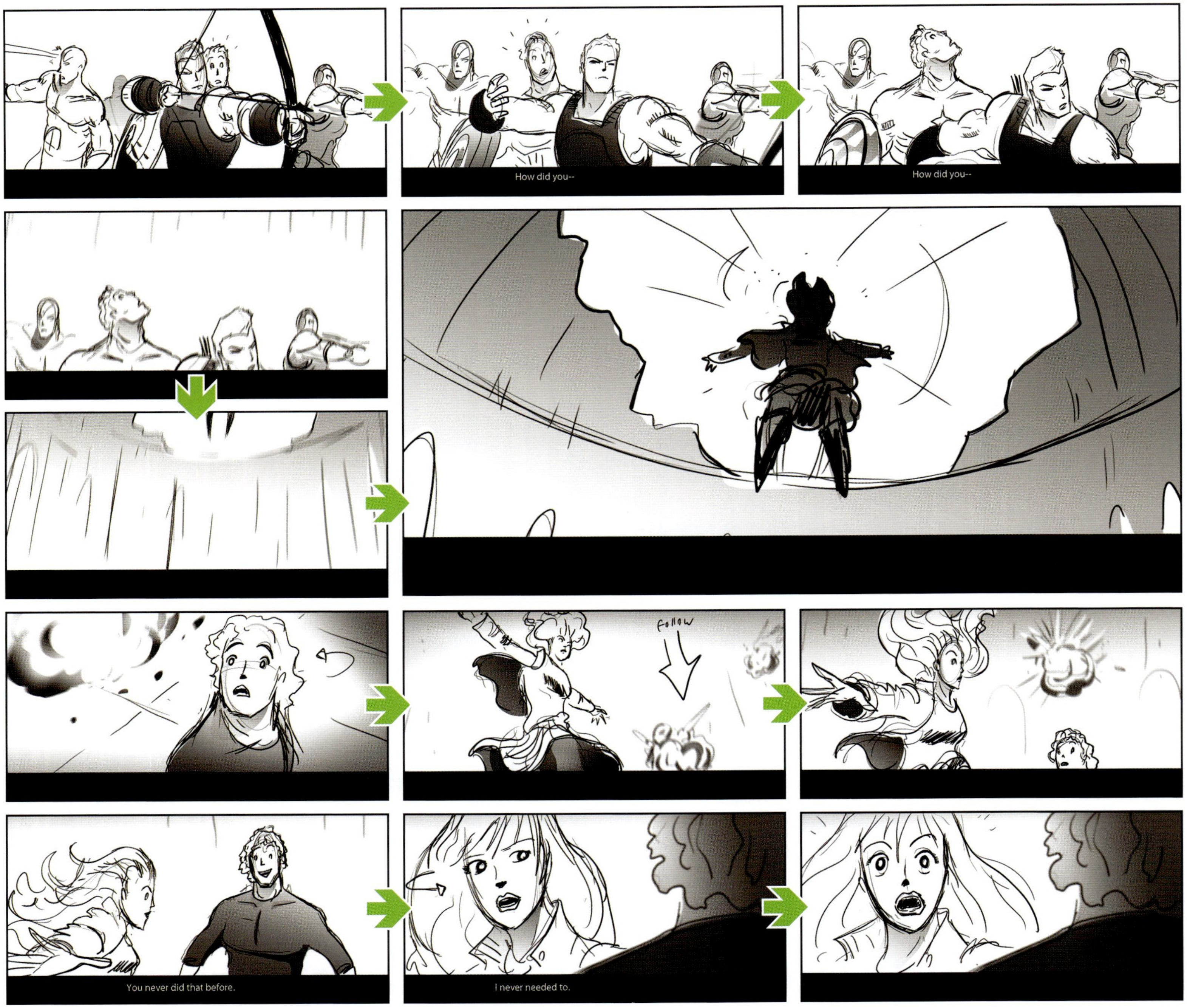
How did you--
How did you--
follow
You never did that before.
I never needed to.

POW
POW
PANG!

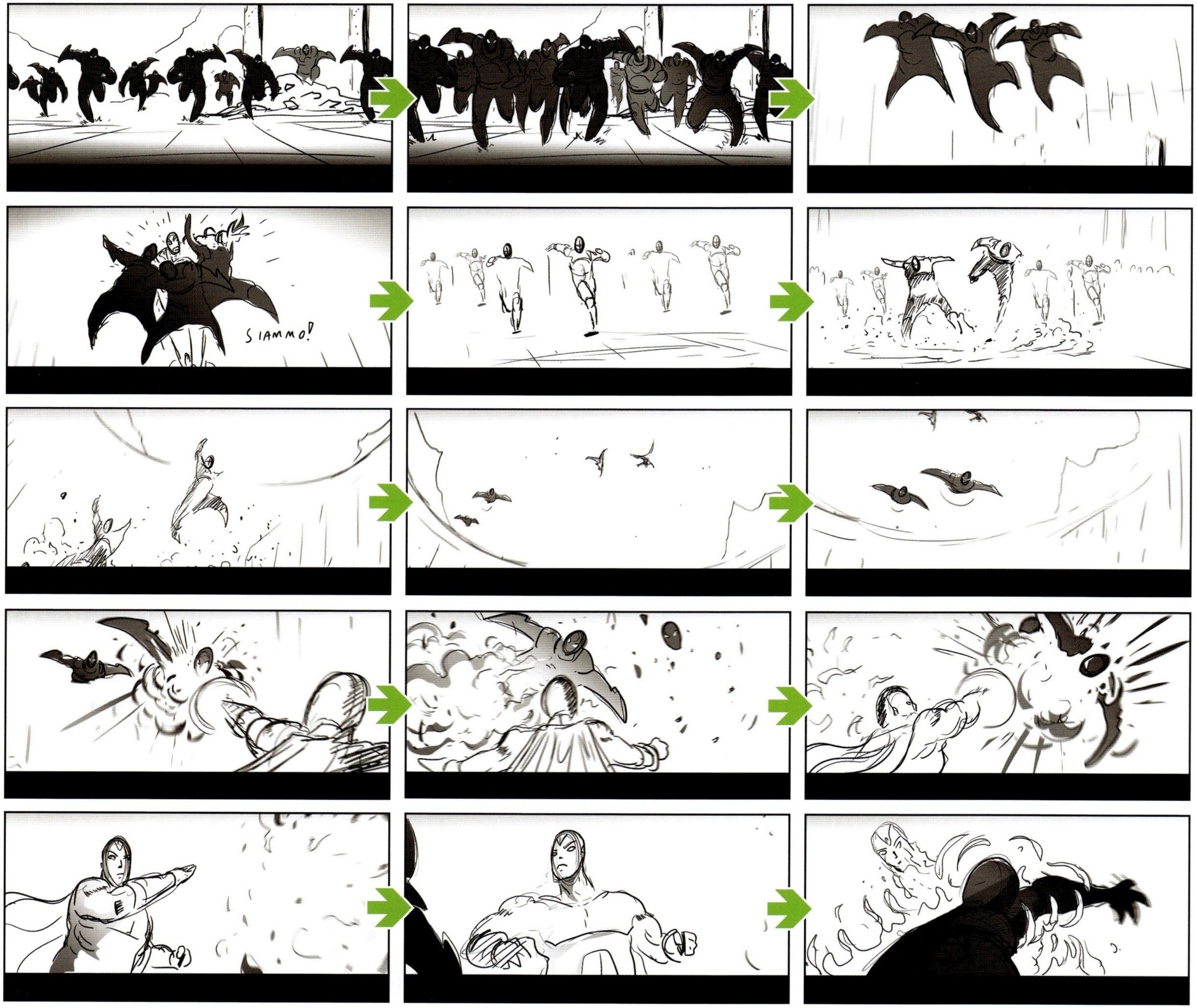
SIAMMO!

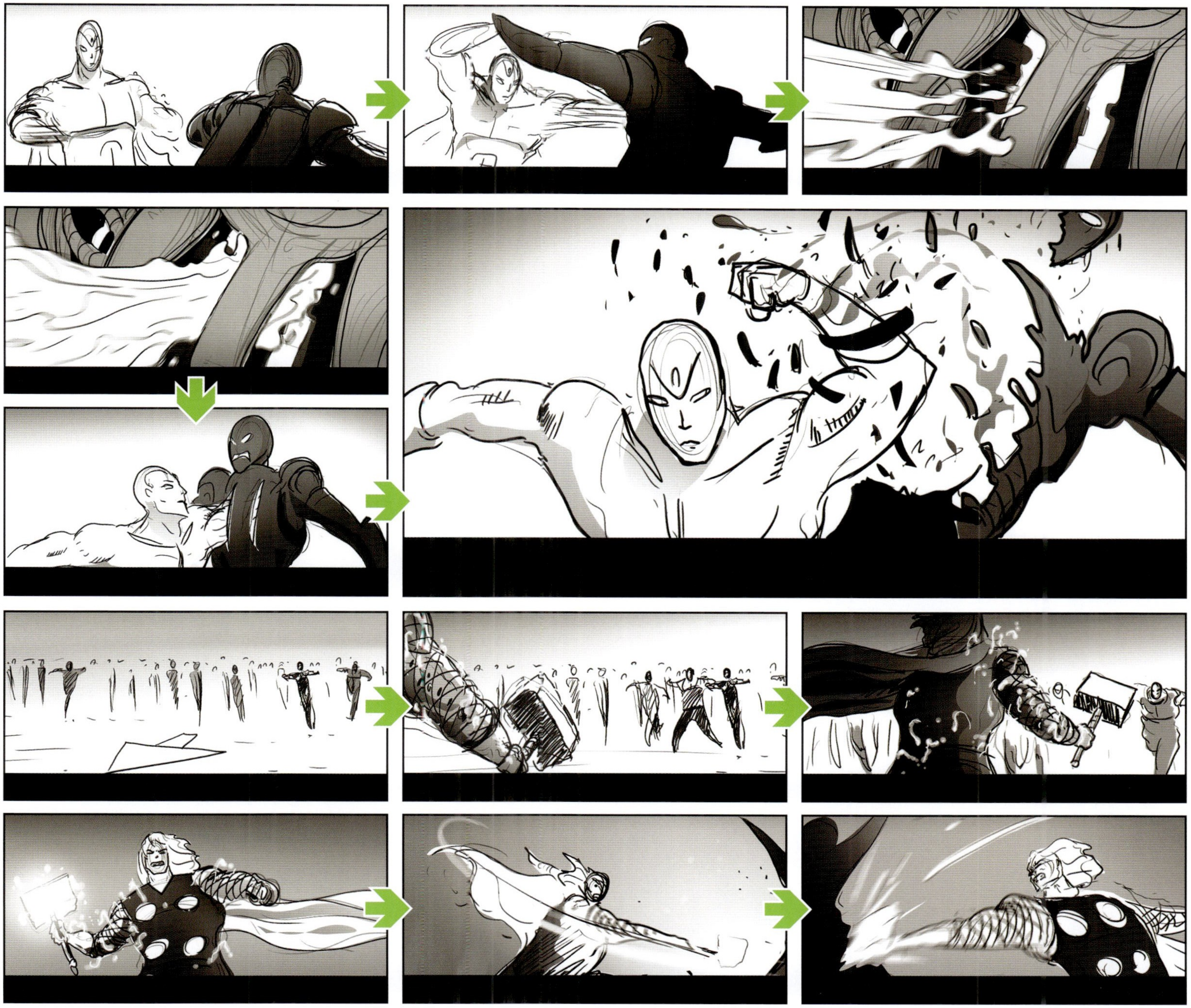

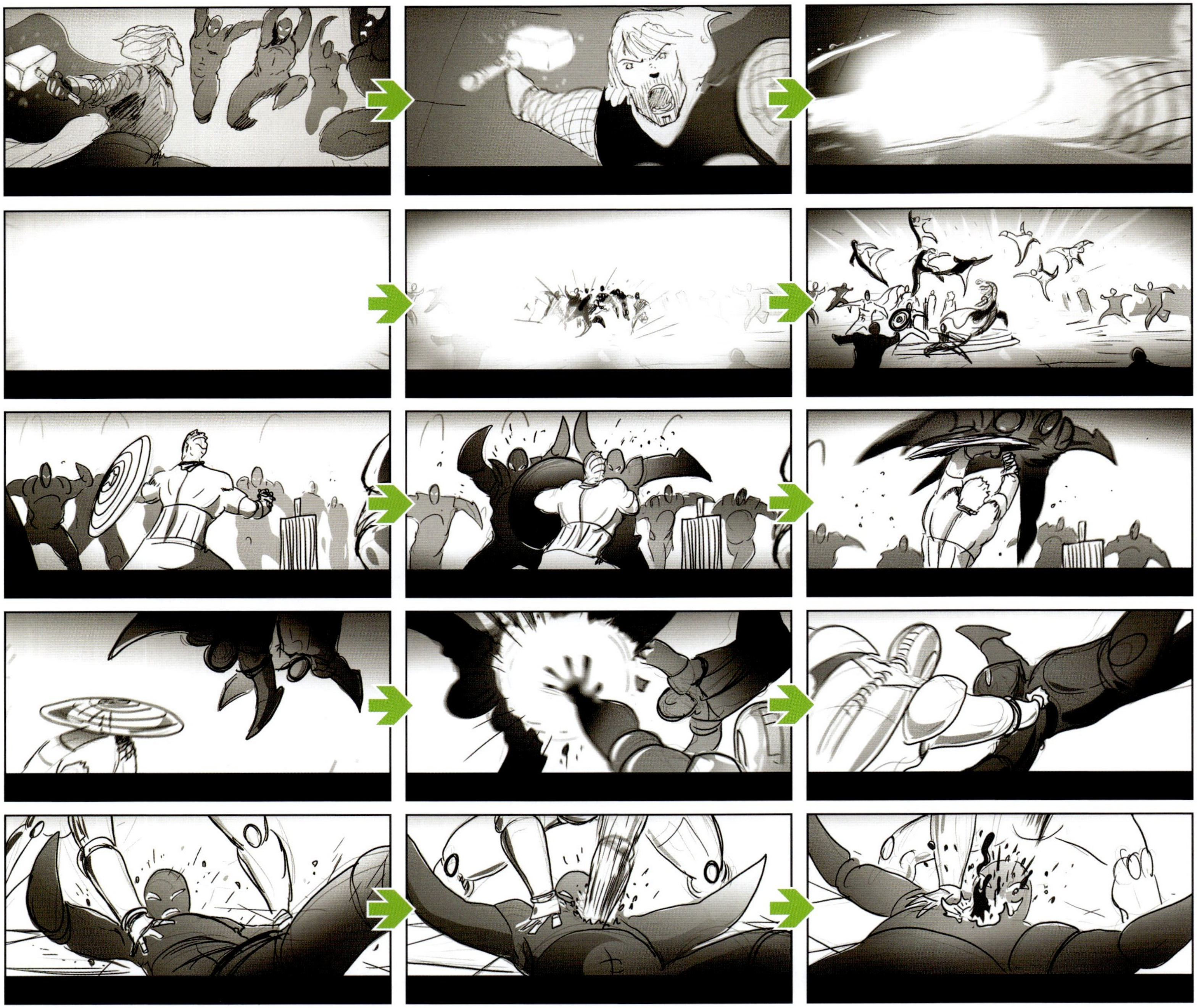

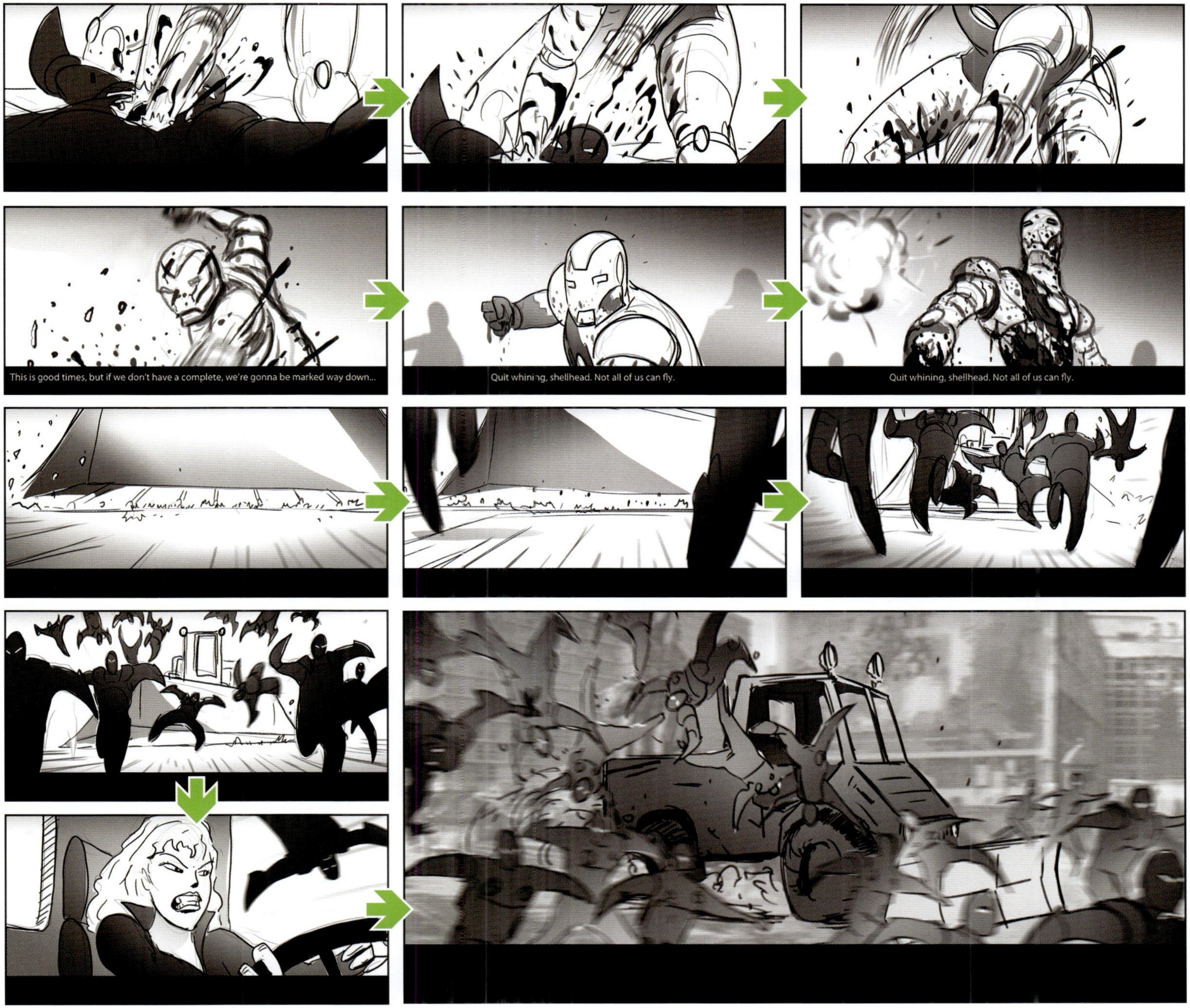
This is good times, but if we don't have a complete, we're gonna be marked way down...
Quit whining, shellhead. Not all of us can fly.
Quit whining, shellhead. Not all of us can fly.

Charlie Wen keyframe.

Charlie Wen keyframe.

Andy Park keyframe.

EPILOGUE: NEW AVENGERS FACILITY

Following the events in Sokovia, the team regroups at an auxiliary Avengers enterprise to lament its losses and discuss the future. This facility, similar in architectural style and tone to Avengers Tower, is located a bit farther off the grid, rather than front-and-center in Manhattan. This construct features a sprawling campus with training grounds, meeting rooms, surveillance technology and a plethora of other conveniences reminiscent of the old S.H.I.E.L.D. facilities—obviously upgraded with a Tony Stark flair.

Bob Cheshire concept art.

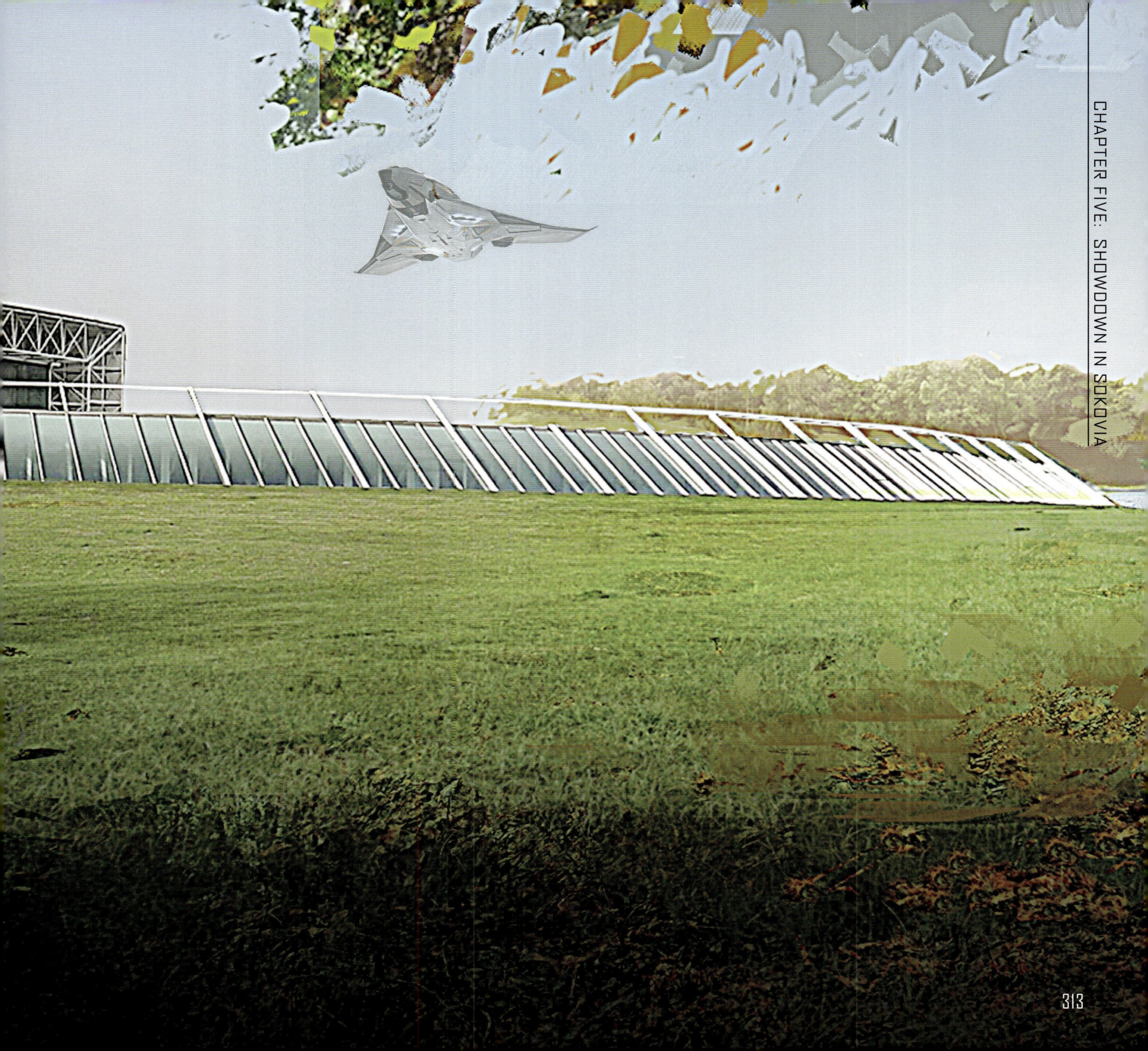

Concept art by Pete Thompson and Bob Cheshire.

Bob Cheshire concept art.

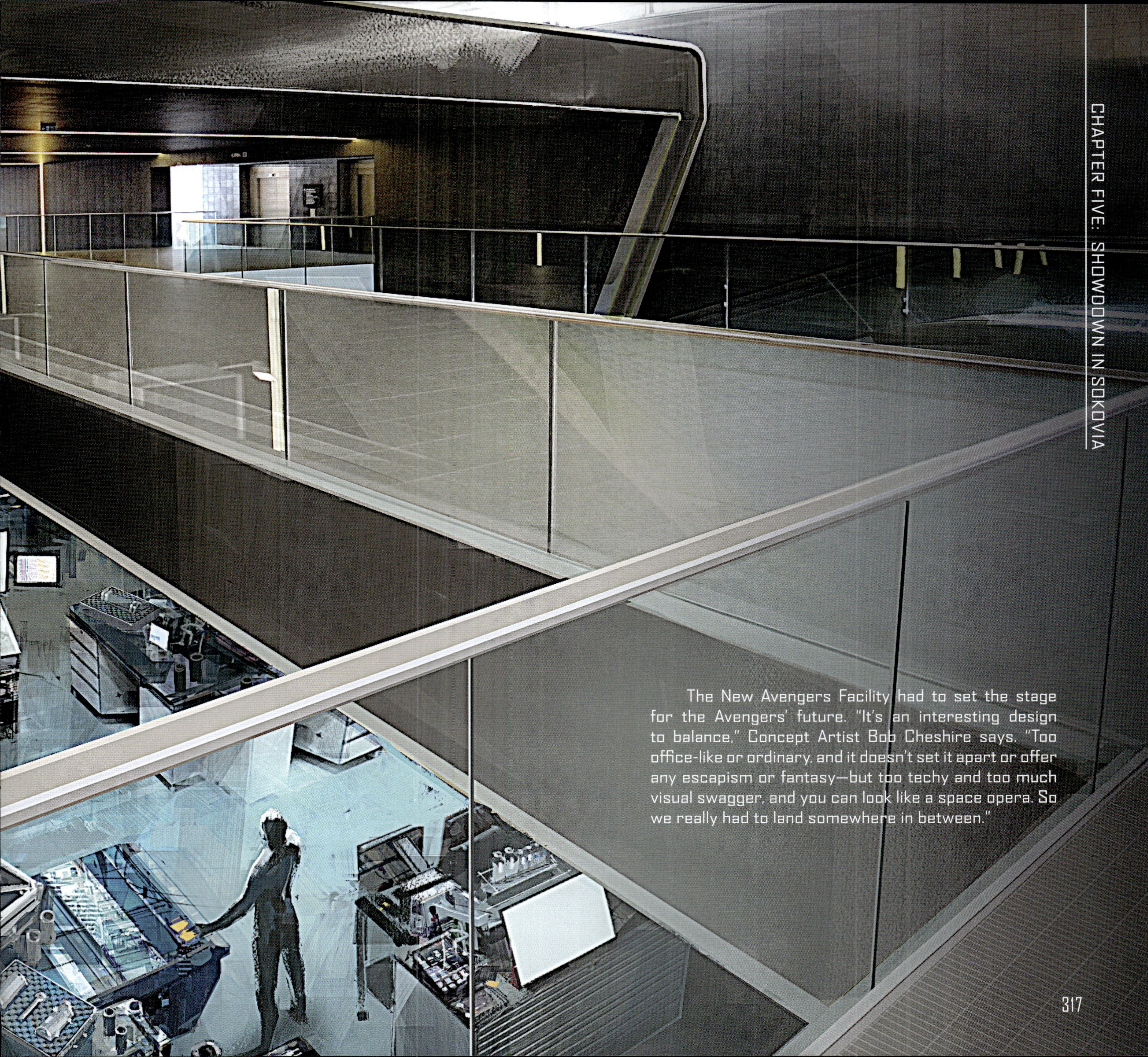

The New Avengers Facility had to set the stage for the Avengers' future. "It's an interesting design to balance," Concept Artist Bob Cheshire says. "Too office-like or ordinary, and it doesn't set it apart or offer any escapism or fantasy—but too techy and too much visual swagger, and you can look like a space opera. So we really had to land somewhere in between."

Pete Thompson concept art.

NICK FURY

Jeremy Latcham explains there's far more to Fury than S.H.I.E.L.D. "The world that he was master of might have changed, but he's a smart guy—he's always in charge," Latcham says. "That's one of the things that makes Fury such a great character: He's always going to do the right thing. Sometimes you don't agree with his methods. Sometimes the way to get there is a little sloppy; sometimes the way to get there is a little messy. But Fury at the end of the day is a good guy; he is a beacon of hope and light in the middle of everything."

Jack Dudman concept art.

MARIA HILL & TRAINEES

Maria Hill is another invaluable asset to the Avengers, which is undoubtedly why Tony Stark hired her in the conclusion of *Captain America: The Winter Soldier*. "Maria Hill is smart, she's a tactician, and she's an Operations person with a rolodex of contacts," Latcham says. "She's now running procedures. I mean, the Avengers are a real organization now—it's a first-class, prime-time organization."

Jack Dudman concept art.

CHAPTER SIX

MARKETING AVENGERS: AGE OF ULTRON

The Avengers were revealed for the first time as a full team in 2011 in a set of posters released at San Diego Comic-Con. This six-poster set—painted by Concept Artist Andy Park, and Co-Heads of Visual Development Ryan Meinerding and Charlie Wen—set the bar for exciting reveals and had fans buzzing in anticipation. When the sequel, Marvel's *Avengers: Age of Ultron*, was announced, Writer/Director Joss Whedon, President of Marvel Studios Kevin Feige and Executive Producer Jeremy Latcham sat down with Meinerding to come up with a concept that would not only serve the same purpose as the first set of posters, but also—in the vein of the sequel itself—take the hype to the next level. Meinerding, Wen and Park turned six posters into eight, incorporating the film's new characters: Scarlet Witch, Quicksilver, an army of Ultrons and the faintest tease of Vision. "The posters are meant to reflect the look and feel of traditional comic-book covers transformed into illustrations that represent the actualization of these larger-than-life characters from Marvel's Cinematic Universe," Park says. "The posters are always particularly challenging due to the fact that each poster connects to reveal a bigger and more powerful picture." As difficult as it was to have three artists create one unified image in separate units, the workflow wasn't the only obstacle this time around. "The addition of the Avengers struggling against the Ultron Sentries presented a unique challenge," Meinerding says. "In our work, we are typically showing the heroes victorious, so working backwards to match the overwhelming odds seen in the film was an interesting experience from start to finish."

MARVEL
AVENGERS
AGE OF ULTRON
May 1.2015

MARVEL
AVENGERS
AGE OF ULTRON
May 1.2015

MARVEL
AVENGERS
AGE OF ULTRON
May 1.2015

MARVEL
AVENGERS
AGE OF ULTRON
May 1.2015

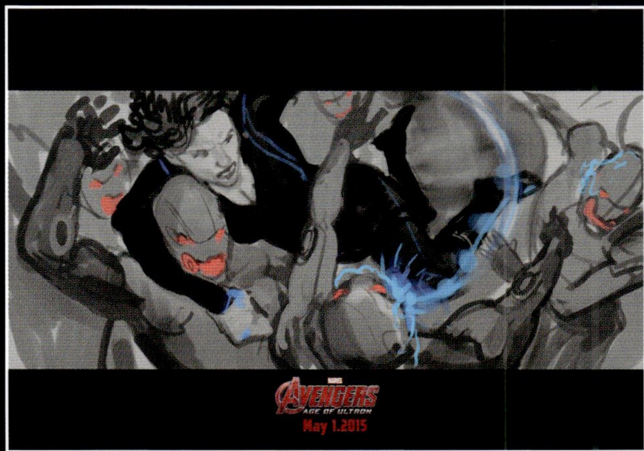

Concepts for the San Diego Comic-Con collectible posters by Andy Park (Scarlet Witch & Black Widow), Ryan Meinerding (Vision) and Charlie Wen (Thor & Hulk).

Concepts for the San Diego Comic-Con collectible posters by Ryan Meinerding, Charlie Wen and Andy Park.

Concepts for the San Diego Comic-Con collectible posters by Ryen Meinerding, Charlie Wen and Andy Park.

Final Comic-Con poster art by Ryan Meinerding, Charlie Wen and Andy Park.

MAY 1, 2015
RYAN MEINERDING

MAY 1, 2015

MAY 1, 2015

MAY 1, 2015

RYAN MEINERDING
MAY 1, 2015

RYAN MEINERDING
MAY 1, 2015

MAY 1, 2015

RYAN MEINERDING
MAY 1, 2015

CONTRIBUTOR BIOS 2015

Writer/Producer/Director **Joss Whedon** is a veteran of film, television and comics renowned for his witty dialogue, genre-blending sensibilities and strong female characters. An Emmy-nominated, third-generation talent whose father and grandfather both wrote for television, Whedon got his start as a writer on the *Roseanne* sitcom in 1989 and soon moved on to film where his writing credits included *Buffy the Vampire Slayer, Alien: Resurrection* and the Oscar-nominated *Toy Story*. Whedon moved back to television, where he converted 1992's lackluster *Buffy* film into the critically acclaimed *Buffy the Vampire Slayer* TV series (1997- 2003) and its vampire-hero spin-off series, *Angel* (1999-2004). Whedon's sci-fi Western series *Firefly* (2002) was short-lived, but its popularity on DVD led to Whedon writing and directing a Universal feature film based on its characters, *Serenity* (2005). Whedon returned to television in 2009 with *Dollhouse* and explores terror in the 2010 feature film *Cabin in the Woods*. A lifelong comics fan, he entered the business with the 2001 Dark Horse mini-series *Fray*, featuring the Slayer of a dystopian future. He later co-wrote a *Serenity* mini-series for Dark Horse (with sequels to follow), helped plot IDW Publishing's *Angel: After the Fall* series picking up where the *Angel* TV show left off, and serves as co-writer and executive producer of Dark Horse's *Buffy The Vampire Slayer Season Eight* series, a canonical continuation of the TV heroine's adventures. At Marvel, Whedon is best known for teaming with John Cassaday on a popular *Astonishing X-Men* run (2004-2008) and taking over *Runaways* after series creator Brian K. Vaughan left the book. Whedon's other Marvel credits include *Giant-Size X-Men #3* (2005) and *Stan Lee Meets Spider-Man #1* (2006).

Over the past decade, Producer and Marvel Studios President **Kevin Feige** has played an instrumental role in a string of blockbuster feature films adapted from the pages of Marvel comic books. In his current role, Feige oversees all creative aspects of the company's feature film and home entertainment activities. In addition to producing *Marvel's Avengers: Age of Ultron*, he is currently producing *Ant-Man*. His previous producing credits for Marvel include *Iron Man 3*, which became the second-largest box office debut in Hollywood history behind the critically acclaimed *Marvel's The Avengers*, which Kevin also produced along with *Guardians of the Galaxy, Captain America: The Winter Soldier, Thor: The Dark World, Thor, Captain America: The First Avenger*, *Iron Man 2* and *Iron Man*.

Executive Producer and Marvel Studios Co-President **Louis D'Esposito** served as Executive Producer on the blockbuster hits *Iron Man, Iron Man 2, Thor, Captain America: The First Avenger*, *Marvel's The Avengers, Iron Man 3, Thor: The Dark World, Captain America: The Winter Soldier* and most recently *Marvel's Avengers: Age of Ultron*. He is currently working on *Ant-Man*, as well as collaborating with Marvel Studios' President Kevin Feige to build the future Marvel slate. As Co-President of the studio and Executive Producer on all Marvel films, D'Esposito balances running the studio to overseeing each film from its development stage to distribution. Beyond his role as Co-President, D'Esposito also directs unique projects for the studio, including his one-shot titled *Agent Carter* starring Hayley Atwell, and the short film titled *Item 47*. The project was released as an added feature on *Marvel's The Avengers* Blu-ray disc. D'Esposito began his tenure at Marvel Studios in 2006. Prior to Marvel, D'Esposito's executive producing credits include the 2006 hit film *The Pursuit of Happyness* starring Will Smith, *Zathura: A Space Adventure* and the 2003 hit *S.W.A.T.* starring Samuel L. Jackson and Colin Farrell.

Executive Producer **Victoria Alonso** is Executive Producer for Writer/Director Joss Whedon's *Avengers: Age of Ultron* for Marvel Studios, where she serves as Executive Vice President of Visual Effects and Post Production. She executive produced James Gunn's *Guardians of the Galaxy*, Joe and Anthony Russo's *Captain America: The Winter Soldier*, Alan Taylor's *Thor: The Dark World*, Shane Black's *Iron Man 3*, as well as *Marvel's The Avengers* for Joss Whedon. She also co-produced Marvel's *Iron Man* and *Iron Man 2* with Director Jon Favreau, Kenneth Branagh's *Thor* and Joe Johnston's *Captain America: The First Avenger*. Alonso's career began at the nascency of the visual effects industry, when she served as a commercial VFX producer. From there, she VFX-produced numerous feature films, working with such directors as Ridley Scott (*Kingdom of Heaven*), Tim Burton (*Big Fish*) and Andrew Adamson (*Shrek*), to name a few.

Executive Producer **Jeremy Latcham** is the senior vice president of production and development at Marvel Studios, where he served as Executive Producer on the 2012 blockbuster hit *Marvel's The Avengers*, which shattered box office records, and the 2014 epic *Guardians of the Galaxy*. Latcham served as Associate Producer on the 2008 critically acclaimed blockbuster *Iron Man* and as Co-Producer on the hit 2010 follow-up *Iron Man 2*. A graduate of Northwestern University, Latcham began his career at Miramax and Dimension Films and also worked at the Endeavor Agency. In 2004, he joined Marvel Studios where he has also held the titles of Vice President, Director of Development, and Creative Executive. In 2011, Latcham was featured as one of "Hollywood's New Leaders" by *Variety*.

Co-Producer and Vice President of Physical Production **Mitch Bell** started with Marvel Studios in 2010. He oversaw production and was Associate Producer on *Captain America: The First Avenger, Iron Man 3* and *Captain America: The Winter Soldier*. Bell was Executive Producer on several Marvel one-shots including *Item 47* and *Agent Carter*, and is working on *Captain America: Civil War*. Prior to joining Marvel Studios, Bell was a freelance production supervisor with over 20 years of experience in both features and television. Originally from Fort Collins, Colorado, Bell moved to Los Angeles in the early '90s and started his career as a production assistant at Imagine Films.

Production Designer **Charles Wood** began his entertainment-industry career in 1991 as a Visual Effects Art Director on such projects as *The Fugitive*, Peter Weir's *Fearless, Under Siege* and Sam Raimi's *Army of Darkness*. Segueing to design work, he has since collaborated on projects ranging from big studio movies to independent films. His credits include James Gunn's *Guardians of the Galaxy, Thor: The Dark World*, Joe Carnahan's *The A-Team*, Michael Apted's *Amazing Grace, Wrath of the Titans, Fool's Gold*, Tony Bill's *Flyboys*, F. Gary Gray's *The Italian Job, Get Carter* and *Mortal Kombat: Annihilation*. Wood earned an Emmy Award nomination in 2000 for the TV movie *Geppetto* and a 2007 Satellite Award nomination for *Amazing Grace*.

Costume Designer **Alexandra Byrne** trained as an architect at Bristol University before studying theatre design on the Motley Course at the English National Opera under the legendary Margaret Harris. She has worked extensively in television and theatre, both as a set and costume designer. Her television credits include Roger Michell's *Persuasion*, for which she received the BAFTA Award for Best Costume Design, and *The Buddha of Suburbia*, for which she received a BAFTA nomination and RTS award. In theatre, Byrne received a Tony nomination for Best Set Design for *Some Americans Abroad*, which transferred from the Royal Shakespeare Company to the Lincoln Center in New York. Following her work in theatre, Byrne designed the costumes for Kenneth Branagh's *Hamlet*, for which she gained her first Oscar nomination. Other credits include *Phantom of the Opera, Sleuth* and *The Garden of Eden*. She received two further Oscar nominations for her costumes in *Elizabeth* and *Finding Neverland*. *Elizabeth, The Golden Age* finally won her the Oscar. Byrne worked with Kenneth Branagh again on *Thor*, her first production with Marvel, and won the Saturn Award. She then worked with Joss Whedon on *Marvel's The Avengers*. After designing costumes for Warner's *300, Rise of an Empire*, Byrne returned to Marvel for James Gunn's *Guardians of the Galaxy* and *Marvel's Avengers: Age of Ultron*. Byrne is married to the actor Simon Shepherd, and they have four children.

Tim Hill concept art.

CONTRIBUTOR BIOS 2015

Director of Photography **Ben Davis**'s feature film credits include Jonathan Liebesman's *Wrath of the Titans*, John Madden's *The Best Exotic Marigold Hotel* and *The Debt*, Mikael Håfström's *The Rite*, Stephen Frears' *Tamara Drewe*, Gerald McMorrow's *Franklyn*, Sharon Maguire's *Incendiary* and Peter Webber's *Hannibal Rising*. Davis has collaborated extensively with director Matthew Vaughn on *Layer Cake*, *Stardust*, and *Kick-Ass*. Davis' work can also be seen in the short film, *The Tonto Woman*, which received an Academy Award® nomination in 2008 for Best Live Action Short Film. Davis' recent credits include Martin McDonagh's *Seven Psychopaths*, starring Sam Rockwell, Christopher Walken, Woody Harrelson and Colin Farrell; Dan Mazer's *I Give It A Year*; Pascal Chaumeil's *A Long Way Down*; and Rowan Joffe's *Before I Go to Sleep*, starring Nicole Kidman and Colin Firth.

Head of Visual Development **Ryan Meinerding** has only been active as a freelance concept artist and illustrator in the film business since 2005, but his work is already drawing the kind of raves reserved for veterans of the industry. After earning a degree in industrial design from Notre Dame, he transitioned to Hollywood and worked on *Outlander*. Subsequent to *Iron Man*, he worked on *Transformers: Revenge of the Fallen* and illustrated costumes on *Watchmen*. While working on *Iron Man 2*, Meinerding contributed the design for the new Iron Man armor in the comic-book series *Invincible Iron Man*, continuing to cement the strong bonds between Marvel Studios and Marvel Comics. He was part of the *Iron Man* crew nominated for the 2009 Art Directors Guild Excellence in Production Design Award for Fantasy Films; was one of the main concept designers for *Thor*; and served as Visual Development Co-Supervisor on *Captain America: The First Avenger* and *Marvel's The Avengers*, and Head of Visual Development on *Iron Man 3*, *Captain America: The Winter Soldier*, and *Avengers: Age of Ultron*.

Head of Visual Development **Charlie Wen** has held a variety of positions in the entertainment industry, ranging from concept designer to art director, on everything from feature films to video games and animation. Wen's client list reads as a virtual who's who of the industry, including Disney, Digital Domain, Dreamworks, Legendary Pictures, Marvel Studios, Darkhorse, Rhythm and Hues, Imagi Studios, Wizards of the Coast, and Sony Computer Entertainment of America. In 2005, he created Kratos and helped establish *God of War* as a monolithic action-adventure title for Sony PlayStation. Outside the production environment, Wen has given lectures on figure drawing and character design at many distinguished studios and universities. After helping establish the main character designs in *Thor*, he holds the title of Head of Visual Development at Marvel Studios, working on Marvel's *Captain America: The First Avenger*, *Marvel's The Avengers*, *Iron Man 3*, *Thor: The Dark World*, *Guardians of the Galaxy*, *Captain America: The Winter Soldier*, *Marvel's Avengers: Age of Ultron* and *Ant-Man*.

Property Master **Barry Gibbs** has worked in film since 1981, when he started his career as a stagehand with model units on *Krull* and *Supergirl*, with The Rank Organisation at Pinewood Studios. He shortly moved to props, where his first jobs included Ridley Scott's *Legend* and the Bond film *A View to a Kill*. Gibbs gained experience in the disciplines of set dressing and standing by on set, then went freelance in 1985 with Julien Temple's *Absolute Beginners*. Three years later, he had the first offer of Prop Master on Roald Dahl's *Danny the Champion of the World*. At that time, he split his efforts between feature films and commercials. This continued until 1993, when Gibbs went to Ireland for *Circle of Friends* with Production Designer Jim Clay. Since then, he has worked on *Captain Corelli's Mandolin*, *About a Boy*, *Love Actually*, *Timeline*, *The Golden Compass*, *Quantum of Solace* and *Inception*, among others. Gibbs' avid interest in manufacturing keeps him involved with and running large prop shops with amazing teams of technicians. He was given the opportunity to work for Marvel on *Captain America: The First Avenger*, *Thor: The Dark World*, *Guardians of the Galaxy* and *Marvel's Avengers: Age of Ultron*.

Visual Effects Supervisor **Christopher Townsend** was the overall VFX Supervisor on Marvel's *Iron Man 3* with Writer/Director Shane Black. Townsend grew up in England, then traveled and worked throughout Asia and Australia before moving to the USA in 1994 to work at Industrial Light & Magic. He worked as an artist and supervisor on many influential movies, including *Star Wars* (both the rerelease of the original, *A New Hope*, and the new trilogy), *Mission: Impossible*, *The Lost World: Jurassic Park*, *A.I.: Artificial Intelligence*, *Hulk*, *Day After Tomorrow*, *The Island*, and the Academy Award-winning *Pirates of the Caribbean: Dead Man's Chest*. In 2007, he became a freelancer and was the VFX Supervisor on Walden/New Line's *Journey to the Center of the Earth*, which made it to the Academy VFX Bakeoffs; it was the first ever stereoscopic motion picture shot and released in HD. He supervised on location for Fox's *X-Men Origins: Wolverine*, oversaw the VFX in Europe for Warner Bros' *Ninja Assassin*, supervised on Fox's *Percy Jackson and the Lightning Thief*, and again made it to the Bakeoffs in 2012 as the VFX Supervisor for Marvel's *Captain America: The First Avenger*.

Concept Artist **Andy Park** began his career illustrating comic books on titles such as *Tomb Raider*, *Excalibur* and *Uncanny X-Men* for companies such as Marvel, DC and Image Comics. In 2004, he began working as a concept artist in video games and television. He was one of the leading artists creating the worlds and characters of the award-winning *God of War* franchise for Sony Computer Entertainment of America. Park joined the Visual Development Department at Marvel Studios in 2010 as a visual development artist, designing characters and keyframe illustrations for *Marvel's The Avengers*, *Captain America*, *Iron Man 3*, *Captain America: The Winter Soldier*, *Thor: The Dark World*, *Guardians of the Galaxy*, *Avengers: Age of Ultron* and the upcoming *Ant-Man* and *Captain America: Civil War*.

Concept Artist **Rodney Fuentebella** has degrees in design from UCLA and product design from the Art Center College of Design. Born in the Philippines and raised in San Francisco, he has worked on various projects for Electronic Arts, Atari, Rhythm and Hues, Dreamworks Animation and WIRED magazine, as well as various other entertainment and commercial projects. In film, he worked as a concept artist at Rhythm and Hues before joining the Visual Development team at Marvel Studios. Fuentebella has created key-art illustrations and character designs for various projects including *Captain America: The First Avenger*, *Marvel's The Avengers*, *Iron Man 3*, *Captain America: The Winter Soldier*, *Guardians of the Galaxy*, *Avengers: Age of Ultron*, *Ant-Man* and other upcoming Marvel Studios films.

Concept Artist **Josh Nizzi** graduated from the University of Illinois with a degree in graphic design. He spent the next nine years working in video games as an art director, concept artist, modeler and animator on games like *Red Faction 1 & 2*, *The Punisher*, *MechAssault 2* and *Fracture*. Since then, Nizzi has been an illustrator for feature films such as *Transformers 2, 3 & 4*, *The Amazing Spider-Man*, *Iron Man 3*, *Django Unchained* and *The Wolverine*. He continues to work on video game projects as well as venturing into toys, comics and television.

Storyboard Artist **Bryan Andrews**, known in the industry for his uncanny ability to board scenes of high drama with uniquely inspiring takes on action storytelling, has been impressing science-fiction action fans for almost a decade since his Emmy Award-winning contributions to animated series *Star Wars: Clone Wars* and *Samurai Jack* ("The Four Seasons of Death"). Citing influences that range from Steven Spielberg, Ray Harryhausen and Akira Kurosawa to Frank Frazetta, *Gatchaman* and *Macross*—and an avid student of not only the visual language of cinema, but also of rapier fencing, and such Chinese martial arts as Wushu and Wing Chun—Andrews has brought his trademark flair for dramatic action storytelling to both the small and silver screens.

Bob Cheshire concept art.

A C K N O W L

Nick Ainsworth
Victoria Alonso
Bryan Andrews
Paul Bettany
Alexandra Byrne
Roberto Fernández Castro
Jose Fernández Castro
Paul Catling
Paul Chandler
Bob Cheshire
Ben Davis
Louis D'Esposito
Robert Downey Jr.
Jack Dudman
Chris Evans
Kevin Feige
Rodney Fuentebella
Barry Gibbs
Renata Gilbert
Chris Hemsworth
Josh Herman
Tim Hill
Industrial Light & Magic
Samuel L. Jackson
Kevin Jenkins
Scarlett Johansson
Claudia Kim

D G M E N T S

Thomas Kretschmann
Jeremy Latcham
Laura Lilley
Stephan Martinière
John McCoy
Ryan Meinerding
Josh Nizzi
Elizabeth Olsen
Andy Park
Jeremy Renner
Chris Rosewarne
Mark Ruffalo
Phil Saunders
Andy Serkis
Cobie Smulders
James Spader
Jackson Sze
Aaron Taylor-Johnson
Pete Thompson
Chris Townsend
Darrell Warner
Ivan Weightman
Charlie Wen
Joss Whedon
Charlie Wood
Stephen Wong

IRON
MAN
CAPTAIN
AMERICA
THOR
BLACK
WIDOW
HULK

ARTIST CREDITS

Ryan Meinerding
Pages 2-5, 22-27, 30-31, 78, 138-139, 141, 152, 154-156, 158, 162, 165, 174-177, 190-191, 198-199, 204-205, 209, 218-219, 225, 230-231, 250-259, 262-263, 274, 322-329, Cover, Slipcase

Jackson Sze
Pages 6-7, 188-189, 290-291

Bryan Andrews
Pages 15, 98-101, 298-305

Paul Chandler
Pages 16-19, 111, 226-227, 279-280, 284-285

Bob Cheshire
Pages 20-21, 72-73, 89, 102-103, 232-233, 228-229, 236-239, 284-249, 276-279, 312-317, 332-333

Charlie Wen
Pages 28, 133, 135-137, 140, 145-147, 157, 159-161, 164, 168, 208, 213, 224-225, 263-267, 306-309, 322-323, 325-329

Jack Dudman
Pages 28-29, 56-57, 75-77, 81, 124-125, 180-181, 234-235, 238, 320-321

Andy Park
Pages 32-33, 40-42, 79-80, 82-83, 96-97, 130-132, 134-135, 151, 153, 168-169, 186-187, 214, 244-245, 260-261, 270-271, 292-295, 310-311, 322-323, 325-329

Josh Nizzi
Pages 34-37, 46-47, 50, 52-55, 66, 196, 200-203, 210, 212, 216-217,

Chris Rosewarne
Pages 38-39, 43, 58-65, 194

Rodney Fuentebella
Pages 44-45, 48-50, 66-67, 150, 166-167, 170-171, 178-179, 211, 220-223, 246-247, 281, 296-297

Josh Herman
Pages 51, 153, 164, 193, 216, 273

Pete Thompson
Pages 68-71, 118-119, 122-123, 194-195, 286, 288-289, 314-315, 318-319

Nick Ainsworth
Pages 74, 115, 172-173

Darrell Warner
Pages 75

Tim Hill
Pages 84-89, 91-93, 240, 282-283, 330-331

Kevin Jenkins
Pages 90-91, 94-95

Stephen Wong
Pages 104-107, 114-115, 118-119, 127, 129

Roberto Fernández Castro
Pages 108-111, 120-121, 126, 128, 182-183, 264-265

Paul Catling
Pages 110, 241

Ivan Weightman
Pages 112-113, 243

Stephan Martinière
Pages 116-117

Phil Saunders
Pages 142-144, 147-149, 152, 161, 163, 206-207, 211, 215, 272-275

Renata Gilbert
Pages 180

Laura Lilley
Pages 180

John McCoy
Pages 192-193, 195-196, 276, 287

Industrial Light & Magic
Pages 184-185, 197, 266, 268-269

Jose Fernández Castro
Pages 242